CHRISTOPHER BUSH
THE CASE OF THE TREBLE TWIST

CHRISTOPHER BUSH was born Charlie Christmas Bush in Norfolk in 1885. His father was a farm labourer and his mother a milliner. In the early years of his childhood he lived with his aunt and uncle in London before returning to Norfolk aged seven, later winning a scholarship to Thetford Grammar School.

As an adult, Bush worked as a schoolmaster for 27 years, pausing only to fight in World War One, until retiring aged 46 in 1931 to be a full-time novelist. His first novel featuring the eccentric Ludovic Travers was published in 1926, and was followed by 62 additional Travers mysteries. These are all to be republished by Dean Street Press.

Christopher Bush fought again in World War Two, and was elected a member of the prestigious Detection Club.

He died in 1973.

CHRISTOPHER BUSH

THE CASE OF THE TREBLE TWIST

With an introduction
by Curtis Evans

DEAN STREET PRESS

For

VERA MORGAN

WITH THANKS

INTRODUCTION

Rosalind. If it be true that good wine needs no bush [i.e., advertising], 'tis true that a good play needs no epilogue. Yet to good wine, they do use good bushes, and good plays prove the better by the help of good epilogues.

–SHAKESPEARE, Epilogue, As You Like It

THE decade of the 1960s saw the sun finally begin to set on that storied generation which between the First and Second World Wars gave us detective fiction's Golden Age. Taking account of both deaths and retirements, by the late Sixties only a bare half-dozen pre-World War Two members of the Detection Club were still plying their deliciously deceptive craft: Agatha Christie, Anthony Gilbert (Lucy Beatrice Malleson), Gladys Mitchell, John Dickson Carr, Nicholas Blake and Christopher Bush, the subject of this introduction. Bush himself would pass away, at the age of eighty-seven, in 1973, having published, at the age of eighty-two, his sixty-third Ludovic Travers detective novel, *The Case of the Prodigal Daughter*, in the United Kingdom in the spring of 1968.

In the United States Bush's final detective novel did not appear until late November 1969, about four months after the horrific Manson murders in the tarnished Golden State of California. Implicating the triple terrors of sex, drugs and rock and roll (not to mention almost inconceivably bestial violence), the Manson slayings could not have strayed farther from the whimsically escapist "death as a game" aesthetic of Golden Age of detective fiction. Increasingly in the decade capable of producing psychedelic psychopaths like Charles Manson and his "family," the few remaining survivors of the Golden Age of detective fiction increasingly deemed themselves men and women far out of time. In his detective fiction John Dickson Carr, an incurable romantic, prudently beat a retreat from the present into the pleasanter pages of the past, setting his tales in bygone historical eras where he felt vastly more at home. With varying success Agatha Christie made a brave effort to stay abreast of the times (*Third Girl, Endless Night*), but ultimately her strivings to understand what was going on around her collapsed into the utter incoherence of *Passenger to Frankfurt* and *Postern of Fate*, by general consensus the worst mystery novels that Dame Agatha ever put down on paper.

In his detective fiction Christopher Bush, who was not quite two years older than Christie, managed rather better than the Queen of Crime to keep up with all the unsettling goings-on around him, while never forswearing the Golden Age article of faith that the primary purpose of a crime writer is pleasingly to puzzle his/her readers. And, in contrast with Christie and Carr, Bush knew when it was time to lay down his pen (or turn off his dictation machine, as the case may be), thereby allowing him to make his exit from the stage on a comparatively high note. Indeed, Christopher Bush's concluding baker's dozen of detective novels, which he published between 1957 and 1968 (and which have now been reprinted, after more than a half-century, by Dean Street Press), makes a generally fine epilogue, or coda, to the author's impressive corpus of crime fiction, which first began to see the light of day way back in the jubilant Jazz Age. These are, readers will find, "good bushes" (to punningly borrow from Shakespeare), providing them with ample intelligent detective entertainment as Bush's longtime series sleuth Ludovic Travers, in the luminous twilight of his career, makes his final forays into ingenious criminal investigation.

*

In the last thirteen Ludovic Travers mystery novels, Travers' *entrée* to his cases continues to come through his ownership of the Broad Street Detective Agency. Besides Travers we also regularly encounter his elegant wife, Bernice (although sometimes his independent-minded spouse is away on excursions of her own), his proverbially loyal secretary, Bertha Munney, his top Broad Street op, Hallows (another one named French, presumably inspired by Bush's late Detection Club colleague Freeman Wills

Crofts, pops up occasionally), John Hill of the United Assurance Agency, who brings Travers many of his cases, and Scotland Yard's Inspector Jewle and Sergeant Matthews, who after the first of these final novels, *The Case of the Treble Twist* (in the U.S. *Triple Twist*), are promoted, respectively, to Superintendent and Inspector. (The Yard's ex-Superintendent George Wharton, now firmly retired from any form of investigative work whatsoever, is mentioned just once by Ludo, when, in *The Case of the Dead Man Gone*, he passingly imparts that he and Wharton recently had lunch together.)

For all practical purposes Travers, who during the Golden Age was a classic gentleman amateur snooper like Philo Vance and Lord Peter Wimsey, now functions fully as a professional private eye—although one, to be sure, who is rather posher than the rest. While some reviewers referred to Travers as England's Philip Marlowe, in fact he little resembles the general run of love and leave 'em/hate and beat 'em brand of brutish American P.I.'s, favoring a nice cup of coffee (a post-war change from tea), a good pipe and the occasional spot of sherry to the frequent snatches of liquor and cigarettes favored by most of his American brethren and remaining faithful to his spouse despite encountering a succession of sexy women, not all of them, shall we say, virtuously inclined.

This was a formula which throughout the period maintained a devoted audience on both sides of the Atlantic consisting, one surmises, of readers (including crime writers Anthony Berkeley, Nicholas Blake and the late Alan Hunter, creator of Inspector George Gently) who preferred their detectives something less than hard-boiled. Travers himself sneers at the hugely popular (and psychotically violent) postwar American private eye Mike Hammer, commenting of an American couple in *The Case of the Treble Twist*: "She was a woman of considerable culture; his ran about as far as Mickey Spillane" [a withering reference to Mike Hammer's creator]. Yet despite his manifest disdain for Mike Hammer, an ugly American if ever there were one, Christopher

Bush and his wife Florence in the spring of 1957 had traveled to New York aboard the RMS *Queen Elizabeth*, and references by him to both the United States and Canada became more frequent in the books which followed this trip.

Certainly *The Case of the Treble Twist* (1957) features tough customers and an exceptionally cruel murder, yet it is also one of Bush's most ingeniously contrived cases from the Fifties, full of charm, treacherous deception and, yes, plenty of twists, including one that is a real sockaroo (to borrow, as Bush occasionally did, from American idiom). Similarly clever is *The Case of the Running Man* (1958), which draws, as several earlier Bush books had, on the author's profound love and knowledge of antiques. By this time Bush and his wife, their coffers having burgeoned from the proceeds of his successful mysteries, resided in the quaint medieval market town of Lavenham, Suffolk at the Great House, a splendidly decorated fourteenth-century structure with an elegant Georgian-era façade which he and Florence purchased in 1953 and resided in until their deaths. The dashing author, whom in 1967 *Chicago Tribune* mystery reviewer Alice Crombie swooningly dubbed "one of the handsomest mystery writers on either side of the Channel or Atlantic," also drove a Jaguar, beloved by James Bond films of late, well into his eighties.

The Case of the Running Man includes that Golden Age detective fiction staple, a family tree, but more originally the novel features as a major character a black American man, Sam, the devoted chauffeur of the wealthy murder victim. Sam, who reminds Ludovic Travers of Rochester, "Jack Benny's factotum of television and radio," is an interesting and sincerely treated individual, although as Anthony Boucher amusingly pronounced at the time in the *New York Times Book Review*, he speaks "a dialect never heard by mortal ear"—an odd compounding of "American Negro" and London cockney.

The Case of the Careless Thief (1959) takes Ludo to Sandbeach, "the Blackpool of the South Coast," as the American jacket blurb puts it, with "a dozen hotels, a race track, a dog track, a music hall and two enormous dance halls." Anthony Boucher deemed this hard-hitting, tricky tale, which draws to strong effect on contemporary events in England, "one of Ludovic Travers' best cases." Likewise hard-hitting are *The Case of the Sapphire Brooch* (1960) and *The Case of the Extra Grave* (1961), complex tales of murderous mésalliances with memorably grim conclusions. The plot of *The Case of the Dead Man Gone* (1961) topically involves refugee relief groups, while *The Case of the Heavenly Twin* (1963) opens with a case of a creative criminal couple forging American Express Travelers Checks, concerning which Americans of a certain age will recall actor Karl Malden sternly enjoining, in a long-running television advertising campaign: "Don't leave home without them." In contrast with many of his crime writing contemporaries (judging from the tone of their work), Bush actually learned to watch and enjoy television, although in *The Case of The Three-Ring Puzzle*, a tale of violently escalating intrigue, Travers dryly references Scottish philosopher Thomas Carlyle's famous observation that England's population consisted of "mostly fools" when he comments: "I guess he wasn't too far out at that. But rather remarkable an estimate perhaps, considering that in his day there were no television commercials."

Of Bush's final five Ludovic Travers detective novels, published between 1964 and 1968, when the Western World, in the eyes of many, was going from whimsically mod to utterly mad, the best are, in my estimation, the cases of *The Jumbo Sandwich* (1965), *The Good Employer* (1966) and *The Prodigal Daughter* (1968). In *Sandwich* a crisp case of a defrauded (and jilted) gentry lady friend of Ludo's metamorphoses into a smorgasbord of, as the American book jacket puts it, "blackmail, black magic, a black sheep, and murder." It all culminates in a confrontation on a lonely Riviera beach in France, setting of some of Ludovic Travers' earliest cases, between Ludo and a desperate killer, in which Bernice plays an unexpectedly active part. Ludo again travels to France in the highly classic *Employer*, which draws most engagingly on the sleuth's (and the author's) dabbling in the world of art and is dedicated to his distinguished Lavenham artist friends, the couple Reginald and Rosalie Brill, who resided next door to Bush and his wife at the fourteenth-century Little Hall, then an art student hostel for which the Brills served as guardians. In *The Guardian* Francis Iles (aka Golden Age crime writer Anthony Berkeley) pronounced that *Employer* represented Bush "at his most ingenious."

Finally, in *Daughter* Travers finds himself tasked with recovering the absconded teenage offspring of domineering Dora Marport, sober-sided head of the organization Home and Family, which is righteously devoted to "the fostering, so to speak, of family life as the stoutest bulwark against the encroachment of ever-more numerous hostile forces: sex and violence in literature, films and on television; pornography generally, and the erosion of responsibility and the capability for sacrifice by the welfare state." Can Travers, a Great War veteran who made his debut in detective fiction in 1926, bridge the generation gap in late-Sixties London? Ludo may prefer Bach to the Beatles, but in this, the last of his recorded cases, he proves more "with it" than one might have expected. All in all, *Daughter* makes a rewarding finish to one of the longest-running and most noteworthy sleuth series in British detective fiction.

Curtis Evans

1. PREVIEW

THERE was something unique about the Case of the Treble Twist. It isn't often one gets a preview of a case or hovers round its fringes four years before it breaks, but that was just what happened. But perhaps *preview* is too embracing a word. It was more like entering a room where a game of chess is about to begin, and seeing the protagonists take their seats, and then, before even an opening move is made, having to go out again and leave the whole thing. And later, of course, ringing up someone who has seen the game and asking for the result. Yet even that analogy isn't perfect. I might have seen the pieces being laid out on the board but it was four years, as I said, before I knew who'd won, and lost, the game.

It happened like this. Some four years ago on a dirty night of October, I'd been working late with Norris, my manager at the Broad Street Detective Agency. The income-tax people had queried some of our expense accounts and we'd been trying to straighten the matter out, and the consequence was that I'd had to ring Bernice, my wife, and say I shouldn't be in for the evening meal. Bertha Munney, who was staying late, too, went out for sandwiches and a couple of bottles of beer. It was nine o'clock by the time we reckoned we had the whole thing well in hand. I hopped the first bus that was going in the general direction of Trafalgar Square. I had an evening paper in my pocket and it was because I got tied up in a short crime story that I overshot my stop and found we were nearing Piccadilly Circus. As I got out, just round the bend into Regent Street, I practically barged into a very old friend, Chief-Inspector Jewle. We had a quick word or two and then he suggested a drink at the Café Rond. I said I could do with it.

The big downstair bar wasn't more than a third full and we took our drinks to a comparatively quiet corner. I began talking shop.

"Any thing special on hand at the moment?"

"Well—yes and no," he said. "You read about that diamond snatch a week or two ago?"

"That twenty-thousand-pound job at Belsize Park?"

"That's the one. Never a clue so far. And never an idea where the stuff was planted. All we think is, it hasn't got out of the country."

It was the fences, he said, and scowled at his glass before he lifted it. You could get the little fry and occasionally the big fry, but to rope in a really high-class fence—well, that'd be the day. Wheels within wheels, he told me. Sometimes the stuff went through one or two little hands before reaching the big fellow behind the scenes: the one who could place the stuff safely and finally and collect the real money.

I think it was about the first time I'd seen Jewle looking worried. He's placid, almost phlegmatic, like a lot of big men, and I was wondering if there was anything highly personal in what he'd been telling me, as I picked up the two glasses and went to the bar for a refill. When I came back he was looking more himself. He leaned forward after he'd taken a first pull at his glass.

"Suppose you've never heard a whisper of anyone named Hope?"

I think I grinned a bit foolishly. The question was unexpected and it had, for me at least, no context. He didn't give me time to answer.

"Something came in from a stoolie. We've heard it before and couldn't run it down. Not Hope, exactly. More like the Band of Hope."

My question was at a venture. All I wanted was to get oriented.

"Is this to do with what we were talking about? Fences, and where those Belsize Park diamonds went?"

"What else?" he said, as if all along I ought to have known. "We've heard a whisper or two before but not enough to go on. This latest whisper is just another one. Stuff is either being passed through a channel connected with someone called Hope, or else the big fellow himself is called Hope. And that'd be too much to hope for. Pardon my joke."

"The stoolie is reliable?"

"Only small fry," he said, "but he's passed on some useful tips in his time. This one's a bit too cryptic. He overheard a conversation. The name Hope was mentioned, that's all. If it hadn't cropped up before we'd have wiped it off as a dead loss. That, and where the conversation took place. Ever hear of Harry Tibball's Gymnasium in Mayworth Street?"

I told him I'd only even the vaguest of ideas as to the whereabouts of Mayworth Street.

"Turning out of Wardour Street," he said. "As near the plumb centre of Soho as you can get. Harry's in a double line of business there. A nice little restaurant that calls itself The Collano. That was the name when he bought it three years ago and he didn't change it. Then round behind, if you cut in further back in Mayworth Street, he has this gymnasium. Converted it from an old mews. Cost him a packet. Some of the top-notchers train there. Everything laid on. Must have cost a packet, as I said. That's what worries me about Harry."

"Where the money came from?"

"That, and a few other things. Harry started life as Harry Tellemann. His old father had a small restaurant in Aldgate. Harry outgrew it and blossomed out for himself. Married a girl with money—Solly Cowan's daughter. Solly had a big furniture store in the New Kent Road. Left her quite a bit but not enough to account for what Harry's been spending. She's dead, by the way. Left an only daughter, a smart girl called Gloria. Harry had her educated up to the nines but they tell me all the rough edges aren't off yet."

I couldn't help smiling.

"Been digging a bit deep, haven't you?"

"We get around," he said, and grinned back. "I could write Harry's biography if I only had the time. Except for the missing pieces. Harry's had three restaurants before The Collano and we've tried to work out just what profit he made on each before moving up. We got the Inland Revenue people in, strictly on the quiet, but he had the answers. A big win or two on the dogs or a race track. Nothing you could disprove. All that fraternity pops into the gym now and again and Harry gets the inside dope—so he says."

He stopped short there as if an idea had struck him. He was looking down at the empty glass and I asked him if he'd have a last one. He didn't hear me the first time and then he said he wouldn't. He looked at his watch.

"That gym doesn't close down till ten-thirty. Like to go along and have a look?"

I had to say it was far too late. I ought to have been home long since.

"Any other night you care to fix it."

"Guess I'm getting a bit hot under the collar about this business," he told me. "What about tomorrow night? Tell you what. We'll have dinner at The Collano and then slip along to the gym. What do you think?"

"And what am I supposed to do besides eating a free meal?"

"Just company," he told me with a grin. "Ostensibly you'll be standing me the meal. They don't know me in the restaurant but it's just as well to be seen in high-class company. In case."

"Good," I said. "I'll wash behind my ears. And where do we meet, and when?"

"What about here, at seven o'clock?"

I told him that'd suit me fine.

I was early that night but he was earlier still. As we walked towards Mayworth Street, zig-zagging through the criss-cross of Soho roads and passages, he was telling me what had been at the back of his mind.

"I've never actually been inside either Tibball's gym or his restaurant, as you've probably guessed. All I've had to go on is reports, and that's why I think the time has come for a personal look-see. A couple of our men are doing their training there for the championships."

"Planted?"

"Oh no. The gym's handy for them, that's all." In the light of the street-lamp I saw him smile. "That didn't stop me from taking a sort of fatherly interest. And that's our excuse for having a look round the gym tonight."

"Tibball will know you, of course."

"Will he?" he said. "Think it out. They haven't had *my* photo in the *Radio Times*, and Tibball hasn't the foggiest notion that we're interested. If he has, then someone's slipped up, and I'm pretty sure that hasn't happened."

"And what's the interest in the restaurant?"

"Just to get the feel of the place."

He stopped for a moment.

"You have hunches, don't you? Well, I've one about the Tibball set-up. If Tibball's moved up to the top circles, and I think he has, then he's working through a perfect bit of machinery which he's built up for the job."

He moved on. Another few yards and we were in the middle of Wardour Street. The first turning west and there was Mayworth Street, and as soon as we turned into it I could see the restaurant, and THE COLLANO picked across its front in flickering red and green lights. Jewle drew me to another halt.

"The table's booked in your name, by the way—name of Vick." I didn't get it for a moment. Then I did. Ludovic Travers. Ludovic. Vick.

"A funny thing about that," he went on. "I looked up the records trying to get a name and damned if there wasn't an amateur light heavyweight named Vick and just about your time." We moved on to the restaurant. Its double-windowed front was like a score of others in Soho, and so was its interior: a tiny, cramped cloak-room-hall, a short passage and the smallish dining-rooms beyond.

Stairs led up to still more rooms. Quite a lot of space, you might say, divided up into small compartments. But the rooms themselves weren't cramped. Tables were well spaced. The concealed lighting was good. Napery and glass and cutlery were immaculate.

An elderly waiter took our coats and hats. Few people were dining and there was no shifting of legs as we made our way to a corner table. Jewle had his back to the room but a mirror was in front of him. I sat with a good view of the passage and the entrance hall. Two or three minutes and the waiter had taken our order. The drinks waiter brought a couple of tall, frosted lagers.

"Quite a good-class place," I said to Jewle. "Nice to sniff the same old Soho smells."

The lager was good. The meal doesn't matter, though it was far from superlative. It was what happened during that fifty minutes that, years later, was to flash across my mind's eye as if a film of that evening had miraculously been run off.

Jewle's eyes were lifting all through the meal to that mirror in front of him. Quite a few people had come in since we had first sat down and he hadn't missed one of them. And then came a special arrival: a couple of Americans in what I guessed to be the late thirties, and an English girl who looked in the early twenties. I had so good a view of them because their entrance was something special. They'd reached the end of the passage and the foot of the stairs when the restaurant manager suddenly appeared, and I wasn't twenty feet away from them.

"Evening, Miss Gloria." The tallish, dark manager was smiling and his bow was somehow obsequious. He bowed again. "Madame. Sir."

"Where are we, Fred?"

He'd snapped a finger at a waiter and was helping the ladies with their wraps.

"The usual table, Miss Gloria. Let me take your coat, sir."

"Nice little place you've got here," the American said. "Sort of homey."

"I think it's cute." That was his companion, looking round the room all starry-eyed. She even looked at me.

"Glad you like it," the manager said. "And I hope you'll enjoy the dinner. This way, madame."

He bowed the party towards the stairs and followed them up. There was a little flurry of whispers at the tables in our room. Maybe the party had been taken for film stars.

"Tibball's daughter," Jewle told me quietly. "A smart-looking piece. Lacking that certain something, don't you think? That's one thing you can't buy—class."

"True enough," I said. "And she ought to get a good elocutionist. Too much cockney in that voice of hers."

Jewle's lip drooped.

"It's the one she was born with. The more they try the more you can spot 'em."

He went on with his meal. I began trying to hold in my mind the picture of Gloria Tibball. She was of average height and with a rather full figure. When I'd first seen her nearing the end of the passage, I'd thought she was a blonde, but when she stood in the full light I saw that her hair was a kind of bronze. Her individual features I couldn't recall, but there'd been no doubt about the good looks. And yet, I was telling myself, I doubt if even in my wild-oat days she'd have been my cup of tea. Not that quite a lot of people wouldn't find her mightily attractive.

Jewle might have been reading my thoughts.

"Don't get any ideas. Our Gloria's booked."

"I'm heartbroken," I said. "Who's the lucky man?"

Jewle did a quick switch.

"Notice that manager. His name's Harban. Fred Harban."

He gave one of those dry smiles of his. "He's Tibball's son-in-law."

I didn't get it for a moment.

"You mean all that 'Evening, Miss Gloria' was sheer eyewash?"

"What else?" he said. "They got married a year ago."

"Bit of a come-down, wasn't it?"

"Depends how high you started from," he told me. "Tibball's father and Harban's were practically neighbours and Harban's been with Harry for years. Not that we've anything on him—not as yet."

The half-whisper was suddenly even lower.

"Look at that chap who's just coming in."

He was a youngish man, probably about thirty: just above medium height, dark-haired and with tiny side-burns that came half-way along his ears. He carried himself well and there was something almost condescending as he ran a cool eye over the room. A waiter saw him and came up with a smile to take his overcoat. They began talking quietly: so quietly that from where I sat they mightn't have been talking at all. Then the waiter waved a suggestive hand towards the stairs.

"Conward. Frank Conward," Jewle told me. "Tibball's general factotum. Drives the car, squires the daughter—anything that comes along."

"Looked a bit assured?" I said. "And, wait a minute. Haven't I heard the name somewhere?"

"An ex-public-school boy," he told me. "Got in a spot about a year ago, breaking and entering his uncle's town flat. That's what we called it. The magistrate thought differently. His family's cut him off."

We didn't stay for coffee. I paid the bill and we collected our hats and coats. We made our way towards Wardour Street and Jewle suddenly halted.

"Would you mind waiting a minute or two? A telephone call I ought to make."

Five minutes later I saw him coming back. I went to meet him but it turned out a waste of time. We were to go back along Mayworth Street.

"Sorry to hold things up," he said. "But I had a brainwave. Rumour has it that Tibball's running a high-class poker game somewhere. Thought it might be as well to pick up Gloria and her friends when they leave."

"She's the decoy?"

"Don't know," he said. "What we do know is that she keeps putting in occasional weeks at various first-class hotels. Why should she do that if she isn't making contacts?"

I was shaking my head as we moved on.

"Curious," I said. "Everything so respectable on the surface. Almost bourgeois. And then these queer sort of undercurrents."

"Just tinsel," he gave a wry sort of smile. "Tinsel. Or froth. Like washing dirty hands with scented soap. The grime's underneath. And here we are. Don't forget you're the modest amateur. Just string along."

We'd cut back through a narrowish passage and then sharp right to another one, much more narrow. Ahead of us was a long, two-storied building, both floors of which were lighted up. The same flickering green and red lights said that it was the Mayworth gymnasium and sports club.

We were held up by a uniformed commissionaire just inside the door: an ex-heavyweight pug with a quiet voice that was a slurred whisper.

"Tommy Clark working tonight?" Jewle said. "We're friends of his."

The pug opened the door of the small entrance hall and looked through.

"Think he's there. He hasn't come out."

He waved a hand to pass us through. Jewle slipped something in it. The pug reached round us to open the door.

It was a long room, well-lighted. It had the same old smells: sawdust, liniment and sweat, with a flux of varnish from some of the newer fitments. It was just short of nine o'clock and every-thing was in full swing. In a ring to the left a coloured lightweight and a lanky white boy were having a work-out. Half a dozen men were watching, and they might have been puppets, all of them, with the only sound the stamp of feet and the faint thud of the gloves. Another coloured boy was shadow-boxing in the far corner, and now and again he'd break off to take a turn at the bag. Four men in shorts and vests were working on the horizontal bar and everywhere were single men at the bag or skipping or having a spell at the parallel bars or the horse. "That's Clark, over by the far door," Jewle said.

It was an immense room, as I said, and Clark must have been thirty yards from where Jewle had spotted him. He was a superbly built fellow in his early twenties, and the sweat shone on the taut muscles as his fists gave the quick one-two on the heavy bag. We were almost on him before he saw us.

"Hallo, Tommy. How's the weight coming?"

Clark gave a modest grin.

"Can't grumble, sir. I was just going to knock off."

"And how's Smithers feeling?"

"Pretty good, sir. He'll be in tomorrow night."

We went up the stairs together to the changing rooms. That upper storey had everything: showers, massage rooms, office rooms and even a buffet with sandwiches and fruit and hot and cold soft drinks.

"You carry on, Tommy," Jewle said. "We only dropped in for a look round. Don't want you to catch cold."

A door opened just ahead of us and a man came out. He caught sight of us. He was still for a moment, then slowly moved towards us. He was a big man, rather spare in build, but tallish and well-muscled. His hair was thin and had streaks of grey. The face was full and the lips thick and protuberant. The look was enquiring and the smile had an ersatz warmth.

"Good evening, gentlemen."

The voice was surprisingly soft. There was a thickish quality about it as if it came from a squeezed larynx.

"We're friends of Tommy Clark here. My name's Jewle. This is Michael Vick."

"I'm Harry Tibball." He smiled again as if the information was more than enough. The smile switched to Clark.

"Tommy's a good boy," he said. "I've been watching him. It'll take a good 'un to beat him. All he wants is a little bit more to that left hand."

Clark hesitated. He didn't know quite how to make his exit. Then he gave a sheepish kind of smile.

"Think I'll take a shower."

"That's right, Tommy boy." Tibball gave him a fatherly nod. Clark moved off. Tibball switched his look to Jewle.

"He's a friend of yours, you said?"

The voice was still as soft. It had the suspicion of a lisp. The smile was still at the mouth, but the eyes were a cold grey.

"I'm his Inspector," Jewle said. "Probably be having a bet on him on the quiet. That's why I wanted to hear how he was coming along."

"A good boy," Tibball said. "I like 'em a bit tougher, but he's good."

The look switched to me.

"I didn't catch your name, sir. Vick, was it?"

"Michael Vick," Jewle cut in. "Amateur light-heavy champion long before you were in the game."

"Wouldn't have thought it," Tibball said. "Not with those peepers." He laughed. "Pardon me taking a liberty."

"Not at all," I said. "When your eyes go it's time to quit the game."

"True enough," he said, as I hooked off the horn-rims and gave them a quick polish. "But I'd have thought you'd have been more in the heavyweight class."

"Always spare like this," I said. "No use working for weight if it isn't natural."

"Too true," he said. He held out a hand. The one I took was cold and yet somehow moist.

"Drop in when you like, gentlemen," he told us. "Always glad to see new faces."

He turned back to the door from which he'd emerged. He waved a hand and the stone in the ring on his little finger flashed in the light. The door closed on him. Jewle stood for a moment looking about him, then he turned.

"Might as well be getting along."

We went down the wide stairs and across the room with its thud of fists on bags and stamp of feet and the quiet voices and the smell of liniment and sweat. The doorman flicked a finger to his cap as we went through. The cold air outside was so sudden and so clean that it almost hurt my lungs.

We were in Wardour Street before Jewle spoke.

"Well, what'd you think of Harry Tibball?"

"Don't know," I said. "He's smooth, but he's tough."

"He's a fake and he's a liar." There was a viciousness in his tone. "He's got the patter. Even that doesn't ring true." He halted. "Know what?" He held out a hand with spread fingers. "I'd give a couple of those to get my hands on him. He's as rotten as they come."

"You'll get him," I said. "Sooner or later they all slip up. But one thing's puzzling me. That handy-man of his—Conward. Wasn't Tibball drawing attention to himself by having a man like that about the place?"

"Conward hasn't a record," Jewle said. "Smirched a bit, perhaps, but he came out in the clear. The trouble is he's got potentialities. And Tibball isn't keeping him for nothing. It's not like Patsy Drew—the doorman. Patsy got on the downhill slide and ended up doing a warehouse-breaking job. Tibball took him on when he came out. Claimed to be a humanitarian. All for the underdog and all that guff."

"And Patsy's gone straight since?"

He grunted.

"With that mug of his? What else could he do?"

We were at Oxford Street. A taxi drew in at Jewle's hail and I took it. He said he might be going back to Mayworth Street.

"You'll let me know if anything breaks?"

He said he would. But he didn't say it like a man who's chock-a-block with hope.

Curiosity, my besetting sin or my best asset—it depends on how you look at it—couldn't be damped down and it was I who rang Jewle the following afternoon. I didn't get him but he later rang me at the flat.

"Nothing doing last night," he told me. "Gloria and her pals went back to their hotel—the Chattenden. Maybe that's where the fun and games take place. If it's in her room, then there's still nothing doing."

"Bad luck," I said. "But you'll let me know if anything breaks?"

He said he would, for what it was worth. I guessed he had more on Tibball than he'd told me or he wouldn't have been so bitter. Jewle generally takes his suspects merely, so to speak, in the line of business, but Tibball was different or he'd never have got under Jewle's skin.

"Something will come your way," I told him. "Tibball can't be as smart as all that."

Something did come Jewle's way and it came pretty soon. But it didn't do Jewle any good, as you'll see. He had to wait a bit longer for that.

2. PREVIEW (CONTD.)

CHRISTMAS came and went. Then the New Year was in and I still hadn't heard from Jewle. To be perfectly frank, it was only at rarer and rarer moments that I happened to think of the evening we'd spent together, and the only thing about it that was in any way vivid was not a restaurant or a gymnasium, but Jewle's obsession in the matter of Harry Tibball. It was more than a man's passion for his work or a rigidity of principles that made a man dedicated to the protection of the public who paid him. Jewle must have had scores of suspects on his books for this crime and that, but they counted for little compared with just the one man against whom he was waging a personal war.

I could grant that I didn't know all the facts. However friendly we might be, and however much he knew he could trust me, Jewle would never tell me all he knew or suspected about Tibball. He'd told me enough during that evening to justify at least the evening itself. But, as I said, the whole thing was receding more and more to the back of my mind. When I read the papers I might look for Tibball's name or wonder about some new jewel robbery or snatch, and then I'd forget the whole thing.

Even the faces of those I'd seen for the first time that night were getting more and more vague, and, except for Patsy Drew and, possibly, Frank Conward, I doubted if I'd have recognised any of them on the street. About Conward there was something curiously unforgettable: a kind of sleek insolence which had somehow impressed itself on my mind far more in the couple of minutes he had been in my view than had Tibball himself, in whose company I'd been for far longer and at closer quarters. The fact was, I'd seen a score of Tibball's kind in my time. Tibball had been in his milieu and his class. Conward had seemed out of his class. I couldn't be right, I admitted, but Conward seemed to me the more dangerous man.

Tibball's son-in-law, Fred Harban, had gone altogether from my mind. Had I been questioned I couldn't have given his height as other than just above average, his hair as dark, his build somewhat slim and his age as under forty, and if you think of that in the terms of, say, a description of a wanted man, it was not much better than useless. Even Gloria was vague. I remembered she was wearing an ermine wrap and that her frock looked expensive too, but any woman who'd seen her for as long as I would have observed far more than that. The face—oval, I think—had practically gone, but I did recall the voice: not that I could reproduce it in any way, but in remembering what Jewle had told me beforehand, that, however lavish the money Tibball had laid out on her, all the rough edges hadn't quite gone. It was her voice, then, that I chiefly remembered, even from the one sentence I'd heard. That's something I've had to train myself to spot at once—the precious, the effected, the arch and the gushing that are trying to be the real thing.

All that receding of things to the back of the mind made a touch of the unexpected when Jewle did ring me one afternoon early in February.

"Did you read about that snatch in Kilburn this morning?" I'd seen it, and no more. It was just one of those wages snatches that seem to be happening almost every week.

"Yes," I said. "I did notice it. Anything special about it?"

"Keep your eye on the papers," he told me, and there seemed to be a kind of exultation in his voice.

"That all you can tell me?"

"Well"—he hesitated—"there's a first-class chance we may tie it up with Mayworth Street. I may be seeing you."

I had another look at the early evening edition. There wasn't a lot about it; in fact, the chief thing that struck me was the almost criminal negligence of those responsible for the conveyance of large sums of money between banks and works. I suppose it's a kind of ingrained conservatism, in spite of the risks that get publicised at every snatch of the kind that comes off. This one was said to be for just over three thousand pounds, the week's wages at an engineering firm, with only a works' clerk and a driver in the small car that was carrying it. That car had been rammed just inside the private road that led to the works. A masked man had coshed both driver and clerk, had snatched the bag that was on the floor between them, and had slipped back to a third car that had had its engine running, and gone off at high speed. This third car, a stolen one, had been found abandoned; the car that had done the ramming was also a stolen one. The whole thing had taken only seconds and, though the main road there was not the busiest, there had been people about and quite a lot of traffic. One man, it was stated, had chased the one who had done the coshing, and had almost reached the car as it shot off.

I thought I should have heard from Jewle that night, but I didn't. And I heard nothing the next day. The papers were silent, too, though that might mean that the Yard thought it best to issue no information and to keep what it knew well under its hat. That's what I guessed—till I saw Jewle. He actually came along to Broad Street. I was with Norris when Bertha rang through to say he was there, and, since he mightn't care to talk in front of Norris, I went out to the reception room.

"You're looking a bit washed out," I said. "Been having a tough time over that Kilburn job?"

It was about the most tactless thing I could have said. Jewle had reached the boiling point and he had to ease his mind on someone or blow a valve. We adjourned to a tea-shop and found a reasonably quiet corner and when our order came he began unburdening his mind. I ought to say beforehand that I claim no credit for the change that came over him by the time he'd told me what he knew. It was only that he'd relieved his mind with some-one he knew would see his points of view. Once he was convinced of that, he was almost his old, quiet, determined self again.

"I thought we had a bit of luck," he said. "The chap who chased that car—a young army officer on leave, name of Vorne—got a look at the cosher. The black handkerchief sort of thing round his face partly slipped as he got into the moving car, so I got a description and something told me the cosher was Conward. You remember Conward, the ex-public-school boy? And I thought I had another bit of luck—keep this well under your hat, by the way. It isn't exactly regular, but I knew where to lay my hands on a photograph—a Press one—taken of Conward at the time of that burglary job at his uncle's. Conward was acquitted and it never was published. So I let Vorne have a look at it and he was prepared to swear the man he saw *was* Conward."

"Those side-burns give him away?"

"Oh no," he said. "Conward wasn't wearing 'em at the time of the photo, and he isn't wearing 'em now. They were just a bit of camouflage between jobs, if you know what I mean. But this is the point. We roped Conward in for questioning. The usual virtuous indignation, of course, though I knew it was all bluff. But it wasn't."

He leaned forward to make a point. I stared.

"He had an alibi?"

"Yes," he said. "A beautiful one. Absolutely unbeatable. Provided by—well, have a guess."

"Tibball?"

He gave that wry smile of his.

"Not bad. But just not right. It was our Gloria. She'd felt like a breath of country air that morning so Conward had been driving her around. They had lunch together at a private hotel near Cockfosters. When that snatch was made they were in the wilds of Hertfordshire. Never a soul who saw them, but why should there be? The car had a full tank, so they didn't stop for petrol."

"Beautiful, as you say. And she knew every detail of the route they'd taken?"

"Everything. All sorts of homely little details." He leaned forward again. "You see how it was worked out? She and he took out the car from Tibball's place at Hampstead. He left her and joined his pal and did the job. Then he hopped a Tube train which took him straight to Cockfosters where he rejoined the car. She'd been driving around and told him the corroborative details."

"Brazen perjury, though you can't prove it."

"I think you're right," he said, "but that won't stop us trying." He leaned back again. "What about another pot of tea?"

"Not for me."

"Well, I'll have a little one for myself," he said and snapped his fingers to the waitress. "Haven't had any lunch and I feel a bit peckish. A roll and butter might help, too."

"Feeling better now you've got everything off your chest?"

"It's not exactly that," he said. "Strictly between ourselves, I've had to take a bit of punishment every now and then from the Higher-Ups about the whole Tibball set-up. I even began thinking I'd got a maggot in my brain like it had been hinted I had. Now they all know different. From now on Tibball's going to get the full treatment."

"A kind of vindication."

"Well, whatever it is, it makes a man feel better. Let's leave it at that."

His order came. He gave a kind of satisfied nod to himself as he began spreading the butter on his roll.

Next came the Sellbrook Gardens snatch. I didn't connect it with Tibball and neither did Jewle. There were as yet no operational hall-marks established about Conward to connect him in any way, and, even if there had been and he was implicated, he'd doubtless have had a superlative alibi. Besides, it was a very big thing, though simplicity itself in execution.

A Mr. and Mrs. J. Hooper Wright had taken a furnished house in Sellbrook Gardens, Kensington, for a couple of months. It's a quiet backwater, quite unspoilt, but handy enough for town. I suppose one might call them Texas oil millionaires, but far from the cruder type. His son, for instance, was an official of sorts at the American Embassy. And that particular night there was a big reception at the Embassy, the Hooper Wrights naturally being there. It was actually one of the chief reasons for the trip to Europe.

The house itself wasn't large and it had a staff of only two—a kind of butler-handyman and a cook housekeeper. Both had been told not to wait up as it would be well after midnight when their employers returned. It was in fact just one o'clock. The Hooper

Wrights occupied separate bedrooms with a bathroom between. No sooner did she enter her room than she was struck down. The husband heard the faint sound and went through, and at once he was struck down, too. Neither saw a thing. The sleeping staff heard nothing.

The husband was the first to recover. He called the police and woke the staff. Except for shock, neither of the Hooper Wrights had suffered any real harm, but the whole of her jewellery had gone. When I say that a reward of £5,000 was offered for its recovery, you can guess its value. The police discovered that an entry had been made via a downstairs room, and the thief or thieves had simply been waiting concealed in the bedroom. No prints were found and there was no proof that it was other than a solo job. I knew nothing about it, by the way, except what I read in the papers.

That robbery was in the third week of March in that same year. I mention it only because it has a bearing on the story that's to follow. What is far more important is the matter of a burnt-out car which was found, while it was still blazing furiously, in the main road just north of Elmhurst in Bedfordshire. Elmhurst isn't its real name, but that's no matter.

The Sellbrook Gardens robbery took place on a Monday. It was the following Friday night when that burning car was seen. With regard to what was subsequently discovered, it was uncannily lucky that the returning empty motor-coach that first saw it should have been carrying a fire extinguisher. The driver and his mate got the fire under control. The body of a man was clumped down across the steering column.

November isn't necessarily the worst month for fog. March is a bad month, especially if the days are sunny. And all that week the days had been sunny with patchy fog forming at night. Patchy fog is the dangerous kind. When visibility is nearing nil then traffic moves warily or stays put, but when fog is patchy a driver is apt to get a false confidence. The road is suddenly clear and he treads on the accelerator. When the fog closes down abruptly again, that's when he's likely to run smack into trouble. And that's what this driver did. He'd hit a telegraph pole at such a speed that the car was a wreck and he himself had been dead before he knew it.

Nothing about that accident got into the London papers. That kind of happening is far too common for that. I didn't know about it till the Monday, and then it was the evening papers that carried a story. It made my eyes pop out of my head. *Harry Tibball was the dead man in the car.*

I was in the flat at the time and it was just before our evening meal, but as soon as I saw that news about Tibball, I made for the phone and tried to get hold of Jewle. I was told he was away on a case. I wondered if it was that burning car job, and the usual curiosity made me want to be sure, so I rang another acquaintance who did happen to be at the Yard and he told me in confidence that it *was* the Elmhurst job that Jewle was on.

But there was something far more startling to come. I saw it in the morning paper. The context was bewildering. I didn't know anything about a burglary or robbery at Elmhurst and yet there'd apparently been one. What that paper said was that there'd been an arrest in connection with that robbery. The man charged with it was a Frank Conward. The arrest had taken place two days previously, that is to say, the very next day after the case of the burning car. Evidently the police had been holding information up.

Conward was remanded, bail being refused. When the case would be tried I didn't know, but probably not for a time. The police might have loose ends to tie up and, if I knew Jewle, there'd be no trial unless the outcome was very, very certain. But I did think it a good moment to give Jewle a ring. He sounded most cheerful.

"Hallo, sir! Nice to hear you again. Sorry I couldn't put you wise to what's been happening."

"Didn't expect you to," I said. "I knew you'd be busy."

"Still am. Won't be long now before the ball starts rolling. Everything's coming along quite nicely."

He was right. Con ward's case was on in very quick time. The full story as reported in the Press and supplemented by what I later heard from Jewle himself, is, in its essentials, this.

Louis Speer, born Luigi Spiro, came to England soon after Mussolini's rise to power. His father had had a jewellery business in Rome and Luigi had carried it on after the father's death. Another brother was in the same line of business in America. Luigi became a naturalised British citizen and changed his name to Louis Speer. His wife died in 1945. The only child, Carlotta, was educated entirely in England, and, as told me by Jewle, who saw her, was good-looking, charming in manner, and reported on as highly competent by her immediate superior in the B.B.C., in whose foreign news broadcasting department she was working at the time of the robbery. She had a little flat in town and usually came home on Saturdays when not detained by work. The home was "Littlecroft", Elmhurst. Many of the fast trains stop at Elmhurst Junction, and that makes the place quickly and smoothly accessible from town.

Speer's office was at 3, Bridge Street, Hatton Garden, and there he also carried on a modest but high-class manufacturing business—special jobs for the trade. He employed only two men. Flamboyance isn't the hall-mark of the diamond industry. Speer, compared with some of the bigger merchants, was in a small way, but his credit was good and his reputation impeccable. His standing was as good in Antwerp, where he occasionally bought stones at the famous Diamond Club. At Conward's trial that last fact became of considerable importance.

And here may I make something clear. I'm trying to keep all this as simple as possible since it's being unfolded, as it were, at a sitting and not in occasional gulps, which was the way the public swallowed it as the trial proceeded. That's why I introduce the minimum of names: only those, in fact, which might have a bearing on the story that's ultimately to come. Take the two men, for instance, whom Speer employed. One was the cutter, a man of fifty or so named Bernard Brittle. The other was a worker in gold and other metals. Work was done to the blueprints of Speer himself or an outside designer. Speer put Brittle in general charge when he himself was absent. Both the men knew that Speer was in Antwerp during the week of the robbery. Both expected him to bring back a parcel of stones. When he returned on the Wednesday, two days before the robbery, neither expected to be told what business Speer had done in Antwerp. They would know that later when some special job or other arose out of it. Not that Speer was necessarily more secretive than his fellows: it's just that publicity is never courted in the diamond trade. What the men did know was that when Speer came back either from the Garden or from Antwerp with a parcel of stones, he never left them in the office safe, but took them home for a private examination and further appraisal.

So much for the Hatton Garden end. At Elmhurst Speer's detached house was at the north of the town, and just down a side road. It was a modest place with a fairly large garden, and run by a housekeeper named Kate Howard and a general maid. Mrs. Howard was just over sixty. Her husband saw to the garden, but had died in the previous January and Speer hadn't as yet engaged another man. Changes would be involved. The Howards had lived in two rooms in the house, but a new man would have to come in from outside.

And so to the Friday night. Speer arrived home at the usual time. His bus from the station dropped him at the end of his road and then he had a walk of about a couple of hundred yards. He spent the hour before dinner in what was known as the study: a kind of private room of his own with french windows opening on the main lawn and flower beds. He had his dinner at seven o'clock. He never drank with it, but at nine o'clock Mrs. Howard, invariably during the winter months, brought him a hot Irish whisky. She did so that night. When she left him, Speer was working at a side table with a large sheet of drawing-paper in front of him. Mrs. Howard went up to her room, at the southeast end of the house, which overlooked the garden. Since her husband's death she had slept badly, and she would read in bed till all hours, hoping for sleep. The maid also went up to her bedroom just after nine o'clock. Both rooms had wireless sets which had to be kept low, since Speer objected to any noise.

It was a moonlight night and, but for the patchy fog, visibility would have been perfect everywhere. It just happened to be quite good in Speer's garden. Mrs. Howard, nerves, as she said, always taut, heard a faint noise from outside. It turned out to be a pail that had been kicked: a pail left on the crazy paving by the french windows of the study. She had bought a couple of rose bushes at the Elmhurst Woolworth's that afternoon and had put them in water till she had time in the morning to plant them.

She heard the noise and went to the window. It was open at the bottom and she pushed it up and looked out. A man, startled too by the sudden noise, was just in front of the french windows and he actually looked up at her. That was why she could identify him as Conward.

"Who are you? What d'you want?"

The man did a queer thing. In a flash he had disappeared, but apparently inside the study. Almost in the same second two men emerged from the study and scurried round the side of the house. In a moment there was the sound of a car starting and, with what Mrs. Howard described as a tremendous roar, it shot off towards the main road. The study and her bedroom were at the back of the house and she didn't see the car.

She put on a dressing-gown and hurried downstairs. The study door was shut but the french windows were wide open. Speer was lying on the floor by the table where he had been working. There was blood on his head. She rang the police. The man on station duty said someone would be along at once. Then she rang the doctor. She went up to the maid's room. Gladys Trent was asleep but she roused her and then she suddenly felt faint. Gladys got some sal volatile from the bathroom and by the time Mrs. Howard had recovered, the police were in the house. Gladys, by the way, had heard nothing till Mrs. Howard woke her.

What the police found was this. While Speer was at dinner the old treacle trick had been used to remove enough glass from the study window for a hand to be inserted to turn the key, and after that the curtains had masked the hole. That job had been done by one man, so Jewle thought, and later both had returned.

It was a kind of safety precaution. Had anything been discovered about the hole in the window, the police would have been there. Speer, when he came round, said he had drunk his whisky and was settling to work again when he heard a sound in the room. He thought it was Mrs. Howard coming back, and that was all he knew beyond a crashing blow on his skull.

The safe door was open. There was something special about that safe. Not long after he bought the house, Speer had had the study panelled in oak and the safe inserted behind the panelling. A concealed boss could be pressed and the special panel could be moved back along a slot to reveal the safe. Such precautions were necessary in view of the value of the stuff that he sometimes brought home. But that night the thieves had been unlucky. Doubtless, through some unknown grapevine, they'd expected a parcel of stones from Antwerp—to the value of £10,000 or so—but Speer had bought nothing in Antwerp. All the safe had held was a certain amount of cash and some oddments of jewellery worth about three hundred pounds.

Conward got four years. Jewle rang me after it was all over. He said he'd clean forgotten to pay me for that dinner at the Tibball restaurant that night, and he proposed taking me out to a really posh place, just to celebrate. It was during the meal that he filled in some details about the events at Elmhurst.

"We had two of the most tremendous pieces of luck," he told me. "The first was knowing who the dead man was. Things were a bit flurried when Mrs. Howard rang the local station. The call had also come in about the burning car and, finally, Fusson—the Inspector—went on to Speer's place and his sergeant took over the car job. And know what the sergeant's name is? Smithers."

I didn't get it.

"You remember Smithers? No, I was forgetting. It was Clark we saw at that gymnasium. Smithers was on duty that night. Anyhow, our Smithers was a younger brother of this Sergeant Smithers, and the sergeant had dropped in at the gym one afternoon to see his brother at work. He'd spoken to Tibball there and that's how he knew who the dead man was. We were got in touch with at once.

"The other thing was almost as lucky. We'd been keeping a discreet eye on Conward and he was seen to call in at the office of a shipping company. To cut it short, he'd booked a passage for America on the *Durania*, which was sailing that very Saturday evening. Nothing suspicious about that, but when we had more than an idea Conward helped do the job, then we warned Liverpool. Conward was actually picked up there on the Saturday afternoon, just as he was going aboard. He was wearing glasses and had on a false moustache, but that was damn silly. He couldn't change his passport.

"The car was a stolen Bentley with false number-plates. It had been lifted the previous night and kept ready. The two must have thought the police would be throwing a net round Elmhurst and that's why they took risks. The idea was for Conward to be driven that night to Liverpool or near enough, and then the car'd be ditched and Tibball would take a train back. Conward had hoped to be taking a parcel of diamonds to America." He chuckled. "The bag he was carrying was his own and it had a pair of beautiful concealed pockets. A nice packet of diamonds should have been in it, but wasn't. There wasn't even any of the missing jewellery."

"Wasn't Conward hurt at all?"

"He'd the luck of the devil. A scratch or two and some bruises and that's all. They were heading north and he'd been driving, so Tibball's side got the full shock of that telegraph post. Conward shoved his body across the wheel, took everything that might have identified Tibball, grabbed the bag and set the car alight. Then he hopped it. How he got to Liverpool we don't know, and shan't unless he tells us. Probably thumbed a lift to Birmingham, say, and took a train from there."

"Poor Conward," I said. "My heart bleeds for him. Nobody ought to have had such bad luck. If that car had really burnt out, you'd still be wondering who the dead man was. By the way, any idea who tipped Tibball off to the likely parcel of diamonds?"

"Don't know," he said. "We've ideas but can't prove them. We've nothing on the two likeliest sources—Speer's two men. Both have clean sheets and Speer spoke well of both of them. Speer isn't too good, by the way. That smack on the skull—with a spanner probably—gave him a very bad shaking. His daughter says he's thinking of retiring. He's in a nursing home at the moment. Selling his house, though, and may be joining his brother in the States."

"And what's happening to Tibball's properties?"

He said he'd heard a whisper that they'd be coming on the market. The daughter, of course, would get anything he left. And that was about all I learned of the affair from Jewle that night. You can't talk crime clean through such a dinner he stood me that night. We even had champagne.

But I was to pick up one or two things later when I happened to run across Jewle. For instance, the mystery was solved of where Tibball got his information about Speer's supposed parcel of stones.

Speer did sell up and go with his daughter Carlotta to America. The man who bought the Bridge Street business began to have suspicions of Brittle. A trap was laid for him and a man was caught working one night at the safe. Brittle was in it and he got twelve months.

The Tibball properties were unsold as one lot but were bought separately. Gloria and her husband dropped clean out and Jewle had no idea of their whereabouts. Sooner or later, he assured me hopefully, they'd pop up somewhere.

"I'd like to have seen the whole set-up under lock and key," he told me, "but you can't have everything in this world. Not that I'm dissatisfied with what we did do. Tibball's out of my hair and Conward's cooked for life. Not bad to be going on with." He grinned. "Funny, isn't it? Used to wake up most mornings wondering about Tibball. Now he rarely even comes into my mind."

"Nor mine," I said. "And I don't know that I'm particularly anxious to see Conward again, or hear about him either."

"You won't," he said. "He's done for. When he comes out he'll probably do another job and that'll put him inside for a real good stretch. And by then I'll probably be a grandfather."

Jewle was wrong. I was even more wrong. But that's to do with the main story.

3. CARLOTTA SPEER

IT WAS a September afternoon, three years later. I was at Broad Street, killing time in the absence of Norris, who'd gone up town to discuss business with one of the big stores. I was killing time, because that's just what it was. Bertha could have run things just as well as I: if a client called she could have taken a message and reported the managing-director as out and fixed, if necessary, an appointment.

The fact is that I was about to take a fortnight's holiday, beginning the following morning. My wife had already left for Sweden with a cultural group to which she belongs, and I hadn't made up my mind how my own fortnight should be spent. In a way it was part of the holiday to have, as it were, the right of self-determination: to have, within fourteen days' space, the freedom to go anywhere, everywhere or nowhere. And in case you're suspecting rifts in our household, let me say that both Bernice and I agree that a short holiday out of each other's company is a binding cement in married life. When one returns to normalcy it isn't normalcy at all. The familiar faces across a breakfast table are somehow new. It's like beginning married life all over again. You feel somehow that whereas things were always pretty good, now they're going to be infinitely and adventurously better.

I was working at a crossword when Bertha came in and I was so absorbed in a clue that I didn't wonder why she hadn't rung through. Bertha's been our secretary-receptionist ever since we took over the Agency and she's like one of the family.

"Might I slip out for half an hour?" she said. "A friend's just rung up who wants to see me. I shan't be longer."

"Be as long as you like," I said, "I'd rather like to go at five."

"Oh, I'll be back long before that," she told me. "I've plugged in the electric kettle and everything's ready for your tea."

"I'll be all right," I said, and, as she went through the door, "By the way, give him my love."

It was a laboured joke and she didn't see it for a moment. Then she blushed furiously, but she was far from displeased.

"You do say some things!" she told me archly. "And don't forget to unplug the kettle."

It was a good retort. I'd done that very thing a week or two back and we'd had to buy a new kettle. I couldn't help smiling as I shifted my quarters to the reception office. What we'd do without Bertha I didn't like to guess.

I made myself a large cup of tea, helped myself to biscuits from the tin in Bertha's desk, and settled down again to my crossword. Then the telephone rang.

"Is that the Broad Street Detective Agency?"

"Yes," I said. "Who's speaking, please?"

I was holding the receiver in one hand and putting my crossword into a drawer with the other. Everything, as you see, was still sort of casual and holiday eve.

"This is Mrs. Harvey Dawson and I'm speaking from the Somerton Hotel. May I speak to—er—someone in charge?"

"You *are* speaking to someone in charge, Mrs. Dawson. My name's Travers"—I spelt it out for her—"I'm a director."

"Oh!" she said, and, "Just a moment, Mr. Travers."

She cupped the receiver. A youngish woman, I was telling myself. American accent but far from aggressively so. A low, rather throaty and far from unpleasant voice.

"Are you there?"

"Yes" I said.

"Then I'd like you to take on a very confidential assignment. For me and my husband really. Unfortunately, he's just recovering from a cold and doesn't wish to go out, so could you see us here?"

"I think that could be arranged," I said. "When do you suggest?"

"Well, what about now?"

"Sorry, but it just can't be done, Mrs. Dawson. The managing-director's out and I'm alone here at the moment."

"This evening? At about eight o'clock?"

"Yes," I said. "I think I could manage that. In your room will it be?"

"Yes. Room 78. The Somerton Hotel. It's just off St. James's."

"I'll find it. And just one preliminary thing, Mrs. Dawson. We like prospective clients to give us at least a rough idea as to what the assignment is. You see, there are certain branches of enquiry which we never undertake. Divorce work, for instance."

"It's nothing like that," she assured me. "It's very confidential, but nothing like that."

"That's fine," I said. "And might I ask, just for the records, why you picked us for this assignment? Were we recommended, for instance, or did you see our advertisement?"

"Oh, the advertisement."

"Thank you, Mrs. Dawson. At eight o'clock, then, at your room at the Somerton Hotel."

So that was that. I'd intended to dine at my club and then begin my holiday by seeing a well-reviewed Italian film, but this interview at the Somerton Hotel might prove just as interesting.

I don't suppose that in the whole course of our existence we'd had more than a couple of American clients, and neither case was very remunerative or particularly interesting. This one sounded as if it might be rather different.

As for that bit about a possibility of our having been recommended, that was just a routine, though necessary, question. It's as well to know as much as one can about a client beforehand. Quite a good few are tricky customers and once or twice we've found that out too late. But a recommendation means that with tact we can make enquiries of the one who did the recommending, if there's the least sign of anything fishy.

Norris wasn't back at five o'clock but Bertha was well on time and I left as planned. I went to the flat, put on a more sedate suit and walked to the club. It was while I was having dinner that I remembered I'd said nothing to Bertha about a possible client. Not that it mattered. If the job didn't eventuate, then nobody need be the wiser. If it did, then Norris should be all the more gratified.

The Somerton is a quiet, high-class little hotel, much favoured, I was to learn, by Canadians. I learned that last fact at the club. The well-informed member whom I'd been suavely pumping was on the board of an hotel group and he told me what hotels were favoured by various nationalities. He said he'd never look for an American at the Somerton. English county—yes: and the Canadians. And why Canadians? He didn't know. Probably some highly personal publicity. Why, for example, did so many visitors from the States favour Brown's Hotel? I knew, but I let him tell me. It was because Teddy Roosevelt had held his wedding reception there.

I didn't come into contact with the clientele of the Somerton. The commissionaire gave me a quick look as I came through the swing door but he saw nothing suspicious and I went across the hall to the stairs. Room 78 was on the first floor and it turned out to be a tiny suite of sitting-room, bathroom and bedroom. Before the bell had hardly stopped ringing, the door opened.

"Mr. Travers?"

"Yes," I said, and he held out his hand. He was Harvey Dawson: a tallish, very thin man, with dark hair and a trim, dark beard.

"Sorry you've had to come all the way here," he said, and took my hat. "As my wife told you, I've had rather a nasty cold." He gave a gaunt sort of smile. "Don't be alarmed. I guess the germs have skedaddled. They ought to—the stuff I've taken. Sit down, won't you?"

It was a pleasant evening and he indicated a chair by the open window that looked out across an open space with some trees.

"You'll have a drink?"

"No, no," I told him quickly. "I always keep a clear head for business."

He laughed, then—"Excuse me a minute." He turned towards the partly open door at the far corner of the room.

"Honey! . . . Mr. Travers is here."

"Coming."

The voice sounded a bit distant.

"You here on holiday or on business, Mr. Dawson?"

"Well, both," he said. "I was in the hotel trade but my health wasn't too good and I sold out."

I didn't tell him so but he didn't look too well. The face was rather sallow and there was too much dark under the eyes. In any case, before I could comment his wife came in, and I was getting to my feet.

She was a tremendous surprise. I put him at at least fifty, but she didn't look a day over thirty. It was extraordinary anticipation on my part, but she reminded me of a Raphael madonna.

Her hair was black, parted in the middle and drawn back behind the head. Two slim earrings in red matched the warm red of the lips. The eyes were dark and intense.

"How d'you do?" She held out a slim hand, then turned to her husband. "Harvey, you haven't given Mr. Travers a drink."

"He wouldn't have one," he told her defensively.

"You sure?" she asked me.

"Quite sure. Nice of you both all the same."

"Then let's make ourselves comfortable," she said, and there seemed to me to be a touch of uneasiness. The voice had no particular quality, but it was pleasant and low-pitched. There was still only a trace of accent.

There was a fireplace with an electric fire in the room but it was far too warm an evening to turn it on. Yet we sat round it as if it had been winter. I was in the middle. She was about five feet six and slimly made. The nyloned legs were crossed and the black skirt of the frock was drawn over her knees, and then she gave me a rather nervous smile.

"Harvey says I'm to do the talking, Mr. Travers, but if there's anything you want to ask him, please do so."

"Fine," I said. "I'll do that."

"Smoke if you feel like it," he told me. "I've given it up. Honey, you find Mr. Travers a cigarette." He looked round. "Never know where that box is."

"No, no," I said. "I smoke far too much as it is."

A couple of nervous people. You expect nervousness when people step into what I'd call the Broad Street consulting room, but here the one at a disadvantage was myself. I felt a little quiver of anticipation, though I could never have guessed in fifty years what I was going to hear.

"I'm not American, Mr. Travers. I expect you've guessed that."

"Should I?" I said, and smiled.

"I'm actually British," she was going on. "Legally, of course, I'm American, on account of being married to Harvey, but I've only been in the States just over three years."

Harvey gave a little cough.

"Perhaps, dear, we ought to let Mr. Travers see our credentials."

She was snapping the coral knob of the black handbag and beginning to take some papers out. I stopped her.

"Please, no. Quite unnecessary, Mr. Dawson. After all, you haven't seen *my* credentials."

"That's nice of you, sir," Harvey said. "I guess we can take each other for granted. Sorry I interrupted you, dear."

"Well, there's one important question," she said. "We're not in your office—I know that, Mr. Travers—but is everything confidential?"

The same old question and the same old answer, and the same old joke.

"Mind you, if you told me you'd committed a murder, I still wouldn't divulge the fact. All I'd do would be not to take your case. If you told me you were going to commit a murder that might be different. I wouldn't take your case and I probably wouldn't keep quiet. Otherwise you need have no fears. Even thumb-screws wouldn't drag anything out of me."

"Mr. Travers is right," Harvey told her. "The goodwill of his business depends on secrecy and mutual confidence."

I said it definitely did.

"It was just a question," she said. "All the same I'm glad it's that way." She moistened her lips, then leaned slightly towards me. I caught a whiff of the scent from her hair.

"Mr. Travers, did you ever hear of a robbery at a house in Elmhurst? Nearly four years ago?"

I almost went back in my seat. I don't know how I managed it, but I don't think I gave anything of a start. I looked at the ceiling and frowned.

"Elmhurst. It rings a bell somewhere." I pretended to have it. "Weren't two men implicated and wasn't one of them killed?"

"Yes," she said. "It was my father's house and he was badly injured by one of the men. My maiden name is Speer. Carlotta Speer."

I half-raised a hand as if for silence and leaned back reflectively in the chair.

"I remember it now. Your father was struck down by one of the men. Later, if I remember rightly, he went to America."

"Yes," she said. "I was working in the foreign broadcast department of the B.B.C.—I *am* Italian by birth, or didn't you know?"

"I don't think I did," I told her unblushingly. "I did wonder something of the sort when I first met you just now. Please take that remark the right way. I mean—well, whatever you are, English, Italian, American, I have an idea you're a very charming person."

"Now that's real nice of you," Harvey said.

"I'm not so sure," she told him, and smiled. "Mr. Travers may be a diplomatist. But about this robbery, and this is the highly confidential thing. I wasn't at home that night. I had a little flat in North London and the police didn't get into touch with me till the next morning, so I wasn't actually present when the robbery took place. I only know what my father told me and what the police discovered. The thieves, for instance, didn't get anything like what they expected."

"I remember that. As a matter of fact, quite a lot about that case is coming back. Wasn't there some talk of your father bringing a parcel of stones back from Antwerp, or somewhere, and hadn't the thieves had a private tip that they'd be in the safe?"

"Yes," she said. And then, rather slowly—"At least, that was the story my father gave out."

"The parcel of stones *was* there?"

"No, not that."

"Excuse me, dear, but shall I put on the light?"

He was right. She was sitting with her back to the window and I could hardly see her face. Twilight had closed down pretty suddenly.

"No," she said. "I like it like this if Mr. Travers doesn't mind. It helps me to think."

"I rather like it, too," I said. "Dark nights come all too quickly. Just carry on in your own way, Mrs. Dawson."

I think it must have been involuntarily that I'd said I'd liked it there in that half-light. There's plenty of traffic along St. James's even at that hour but from where we sat there was scarcely the faintest sound of it. Through the window there was the green of the trees and we might have been miles away from town.

"My father wasn't in a big way of business," she went on, "but he did exceptionally good work and he was implicitly trusted. That was why he had those jewels in his safe that night. They belonged to one of the best families in England and my father had agreed to buy them and to make duplicates. Paste duplicates of course—"

"Excuse me, but wouldn't that kind of work be rather out of your father's line? I mean paste?"

"False stones didn't matter," she told me. "It was the settings that had to be reproduced, even if they were in cheaper metals. They had to be perfect, undetectable replicas."

"I understand."

She gave a little sigh.

"I'm afraid I've begun rather at the wrong end, but it's rather a complicated story. My father went to America, as you know, and worked with his brother at Wensburg. That's in Long Island. What I couldn't understand was why he *should* want to work with my uncle. He ought to have had plenty of money and he could have had a modest place of his own in, say, New York, but when I spoke to him about it, all he'd say was that he liked it that way. And then, a year ago, he died. I think he knew he was very ill indeed, and that's why he told me the truth.

"You see, Mr. Travers, he was a scrupulously honest man. Everything about that jewellery, considering who the owners were, had to be kept very secret. Their good name had to be preserved at all costs, and there hadn't to be any bad publicity, and that's why my father told the police there was nothing of any real value in the safe. And not only that. Unless the owners were prepared to stage a fake burglary, and that was unthinkable, nothing could be recovered from insurance. And that's why my father was a poor man and literally had to work for my uncle. You see, he'd paid the value of the jewels to the owners himself."

"A lot of money?"

"I believe in the neighbourhood of forty thousand pounds. The jewellery was worth more than that but the family appreciated what my father had done and that was the agreed price. You see, duplicates still had to be made to cover the loss, my father supplying the designs from what he remembered. I believe there were also photographs."

"Yes," I said. "Your father was certainly one in a million."

"His good name was at stake," Dawson cut in. "He had to make it clear that he wasn't implicated in the robbery."

"Exactly. But tell me one thing, Mrs. Dawson. Why shouldn't your father have stayed on in business and made those replicas himself?"

"I'm glad you asked that," she said. "He was a very honourable man and he hated telling lies to the police. He knew that sooner or later they'd suspect something from his manner and that's why he left England. He ran away, if you prefer it like that."

"I'm beginning to remember more and more," I said. "Didn't something come out subsequently about one of your father's own men being implicated in that robbery?"

"Yes. A man named Brittle. He occasionally came to the house. I never did trust him. And he certainly knew all about the safe. Harvey Dawson got up and switched on the light. I'd been so absorbed in his wife's story that I hadn't realised how dark the room had suddenly got. The curtains weren't drawn. Apparently we weren't over-looked and it was such a warm night that it was good to have more air."

"I think I've got everything," I said. "What I don't see is what we can do about it."

She hesitated for a moment. Out of the corner of my eye I saw her shift nervously in her chair.

"It's difficult," she said, "but when my father died I didn't see why he should have been virtually ruined and only to enrich the one who took that jewellery. That was the man Conward, the one who got four years. The other man was killed. But the jewellery was never traced. I know that. I made it my business to know it. It wasn't found on Conward when he was arrested. He was making for America and yet he didn't have the jewellery. So don't you think he was changing his plans and going there till things quietened down?"

"Having disposed of the jewellery meanwhile?"

"But how could he? He made straight for Liverpool and he was arrested virtually as soon as he got there."

"You think he put the jewellery in some safe place? Hid it or cached it?"

"We think so," Harvey Dawson said. "That's why we thought it was worth a comparatively small investment trying to find out." I had to smile.

"England's a mighty small country compared with the States, but there's also a mighty lot of country between Elmhurst and Liverpool. I'd rather look for a needle in a haystack, even if I didn't know what haystack."

"Well"—he was doing the smiling now—"we do have an idea where there might be a haystack. Or there's someone who might lead us to it."

"You mean Conward? When he comes out?"

"Yes," he said. "And that's in ten days' time."

His wife gave me no chance to comment.

"Look, Mr. Travers, it's surely worth a chance. We thought so, or we'd never really have crossed the Atlantic. All you'd have to do is follow Conward. If we're wrong, then we're wrong, but you'll get your fees all the same."

"What *are* your fees?" That was Dawson again.

"Probably no more than five pounds a day per man on the job, plus expenses. But aren't we getting a bit ahead? I'd like to know more before I considered accepting the job. For instance, it seems to me that even for what you called comparative money, you're wanting to take a very long chance. Why couldn't there have been a third man who was there to take the jewellery back to town?"

Dawson smiled almost pityingly.

"You can't be serious about that. I'm not in your class as an investigator. All I do is read quite a lot of whodunits, and perhaps that's one of the reasons why I let myself get interested in this business. But a third man! Conward was making for America. It came out in court that his grip had a special fitment to take the jewellery."

"That's something I'd forgotten," I told him. "Don't forget I only read about that case in the papers, and that when I came here I hadn't the least notion why. But one other thing I'd like to know, and in the strictest confidence, Mrs. Dawson. Who were the family that owned the jewellery?"

"I don't know," she said. "That was one part of the secret my father wouldn't divulge. He'd given his word, and that had to include me, too."

"Well, that's that. But now to the really important question. Suppose—and it's one of the biggest supposes I've ever put forward—suppose I recover the jewellery—"

"A bonus of ten per cent of its value."

"I'm not thinking of that, Mr. Dawson, though it sounds highly gratifying. What I'm thinking of is this. My firm's best asset is its absolute probity and I intend to keep it that way. So what's the position in law? Does the jewellery go back to the possibly fine old titled family, who thereupon privately refund the money they received from Mr. Speer? Do you take the jewellery and nothing said?"

"But surely—"

"Just a moment." She interrupted him. "Mr. Travers either trusts us, or he doesn't, to do the right thing. But that isn't the first thing. The first thing is to get hold of the jewellery. After that we can decide what's to be done, but always on one condition. There's to be no publicity. That would mean smirching my father's name."

There had been a certain bitterness in her tone, and then she suddenly smiled.

"Do you know how we thought about this, Mr. Travers? Like a sort of adventure, only you'd be paid for it. Like hunting for buried treasure. Some friends of ours did that in the States. Can't you see it like that? And let the ethics come later?"

"And there's no immediate hurry," Dawson said. "Conward won't be out till ten days' time."

"You're sure of that?"

"Our information was to that effect," his wife said. "Naturally you'd have to check it. It might be disastrous if you failed at the start to make contact."

"I'll do that," I said, and got to my feet. "May we leave it like this? By the way, you'll still be here?"

"Oh yes," she said. "We like it here."

"Then what I suggest is this. We've ten days. Agreed? Then let me have a week to make certain preliminary investigations. This may sound flamboyant, but we have various contacts with what's known as 'the underworld', and we might get some very useful hints on what really happened to that jewellery. You agree?"

"Sounds reasonable," Dawson said.

"Glad you think so. And for that you'll be charged a very modest fee—say ten pounds—if we don't agree to take the case. That'll still give you time to use another firm."

"I'm all in favour," she said. "What about you, dear?"

"Sounds more reasonable than ever. Do we have to sign anything?"

"Just a gentleman's agreement," I said. "If we agree to take the main case, the contract on mutually acceptable terms can be signed later."

A couple of minutes and I was walking towards St. James's. After the quiet of that room the few taxis and buses made a noise that seemed almost deafening. It was somehow like being in another world. And that, it suddenly struck me, was just what it was.

4. BUSMAN'S HOLIDAY

A NEW world it was: a world which included my holiday. A new world because it was the old world—the world of four years ago. Like innumerable other people, I'd made long journeys by plane, and been transported from one world to another with an abruptness that eliminated, as it were, all the old gradual acclimatisations. This was the same thing. If I were to insinuate myself into that case so as to be a part of it, then I'd have to transport myself back in time.

But to go back only a short space of time: to that long hour I'd just spent in that room at the Somerton Hotel. It may have struck you that some of the things I said, especially towards the end, hadn't too much relevancy, and you'd have been right. What I was trying to do was to make time while I came to definite decisions. There were wheels within wheels, to quote a favourite remark of Jewle's—already, you see, I was back in that case—and the wheels I had to watch were highly important from two points of view: that of the firm and that of myself.

A few months back we'd been inveigled by another firm of enquiry agents into taking a case that had certain similarities: to pick up a man just being discharged from jail, to follow him to where he settled down that night, and then report the address to the client. For a fee of ten pounds that seemed money for nothing, but when the man in question was murdered that very night, things were vastly different. Only some artistic prevarication and the luck of the very devil saved us from very serious consequences.

As for the strictly personal side of things, there was no reluctance at all about taking on the preliminaries that I'd mentioned. In fact, once more I'd had an enormous deal of luck. Everything had played into my hands. Let me explain.

Sometimes on a case I think work should be done beyond what that case apparently demands. I always let Norris have his head. He's not only the managing-director, but he's what those words say he is. But that doesn't stop my employing one of our own operatives and paying for him. After all, it's almost like taking money from one pocket and putting it into another, since the expenses ultimately find their way to the client's bill. And, in something like the same way, I could make that preliminary work on that old robbery into a private matter—at least for the next week. Bertha knew nothing about it, thanks to an oversight on my part, and Norris knew still less. Very well then: for a week I could treat myself to a busman's holiday.

I suppose you know quite a lot of fools who proclaim that they're never so happy as when at work. One accepts the term as meaning congenial work. Well, I'm that kind of fool too. Enormous luck, as I've said. At least a week of my holiday was provided for. If at the end of it I decided that the firm might take on the case, then just a little prevarication could be arranged with the Harvey Dawsons and Norris could take over. It mightn't, of course, be so simple as that, but, pleased with myself as I was when I thought of it, I saw no difficulties. Maybe Norris might even ask me to lend a hand in that second week.

So, late as it was already that night, I fetched a bottle of beer from the refrigerator, got a pipe going and settled down to a plan of campaign. The flat would be my headquarters and I hoped to get home every night. That was why I'd told the Harvey Dawsons never to ring the office, and to ring me only at my private number after nine o'clock at night, and then only if anything really important turned up.

The Harvey Dawsons, I said to myself. Quiet, homely people, though she obviously of a better social class than he. But what did I actually know about them? What else did I need to know? The answer seemed just nothing. Speer's daughter was merely a conveyor of information. But what about Speer himself?

Something peculiar at once suggested itself. Carlotta was an only daughter. She had thought so much of her father as to throw up what was presumably a good job and excellent prospects to accompany her father to America. Doubtless he thought as much of her. And yet it hadn't been till he was almost on his death-bed that he'd told her the truth about that jewellery. Why shouldn't he have told her long beforehand? Surely he trusted her sufficiently to tell her something which, once they were in America, was of no vital importance? And something that reflected far from unfavourably on himself? Did he think, say, that a new scandal might break out to implicate himself, if the present owner of the jewellery died and the jewellery, as heirlooms, had to be produced for the executors?

I didn't know, and I couldn't find any answers. Then it struck me that I might as well get into touch with our American agents in New York. The more I knew about Speer, the better, and maybe something might be unearthed that might somehow help at my own end. An air-mail letter would do the trick. It would allow for more information to be given, and leave at least a couple of days for enquiries and then a cabled reply.

I wrote the letter and posted it straight away. It asked for as much information as possible about a late Louis Speer who had a brother in Wensburg, Long Island, in the jewellery business. I'd like the amount of his estate, if he'd left any. And I'd have to have a cabled reply within seven days, however little time that left for enquiries. The account was to be a personal one and sent to my private address, like the cable. But when I came back from posting that letter, I somehow didn't feel like doing any more thinking. The night, we're told, brings counsel. I thought I'd give it a chance.

The fine September spell was continuing and that sunny morning was as perfect as any in the year. But it didn't tinge with gold my matutinal ideas: it merely brought me down to earth. Bright daylight and clear air made me sure of one thing only: that the assignment which, but for some hazy scruples, I might have taken on, was about as crazy a one as I'd run across in the course of a long career.

"Just get the jewellery and then we'll discuss ethics," the lady had said in so many words. Nice thinking, Mrs. Dawson. You're wasting your talents, Mrs. Dawson. You ought to be a delegate to United Nations.

That was the mood I was in, and I still don't find it unreasonable. Go back, for instance, to that night at Elmhurst. Tibball and Conward leave in a desperate hurry, with the almost certainty that the police are already being warned. The car crashes into the telegraph pole. Conward miraculously escapes serious injury, but at any moment a car may come by. It may pass him in the fog and it may not, so he has to work quickly: put the jewellery into the travelling bag, hoist Tibball's body across the wheel, light some paper to start the fire, and be sure the car's alight, and then be off down the road with the bag. But always, of course, watching each way for the lights of a car and ready to nip out of sight through a hedge.

A car behind him may be a police car and he has to judge between that and, say, a lorry. But not yet. Somehow he has to get a few miles away and so dissociate himself from the accident which the oncoming motor coach will probably have seen. But to have parted with the jewellery would have been unthinkable—as yet. If things got more desperate, then it might be cached, but not till then. And when did that final moment of decision come? The answer was—anywhere: anywhere between Elmhurst and Liverpool: well over a hundred miles and maybe with twists and turns.

There was more than that to make the whole assignment sheer stupidity. The police would have made enquiries as to how Conward reached Liverpool, and all Jewle had been able to tell me was that he'd *probably* hitched a ride as far as an intermediate station. In fact, all I did know was that the jewellery hadn't been cached or handed to yet another confederate in Liverpool itself, since Conward had been shadowed from the moment he'd left the station platform.

I had breakfast. I lighted my pipe and had a look at a morning paper. The sun shone invitingly through the window and in the air there was just that little autumnal nip and the faint haze that makes me think of the open country, and golf. For a moment I thought of ringing someone and fixing up a day on one of the fringe courses, and then I changed my mind. Between where I was and Elmhust was plenty of open country. Why not drive out there? It couldn't do any good but, as my old nurse used to say, it'd show willing. And the more I thought about it, the more I liked it. After all, I'd never even been near the scene of the crime. Maybe, I furtively began to tell myself, I might even spot something that the local police, and even Jewle, had overlooked.

I looked up a reference book. Elmhurst had a population of just over seven thousand. It had one pretty good hotel where I could get lunch, and a commercial hotel as well. It also had a weekly newspaper—*The Elmhurst Recorder*. That paper would have done itself well when that robbery broke, and I could have a look at the files. I could visit the very scene of the robbery and the spot where the car had been set alight. And everything would be paid for by the Harvey Dawsons' ten pounds.

I was almost out of the flat when I thought of something. What excuse could I give for nosing around in Elmhurst? For a moment or two I couldn't think of one and then I had an idea. I worked it out and then rang United Assurance and asked to speak to John Hill. The Broad Street Detective Agency makes quite a lot of money out of United Assurance.

Hill was in and I put the proposition up to him.

"I'd like you to do something for me, John. I'm on a rather important case and may have to ask a lot of people a lot of questions. The only reason I can think of for the questions is that they're connected with an insurance case. May I use, purely fictitiously, your company's name?"

I knew John Hill, careful to the point of fastidiousness, so I'd guessed it wouldn't work. But once he was listening, the rest was easy.

"Well, perhaps it would be ill-advised," I admitted. "But put it like this. I won't say outright that I'm on an insurance case. I'll merely infer it. I'll say that if my bona fides seem to be in question, they can ring your company as a general reference. That'll be all right?"

He still didn't like it, even when I said the situation was highly unlikely to arise. He wouldn't be pestered with telephone calls. Think of it as a favour from a friend to a friend. Just a little something to have up my sleeve as reserve. That last may have broken his heart, but he gave what's known as a grudging consent. Before he could start laying down any conditions I babbled hasty thanks and rang off. I gave myself a satisfied nod as I made for the door again. Face the impossible and there's nothing like a good laugh at yourself. Lines of communication now secure, I told myself. Everything set, and Travers on the trail.

If you drive steadily it's an hour and a quarter from town to Elmhurst. I'd been through the place once or twice before on my way to the north, but I'd never even halted there for a meal. Its outskirts were the usual sprawl: semi-detached houses and bungalows to the south and a tailing off to better-class residential roads to the north-west. It had a large market square, used, except on market day, as a car park. That square was the main shopping centre and the hub of the Elmhurst wheel. One of its spokes was Rickway Street and about fifty yards along it were the offices of the *Recorder*.

It was a slack morning. One side of the grilled counter was marked advertisements: the other was Enquiries, and a couple of youngish women were in charge. I handed Miss Enquiries a private card, and Miss Advertisements at once stopped tapping her typewriter and looked on.

"I'm a research specialist," I said, "and I'd be very grateful if I could look at your files for 1953."

I was evidently something unique. She gave me almost a startled look, asked me to wait a minute and went through the door just behind her, the card with her. In just about the minute I was shown through the same door into a room with one long table at which two men were working, and a roll-top desk behind which an elderly bald-headed man was standing.

"Mr. Travers?" He held out his hand. "My name's Purdon."

"Sorry to be a nuisance like this," I said, "but I'd be grateful if I could run through your files for 1953."

"I'll clear that table for you. Anything special you're interested in?"

"Well, yes," I said. "I'm doing research work into crime motivations for a psychological institute and it struck us that the crime you had here at that time might have its useful aspects."

Enough words and enough speed and you can get away with murder. He seemed impressed. The ball-point behind him stopped gliding and another typewriter stopped clicking.

"You're starting at the right place," he told me. "I actually covered the whole story myself. Jim Fusson rang me as soon as it broke—"

He halted at my look of enquiry.

"The local inspector of police," he said. "But you'd like to look at the actual files. Just a moment."

He went through another door. When he came back he was carrying a couple of fairly slim files.

"We file quarterly," he told me. "These two will give you practically everything. It starts off at the March."

He left me to it. Anything extra he'd be delighted to tell me, if he could. Ten minutes later tea came in. There was an extra cup sent for. Purdon came to my table with it.

"Found anything specially interesting?"

"Just getting my bearings," I told him. "You've got to soak up quite a lot of atmosphere before you can get clean into this kind of thing. This picture of Mr. Speer. Is it a good one?" I chuckled in hasty confusion. "No reflections on your photographer, of course."

"Quite a good likeness," he said, and had another look at it with me. Speer was a shortish, alert-looking man who hardly looked his fifty years. His hair was black and his eyes dark and deep-set. "Rather foreign looking," I said.

"He was. A naturalised Italian. Been here a good many years."

"Well-known locally?"

"I wouldn't say that. Quite a lot of our better-class residents aren't. They subscribe to local charities and so on, or there may be births, deaths or marriages, but that's about all. This is quite a handy caravanserai for town, you know."

"Exactly. Did he have any children?"

"Just a daughter. There's a picture of her. I think it's in the next issue."

He turned over the pages himself.

"Ah, here it is! And one of the house. And one of the burnt-out car."

"A nice-looking woman, the daughter?"

"Very nice indeed." He grunted. "Looks a bit Italian, don't you think?"

She did. For a newspaper snap it still wasn't a bad likeness, even after four years. I noticed she hadn't changed her hair style. Maybe the Italian look had been a useful asset in her job.

He drifted away again. It was almost noon when I'd read all I wanted to and taken notes, chiefly for show. I now knew the exact locations of the house and of the burnt-out car. After lunch I was proposing to have a look at both.

"What's the best place here for lunch?" I asked Purdon.

"Oh, the Lion. Lunch from twelve-thirty on."

"Will you join me there?"

"Well"—he smiled—"that's very nice of you. I'll have to ring my wife."

"Do," I said. "Perhaps you might be so good as to ring the Lion and book a table for half-past twelve."

He said he'd certainly do it. A smile of thanks meant to include the room, and I made my way out, Purdon at my heels. I had only twenty minutes to kill before lunch.

I moved the car off in the direction of Ypres Road. That was the road in which Speer's house was situated, and its name dated it accurately. It was almost the last side road as I went north, and for the last couple of hundred yards I was tucked in behind a bus. It was going to a place called Puckenford, and it stopped at Ypres Road. I had to keep behind it because of an oncoming bus which was going to Elmhurst station. Both buses moved on but I stayed there. It seemed to me I was seeing a small fragment of what had been Speer's life. From the railway station there was a bus service that ran by his very road. I saw him, in my mind's eye, leaving the station, looking to see if a bus was there, mounting it and getting off almost at where I sat. In the morning there would be the same in reverse.

I looked at my watch. Still ten minutes, so I turned the car into Ypres Road. Speer's was only the third house on the right: a medium-sized place well separated from its neighbours by a largish garden. That road, I saw, would be quiet enough at night and each house an entity. I also saw that the road ran well downhill towards the main road. And it wasn't a cul-de-sac. So Conward would probably have driven the car into the far end of the road and then let it silently coast on its now proper side to near the gate of Littlecroft, ready for the getaway. To try that out I drove past the house and in about another hundred yards took a turn to the right. In another couple of hundred yards I turned right again and I was back at the main road.

Purdon was a very nice fellow. The paper had a managing editor, he told me, but he happened to be away. Purdon was his deputy, and also chief reporter. We had a short drink before the meal and then he mentioned the job I was supposed to be on.

"Between ourselves, I put it a bit impressively," I said. "All newspaper offices aren't as co-operative as yours. What we're trying out is an analysis of crime motives. You might call it an addition to criminal files. Criminals are already classified under various branches of crime and methods within those branches."

"I get you," he said. "If a left-handed man used nitroglycerine on a safe job, you look up the files for left-handed men who tackle safes that way. But what made you think of this particular job?"

"Well, it had its unusual aspects. The job was evidently uncommonly well planned, and yet the thieves got away with practically nothing. We'd like to know just where the slip-up occurred. Another sherry? Or shall we see about lunch."

It was a reasonably good but wholly unimaginative English meal. As soon as the soup arrived I asked him to tell me what he personally saw that night. There seemed nothing new in what he told me, except that he'd been held up for a few minutes at the car fire. When he reached Speer's house, Speer had just recovered consciousness but the doctor didn't want him questioned. But Purdon did get Mrs. Howard's story. The next morning, the Saturday, Purdon went to the house again. Miss Speer was there, but she could contribute little.

"The whole thing must have made quite a stir locally," I said. "You can't have a lot of crime here."

"Very little. We're an agricultural centre and market town. The funny thing is we did have something peculiar only about ten days before that big affair. Connected with it, too, in a remote way."

"I didn't notice it in the files."

"That's because you began with the robbery," he said. "This was before that. An accident to the maid at the Speers'. She had the Thursday off as usual from mid-morning onwards. On her way home that night—her home was in the town—she was knocked down by a car and sustained a broken leg and some rib injuries. Had to go to hospital. The car didn't stop, by the way, and she swore that she'd been knocked down on the actual footpath. The police didn't believe it: that's between ourselves. It was a foggy night and she must have stepped into the road. It's possible the car didn't know what it'd hit, but it didn't stop, as I said, and the police never found it."

"But there was a maid in the house the night of the robbery?"

"Yes," he said. "The Speers got one almost at once."

"But surely that's unusual? I thought the maid situation was absolutely impossible, and there were the Speers with a maid and being able to replace her in no time."

"Maids may be impossible to get in most places," he told me, "but not in agricultural centres like this. No factories to attract the girls and reasonable amenities to keep 'em here. The new girl came from a village quite near here, for instance. Girls in these parts aren't brought up to think that domestic work is degrading. It's very well paid, too, nowadays."

I took his word for it, but I did ask if I might read what had been printed about that accident. So when we left the hotel we walked the short distance back to the *Recorder* office. I learned nothing new except that the maid had been with Speer for three years. A cross-reference to the robbery confirmed what I thought I remembered, that the new maid was called Gladys Trent.

"You wouldn't like to come out with me to where the car was burnt?" I asked Purdon.

He said he'd be delighted. Not a trace was left, though I'd expected a little something, even after four years. The grass and the hedge showed no signs and the telegraph pole had long since been replaced. What did surprise me was the nearness of the scene to Ypres Road. It was a bare fifty yards north along the main road. The Bentley must have hurtled round the corner and practically at once have hit the pole.

"That's why I got held up," Purdon said. "I saw the lights of the motor coach and the police car through the fog and I wanted to have a word with the men who'd put the fire out and arrange for a picture."

"I suppose the men saw no one on the road when they were drawing near the fire?"

"Not a soul. There's a shallow ditch here, as you see. Conward might have crouched in that till the coach passed him, or he might have nipped through the hedge. Plenty of thin spots, as you see."

It was almost three o'clock when we got back and I was thinking of calling it a day. I told Purdon there might be a few more enquiries to make and I'd probably see him again. He was a very good fellow, as I've said, and he couldn't have been more helpful. But there had been times when I'd caught a slightly ironic look in his eye and I had the idea that he didn't take me and my crime motivation altogether for granted. That's why I thought I'd better drop in at the local police headquarters.

Inspector Fusson was out, so I left my name and said I hoped to see him in the morning. My guess was that Purdon would be giving him a ring, which meant that I might have to think up a whole lot of new prevarications, or embellish the old. But what did intrigue me on my way home was that accident to the maid.

I even had the idea that the so-called accident might have been deliberate, and in order to plant Gladys Trent in the house.

Though how Gladys Trent could possibly have contributed to the robbery was something altogether beyond me.

I hate going to bed with an unsolved problem on my mind, and at soon after nine o'clock that night I rang Carlotta Speer. She was in, and I told her at once that I'd been to Elmhurst, just to put myself in the picture, and that I'd heard about the accident to the old maid and the fortuitous arrival of a new one. Might there have been something in it?

She laughed.

"I'm sorry, Mr. Travers, but you're really hopelessly wrong. Alice was always—"

"Alice?"

"Alice Edwards, the maid. She was always the theatrical type. Used to dramatise everything. I'm afraid she suffered from an overdose of cinema."

"And how'd you get the new maid?"

"She rang up. The news of Alice's accident was in the local paper, and she asked if the job was vacant. Kate—that's Mrs. Howard, who was our housekeeper—told her to come and see me and bring her references with her. I was down that week on the Friday night and I saw her next morning. Everything was in order. She'd been working in London and didn't like it and she'd come home to one of the villages near by-—I forget which—and was looking for a job in Elmhurst."

"How'd she turn out?"

"Very well. Mrs. Howard had to show her a lot, of course, but she was very satisfied with her. I gave her quite a good reference when she left. That was almost at once after the robbery. My father was coming to my flat where I could keep an eye on him, and he'd already made up his mind to sell the house. We just left Mrs. Howard there till it was actually sold."

"Well, sorry you've been troubled, as they say. It was a wild idea that Gladys Trent might have been concerned somehow with the robbery."

"She couldn't possibly have been," she told me. "All the same, it's nice to know you're—what is it they say—leaving no stone unturned. Just a moment. My husband is saying something." She cupped the receiver for a moment. "It was only that he doesn't see what the actual robbery has to do with the recovery of you-know-what."

"True enough," I said. "I admit I've merely been getting the feel of things. All the same, *if* that wild notion of mine had had any truth in it and the girl *was* some sort of a confederate, mightn't we-know-what have been handed over to her?"

"But the two men were out of the house. And she was asleep in bed. Just a moment."

She cupped the receiver again. I could hear a little chuckle when she spoke.

"That was my husband again. He says you ought to write a book. A whodunit."

I had to smile.

"A good retort," I said. "Tell him that maybe I will."

5. Fusson—and Others

Like most city dwellers I'm a fairly late bird and, though I dismissed Gladys Trent from the case, I did do quite a lot of thinking before I finally turned in. One of the things I thought about was money. I thought about it in such a way that I actually rang Purdon. It took quite a time to get his number but at last I did get him on the line.

"Sorry to bother you at this unearthly hour, but do you happen to know if Speer banked in Elmhurst?"

"He did," he said. "At my own bank—Barclays. I know, because I'd seen him there occasionally on a Saturday. I expect he'd also have a bank in town."

"Most grateful," I said. "I may be seeing you tomorrow but you ought to know what was behind the question. Speer went to America and I've learned that he died there. But with all the restrictions, how'd he get any money transferred from here to there?"

"That's beyond me," he said. "I'm not an economist. Probably there were ways and means."

"Well, thanks again," I said. "Hope to be seeing you."

The question I'd put to Purdon was more of a cover-up than an asking for information. All the same, I'd been wondering about Speer's money and the big sum he'd handed over for the stolen jewellery. Forty thousand pounds is quite a lot of money, even for a Hatton Garden diamond merchant. Had he been able to find it all out of his own resources, including the sale of his properties and interests? Was the transaction completed before he left England? Since the repayments had been private, I didn't expect to be able to trace cheques, but his bank ought to have records of cash withdrawals.

Why was I worrying myself about all that? To tell the truth, I was looking a very long way ahead, and far too optimistically.

I thought I might discover the identity of the ancient family who'd owned the jewellery, and in that way I'd know as much as anyone else—and even more—when that question of ethics cropped up. You see, in the words of Lear, how foolish and how fond I was: actually thinking in terms of the recovery of that jewellery. But that's how one gets on a case. As soon as you become involved in it, you have to think in terms of success, not failure.

The morning brought, as usual, less optimistic ideas, but I did wake up with one highly pertinent question which I could put to Fusson: one that had a very direct bearing on the case. But first of all I wanted to clear up that business at the bank. That was why

I set off very early for Elmhurst. The bank had only just opened when I arrived there.

I had only five minutes to wait before I was shown into the manager's office. I'd sent in my business card and he was looking a bit perturbed till I assured him I wasn't there on account of anything concerning the bank.

"It does concern it but only very remotely," I said. "I'm making enquiries on behalf of the heirs of the late Mr. Speer, who, I'm given to understand, banked here. He died in America about a year ago, as you may or may not know."

"I did know," he said. "I remember now that my wife told me. She heard it through a Mrs. Howard, who used to be Mr. Speer's housekeeper. I believe Miss Speer wrote to her from America."

"Well, Miss Speer—or rather Mrs. Dawson as she now is— wasn't happy about the insurance paid on what was stolen from Speer's safe that night. Not only does it seem that more was stolen than was thought, but there was also more cash, and Mrs. Dawson wants us to make enquiries. Her father apparently was so ill after the attack on him that he rather let things slide."

"I can understand that," he said. "But we can't check his accounts to see if any cheque or cheques were received from any insurance company. His accounts both here and at Bridge Street were closed when he left for America. It would take a lot of time to look things up and, in any case, it would be out of my province."

"Of course. But tell me, in strict confidence. He kept a reasonable sum of money here?"

"Much larger than most of our customers. People like Mr. Speer draw and deposit very large sums at very short notice. We had a working arrangement with the Bridge Street branch and you might say the accounts were in many ways one. He closed down the account here almost immediately after the attack on him."

"Any big cheques paid in or out in the meanwhile?"

"This is in strict confidence?"

"Most decidedly so."

"Well, as far as I remember it, the robbery was on the Friday night and the next week he left Elmhurst to go to his daughter in town. On the Monday he asked us to have five thousand pounds in cash ready the following day. He usually gave us twenty-four hours' notice for withdrawals of that kind. He had it brought to his house by one of our employees and at the same time gave notice of closing his account here at once and transferring everything to Bridge Street."

"And that wasn't unusual?"

"Not really. Except that he'd have collected the cash here if he hadn't been too unwell to do so. I admit he didn't make such large withdrawals here very frequently."

"Well, I'm very grateful for what you've told me," I said. "It doesn't help, but maybe I can tackle the problem another way without troubling his bank again. And what you've been good enough to tell me shall be kept confidential."

We shook hands and he saw me out. I walked across the road to my car but I didn't move off at once. When I did, I was quite pleased with myself, even if it didn't help with a recovery of the stolen jewellery. What it did do was prove up to the hilt what Carlotta had told me. Speer had shown good faith by at once making a payment for that jewellery. It was a highly confidential matter between him and the owners and that was why he'd taken no risks and paid cash.

A couple of minutes later I was at police headquarters and being shown into Fusson's room.

Fusson was a tall, loose-limbed fellow; red-haired and with a beautifully trimmed ginger moustache. He was about forty by the look of him and first impressions generally weren't to be too far out. I've met few people to whom I took so quickly as to Fusson.

"Well, this *is* a pleasure," he said as he held out his hand. "Our mutual friend Jewle was always talking about you."

"That's the worst of Jewle," I said. "Once you owe him money he has to spread the news around. But I'm glad to meet you. Inspector."

"Well, make yourself at home," he told me. "Have a cigarette? Tea'll be in in a minute."

"Tea! What a life you country fellows have. Practically no crime, living in the lap of luxury—"

"And overpaid," he said. "Don't forget that. And who told you we had no crime? Jim Purdon?"

"So you've had your spies out."

He laughed.

"Jim's my father-in-law. Ah, here's the tea. Help yourself to sugar."

As soon as the door closed I thought I'd better do some explaining.

"I think I'd better own up. That excuse I gave your father-in-law seemed pretty good at the time. No use telling the world your business."

"True enough, sir," he told me, and with a bit of a twinkle. "And what've you got cooked up for me?"

I had to laugh.

"Oh dear!" I said. "This is going to be difficult. Whatever I tell you, I'm not going to be believed. But listen to this, and take it as strictly confidential. I'm down here on that old Speer-Conward case."

"Yes, I guessed that."

I told him the same story as I'd told the bank manager. It was a good story and he seemed to believe it, especially when I mentioned United Assurance and John Hill.

"I thought Speer was hiding something at the time," he told me. "Mind you, the man was ill. That crack on the skull shook him badly. But what's the daughter hope to get? Isn't there some kind of statute of limitations with insurance companies?"

"It isn't exactly that. Her claim is that she can find no record of any compensation being paid at all. She thinks her father, being ill at the time, overlooked the insurance claim, and she doesn't see why the matter shouldn't be reopened."

"What company was it? The one you mentioned?"

"They say they've no record. Still, that's why she's employing my agency," I said. "She knew little or nothing about her father's business. I could find out by elimination if any other company was concerned, but that's only half the battle. When her father was practically on his deathbed he told her he thought there was more to that robbery than had ever come out, and before she could question him further he was really very ill indeed, and he died without her having learnt any more."

"You're reopening the case?"

"Nothing like that," I assured him. "All I want to do is to have a shrewd idea what jewellery was taken and how much cash, and then find out the company who always kept Speer covered and try to arrange a settlement if one wasn't already made. Just as simple as that."

"Sounds to me like hopeless dawn," he said. "Speer said that what was taken was worth roughly about three hundred pounds, plus some cash. He seemed to think it trivial compared with what might have been in the safe that night. A parcel of diamonds, for instance. That's what Conward and Tibball were after."

"Mind if I ask a question or two?"

"Go right ahead," he told me.

"Right. Let's assume that jewellery worth only three hundred pounds was taken. Where is it?"

His smile was a bit reproachful.

"That's a question and a half. It wasn't found on Conward and therefore he dumped it somewhere."

"*Somewhere*'s a pretty spacious word," I said. "You never knew where he took the train for Liverpool?"

"We don't have the foggiest idea. We can't even guess. All we know is that he got off the train at Lime Street and his ticket, like everybody else's, had been collected on the train. But we never bothered to enquire into it. We weren't after the jewellery; we were after Conward. And we got him."

"Let's get a bit closer," I said. "He was picked up on the Saturday afternoon. What was he doing on the Friday night?"

"Hitch-hiking to wherever he took the train. That might have taken him till the Saturday morning."

"But exhaustive enquiries never discovered the driver or drivers who gave him a lift."

"Admitted," he said. "But the enquiries weren't necessarily exhaustive. Why should we worry about how he got to Liverpool? He was what we were after. How he got to where we picked him up was only of minor importance. I admit we'd have been glad to take him with the goods on him, but we had enough for conviction of robbery with violence."

"That bag he had with him. It was a new one of course?"

He gave me a quick look.

"You saw it?"

"Good lord, no," I said. "I'd nothing whatever to do with that case. I had a slight personal interest because of Jewle, as he may have told you. I guessed the bag was new because Conward wasn't accustomed to making trips abroad. But tell me this. I rather gathered that the bag had a false bottom, or something like that. Did it?"

"Not exactly a false bottom. Two concealed compartments in the reinforcing of the strap handles. Like this."

He made a quick drawing.

"Very ingenious," I said. "But those two little compartments couldn't have taken what one thinks of as jewellery."

"I don't know. They'd have taken quite a lot of small stuff like diamond rings or earrings."

"And yet there was nothing in them."

"Admitted," he said. "The hue and cry was out and he knew it. He dumped the stuff or threw it away. His concern wasn't getting the stuff out of the country, but getting himself out. But do you know what those two compartments showed us? That the bag was specially made to conceal the stones: that parcel of diamonds Speer was supposed to have brought home with him." That was beautifully logical and I told him so. But it knocked my own ideas sideways. That bag *had* been specially made, but not to hold a tremendously valuable collection of jewellery. The secret compartments couldn't have held that jewellery! So what was wrong? Was it that Speer had already removed the stones from their settings? I liked that as soon as I thought of it. The stones would be wanted for the new settings, so the old settings had been left at Bridge Street. Doubtless Speer had later handed the settings back to the owners, though their value would be little compared with that of the stones. Tibball and Conward—through Brittle?—had known that only the stones would be at Elmhurst and the bag was made accordingly.

"What were the actual contents of the bag?"

"I've got it here somewhere," Fusson said, and went to a filing cabinet. He came back with a sheet of paper. I ran my eye down the list.

"Just what he needed for the voyage. Did he have a return ticket or a single?"

"A single. Apparently he didn't know how long he'd have to be there and what boat or plane he could take back."

"What's this last item?" I said. "One tube of Stickwell."

"Just a tube of adhesive paste. A proprietary name. Like Duro-fix or Stictite and so on."

"Yes, but what'd he want it for?"

Fusson shrugged his shoulders.

"Heaven knows. He had it. That's all there is to it."

"Might it have been to stick down that false moustache he was wearing when he was picked up?"

"That's right," he said. "I remember now. That's what we thought at the time."

I wasn't so sure, not that I had any ideas of my own. But there it all was. I'd got precious little from Fusson: not that it was his fault, as I told him.

"Looks as if my job's ended before it's begun," I said. "It never was anything, as you said, but pretty hopeless."

"You'll certainly never know what claim to put up to an insurance company. Only Speer knew exactly what was taken from that safe and he'll never tell us now."

"Well, I'll have to make some sort of a show to justify the retainer," I told him. "When I've done that much I think I ought to throw my hand in. No use giving a client false hopes. So what about that Mrs. Howard who was Speer's housekeeper? She might know something, just for the records."

"She's at Puckenford now. Got a little cottage of her own there. Anyone'll tell you where."

"Might do worse than have a word with her. What about the maid?"

"Don't know where she is now," he said. "Mrs. Howard might know, but if it was me, I wouldn't waste time over her. Unless you want it to bulge your account."

"You saw her?"

"Just for a minute or two. Not a bad-looking girl. A blonde. One of the beautiful but dumb types. She was sound asleep when everything happened that night. My guess is she was dreaming of cowboys."

"How'd you find my client—the daughter?"

"Speer's daughter? A very nice lady indeed. Quiet, but very nice." He smiled. "Not the kind to argue about your bill when you send it in."

"Fine," I said. "Remind me to remember you at Christmas."

I looked at my watch.

"Think I'll be getting on. I'd hoped to ask you to have lunch with me but I may be a bit late."

"Don't worry about that, sir," he told me. "There's always another time."

Puckenford was only three miles away. I went north on the main road and there it was. Mrs. Howard's cottage was just off the main road, like the bulk of the village, and the first person of whom I enquired sent me straight to it.

It was a picture-postcard place: detached, small, thatched and with a tiny flagged path to the door. Inside it was meticulously clean. As soon as I mentioned Carlotta Speer's name I was invited in.

Kate Howard looked just about her sixty-odd years. She was a smallish, bustling kind of woman, with keen brown eyes and a friendly manner. She didn't look too robust, but from what had happened that night in Speer's house, I knew she had all the pluck in the world. Her speech was brisk and pleasant, with just a touch of the country.

"You're a friend of Miss Carlotta's, sir?"

I told her the story I'd passed off on Fusson. She kept giving little nods to herself.

"I'm afraid I can't help you," she said regretfully. "Much as I'd like to have helped Miss Carlotta. But I never knew anything of Mr. Speer's business and never wanted to know."

"He was a good employer?"

"There couldn't have been a better. It was like a home from home, and everyone was so kind when my husband died. That's why I never dreamed of taking another place—that, and my pension."

"Do you feel you could tell me all about what happened that night from your point of view?"

I think she was pleased to go over it all again. One or two things were new to me and questions were to arise out of the account she gave me, and that—as far as new information was concerned—was briefly this.

Speer had his meal first. She remained in the kitchen and Gladys Trent took in the food and waited, as one says, at table. Only when Speer had finished his meal and returned to his study did she and Gladys have their own meal. There was no hurry about it. It usually wasn't over till about half-past eight, and then all the washing-up was done. That might have been timed for nine o'clock when Speer's whisky was got ready—a third of a tumbler of Irish whisky, two lumps of sugar and a slice of lemon on top. Mrs. Howard always took it herself to the study, after which she and Gladys went upstairs.

"Why the hot whisky?"

"The master never drank anything with his meals and he was liable to colds," she said. "He thought the whisky staved the colds off, if you know what I mean."

I asked her what the study was like when she came into it after the two men had run out, and again I learned something new. The study door was locked—bolted from the inside—and she had to go round the house to the french windows. She only smiled when I said that was very brave of her.

"From what I read about the affair, Mr. Speer was working at his desk when he was attacked," I said. "Do you know what he was actually doing? He was supposed to be working something out on paper. Wasn't that what he was doing when you brought the whisky in?"

"Yes, he was drawing something but I didn't see what. He was often drawing things. Designs for jewellery, Miss Carlotta said they were. But the funny thing was that the men took the paper he was drawing on with them. It wasn't there when the police came."

She added rather plaintively that she'd thought they hadn't believed her.

"Nonsense!" I said. "I know they believed you. But tell me something else. How did you get on with Gladys Trent?"

"I didn't know her very long, but she was a God-send. Quite a nice, cheerful girl and willing to learn. I had a letter from her later on. She was getting married and going to live in Scotland, I think it was. I missed her company after Mr. Speer closed the house down."

"That was the same week?"

"The next week. Gladys left on the Tuesday night. No point in her staying if the family weren't to be there. I know she was well paid in lieu of notice, because she told me so."

"You knew Mr. Speer was dead?"

"Yes—the poor gentleman. Miss Carlotta sent me a letter from America. It went to the old house and they forwarded it. She said she might be leaving the place where she was and I thought she might write again, but she never did."

"You liked her?"

She smiled.

"She was nice. In every way. A very clever girl, you know. Worked for the B.B.C. But never any airs. Just as natural as you and me."

"And what about Alice? The maid who had the accident. Did you believe that story about her being deliberately knocked down by the car?"

She gave a little laugh.

"I just pretended to believe her because she was so positive about it, but people don't do that sort of thing. Now do they?"

"They certainly don't make it a habit," I said, and smiled. "She's all right now, is she?"

"Quite all right. As a matter of fact, some good came out of it." She gave that little chuckle of a laugh again. "She married the ambulance driver at the hospital. She has a little son now. They're living in Rowley Avenue, near the hospital."

I thanked her and rose to go. I gave her my private telephone number and said she could always ring me there before nine in the morning or after nine at night if she remembered anything which might be of help. She said she would. A Mrs. Somebody-or-Other would always let her use her telephone.

"If you're writing to Miss Carlotta will you remember me to her?" she said as she saw me off at the door. "Tell her I'd love to have her write me even a note."

"I'll certainly do that," I told her. "And thanks again for letting me trouble you."

"Oh dear!" she said. "Whatever will you be thinking of me? I got so wrapped up I never even offered you a cup of tea."

I laughed. Then she laughed. And that's the kind of pleasant time it had been. I was wishing as I waved to her from the car that I could have whisked her inside it and taken her off to lunch with me at the Lion.

By the clock on her little sitting-room mantelshelf it had been well after one o'clock but I found time to turn down Ypres Road again. The surface was good, but it had never been extravagantly made up. It was easy enough to step from the paths to the road itself. Only one thing occurred to me. Littlecroft was on the right-hand side of the road, and, so, unless the fog had been particularly bad and the driver hadn't known where he actually was, Alice had been knocked down on the opposite side of the road from the house. Not, as I saw at once, that that was anything noteworthy. Although she had come from the town and might therefore have been expected to take the right-hand path into Ypres Road, she might almost as easily have taken the other side, especially in the fog, and have expected to cross the road when she was near enough to Littlecroft. Or, better still, maybe she *was* actually crossing the road when she was knocked down.

I had lunch and took my time over it. After all, I was on holiday and, strange to admit, enjoying it. I wasn't getting any further with what one might call the essentials but at least I'd made myself acquainted with backgrounds. And what I was wondering when I came out of the hotel was whether or not I should pay a call on Alice Edwards, and hear her own account of that accident of four years ago.

If I hadn't gone on debating the matter when I was in the car I shouldn't have noticed that green Ford again. I'd noticed it first when I'd been nearing Elmhurst that morning. I'd been tucked in behind a removal van and when it luckily turned off into a side road, I'd waved the Ford on. I'd noticed it had a particularly yellow fog lamp mounted just above the front bumper and that its number was the unusual one of 444. Also it hadn't responded to my wave as I'd shot my car on.

I'd later noticed it when I left Puckenford and it had been behind me when I had turned into Ypres Road. I'd put all that down to mere coincidence. That anyone should be following me was preposterous, and yet when I was in my car and debating the question of Alice Edwards, there was the Ford only two cars from me in the car park. That wasn't unusual either. What was odd was that the man at its wheel was taking surreptitious looks at me from the shelter of a newspaper, and if that isn't the oldest trick in the trade, what is?

Mind you, I wasn't by any means sure. If anything, I thought I was being just a bit melodramatic, and that it was a waste of time to make after all for Rowley Avenue to see if the Ford did follow. And it did follow, just far enough behind me to keep me in view. I didn't stop to ask about Alice Edwards because I realised I didn't know her married name, so I went on to the hospital, circled round it and took a turn to the right which brought me almost out of the town on the south side. The Ford was well over a hundred yards behind me and when I slowed it made no effort to pass. When I moved on at a fairly good lick it still kept well behind, so I pushed on even more quickly and lost sight of it. I didn't see it again, though by the time I'd lost it I wasn't more than fifteen miles from town.

As soon as I was in the flat I rang City Detection and asked to be put through to Bill Fraser. City Detection is a high-class firm with whom we often work, lending them an operative or two, for example, when they're busy and we're slack. They do the same for us.

"A job for you, Bill. I've been working personally on a job, and I think a car's been tailing me. This is the number. Track it down for me, will you?"

"Urgent, is it?"

I said I'd like it any time after nine o'clock that night, and to be phoned to my private address. It was largely a personal matter, I said, and nothing to do with the firm. He said he'd do his best.

I'd nothing particular to do that evening so I dined at the club and was back at the flat well before nine. City Detection rang me dead on time. It was Bill himself who gave me the information.

"That car belongs to a Drive-Yourself firm. Linfolds of Selby Street, just off Portland Place."

"That's interesting," I said. "Do you think it might be possible to find out who today's hirer was?"

"I doubt it," he told me. "If someone was hired to follow you, then he'd either make sure of absolute secrecy by the firm or else he'd give a wrong name. Did he take pains to see you didn't spot the car number?"

"He didn't. Not the pains I'd have taken."

"There you are then. Still, we'll try if you think it's worth it."

I said I didn't think it was. What I'd do was to be on the *qui vive* for anyone who was trying to get on my tail in the morning. That's how we left it, but what I was wondering was if I'd not only been tailed that day but the previous day as well. And why? On behalf, that is, of whom? And since no possible living soul except the Harvey Dawsons knew I was on that particular job, it was, on the face of it, preposterous to think I was being tailed at all. Maybe I wasn't. Maybe it was one of those queer coincidences that happen from time to time. All the same I thought I knew how to find out.

That would be for the morning but it struck me that in the meantime there was something I might ask Jewle. Out of the question something might emerge to throw light on what it seemed was happening, so I did ring Jewle. It was unlikely he'd be at the Yard, so I tried his private address and there he was.

"Travers here," I said. "How are you?"

"Can't grumble," he told me. "Seems a long time since I heard from you. What've you been doing?"

"Just the usual. But I thought I'd tell you about a rather queer thing that happened to me today. But before I do that, isn't an old acquaintance of yours due out of the cage in the very near future?"

He got it almost at once.

"That's right. If you mean our friend Conward. Due out tomorrow week."

"Would that be general knowledge?"

"Don't get you," he said. "It wouldn't be announced in the Press, not unless it was by some rag that had fixed up to publish his autobiography. Any relative or other person interested could easily find out."

"Are you people watching him when he does get out?"

"Why should we?"

"Well, there was a little matter of three hundred pounds' worth of jewellery that he may have put away somewhere. I take it none of it was recovered?"

"Not interested," he said. "If we should bring him in one fine day for some other job and he happened to have some of that stuff on him, he could be charged with unlawful possession. Now I come to remember it, we couldn't even do that. We never had a sufficiently detailed description of the missing stuff. Speer was pretty ill at the time."

"Why I mentioned it was this. I got to thinking about Conward yesterday and it so happens I'm at a loose end—Bernice is away and I'm supposed to be on holiday—so I thought I'd run down to Elmhurst and have a look at the site of that old crime. I didn't have all that much time so I ran down there again today. And I'm pretty sure someone was on my tail."

He laughed.

"Must have been to do with some other case you're on."

"But I'm not. I'm just at the start of a fortnight's holiday."

"It's beyond me," he said. "You never *were* involved in that Speer business."

"In a roundabout way I might have been," I pointed out. "I was with you that night we saw Tibball. He may have made it his business to find out who I was."

He chuckled.

"Where Tibball is, he's far too busy trying to get cool to worry about you or me."

"True enough," I said. "But let me leave you something to think over. Tibball had a daughter. You may have lost sight of her but won't she be the one Conward will get into touch with when he gets out? They used to be literally thick as thieves."

"I'll bear it in mind," he told me. "But we're not interested. Why should we be? If Conward does another job, that'll be different."

That was about all. I went to bed early and set the alarm for half an hour before my usual time.

Before breakfast I went downstairs to the night porter, George, who was just going off duty. George knows all about my job and I've used him before, so I told him there might be a man hanging around the front waiting to follow me when I came out later on.

"Just have a look round in a quiet sort of way," I told him. "If you think you spot him, don't let him get an idea you're interested. He may be propped up against a wall ostensibly reading a paper or he may be waiting in a handy car. If you spot him, ring me from a call-box in the course of the next half-hour."

He rang me in less than half that time. A man was reading a newspaper in a private car—a biscuit-coloured Austin Ten—just round the corner from Bewlay Street. He gave me the car number.

I took my time. It was just short of nine o'clock when I left the flats and walked the few yards to the garage. I got one of the men to back my car out while I gave him the road, and that allowed me to spot the Austin drawn up some fifty yards away.

I drove off warily: that was all one could do in the whirl of traffic. It must have been half an hour before I got to Bridge Street, Hatton Garden. I left my car just short of it and walked the short distance to Number 3. I didn't look back to see if the Austin was parked behind me. There'd be plenty of time for that.

I'd had in mind the need to have a look at Speer's old business headquarters as an essential to the background into which I was trying to insinuate myself, and the luring along of the Austin worked in well. And Speer's old place rather surprised me, though it shouldn't have done. The building itself was a two-storied one, with a special side entrance to the upper rooms. The lower part consisted of what looked like a display window behind which would be a kind of shop. Behind, as I'd learned, would be an office and a workroom. The centre part of the almost dingy display window was grilled, and well behind it on a single, velvet-covered shelf, was a turquoise necklace displayed on a small bust, and a pair of matching ear-rings hanging from tiny stands at the side. Speer's name had been painted out and the name above the window was Harris.

I opened the door and went in. An old-fashioned bell began buzzing and at once a man came in from the back. He was a grey-haired man of over sixty, short and spare. His shirt sleeves were rolled up and he was wearing a green baize apron.

"Mr. Speer in?"

He gaped, then smiled.

"He left here years ago, sir. Best part of four years."

"Oh dear," I said. "That's very unfortunate. I've been away for just over four years and I thought I'd look him up. He did some work for me once. You can't tell me where I can get hold of him?"

"I think he went to America. In fact, I'm almost sure."

"You didn't know him?"

"By sight—yes, sir. Quite a well-known man, Mr. Speer."

"He did good work."

"Yes," he said, and nodded. "He had a very good reputation for specialised work. Not—if you'll pardon me, sir—that we can't do as well. Anything you have in mind, sir, we'll be happy to quote you for."

"I'll bear it in mind," I told him. "You're the owner here?" He smiled.

"Afraid not, sir. But Mr. Harris'll be in this afternoon and could see you. Or if you cared to give me some idea of what it is you'd want done?"

"I'd better talk things over first with my wife. But thank you very much. I'll probably be seeing you again."

"Any time, sir. We're always here."

I almost got to the door, then stopped. I smiled reminiscently. "A man named Brittle used to be here. Is he still with you?" He gave a little laugh. I wondered why.

"Berney Brittle," he said, still smiling. "Afraid he got himself in a bit of trouble, sir. Had to go to jail for a year."

"Really? He always seemed such a reliable sort of man."

"Smarmy as they make 'em," he told me. "He could talk the hind legs off a donkey, Berney could."

"Which just shows you," I said. "I suppose he's left the district now."

"Excuse me laughing, sir, but I just can't help it. You'd never guess what happened to Berney—not in a hundred years. When he came out he turned religious. The Salvation Army took him up. He's one of their prize exhibits, as they say. You know Laverock Street, Clerkenwell? Anywhere round there you're likely to run across Berney, 'specially on a Saturday night when they're having one of their do's."

"Extraordinary!"

He tapped his skull significantly.

"That's what's wrong with Berney. Gone potty. Harmless enough, if you get my meaning." He gave a little cough. "Excuse me, sir, but might I have your name?"

I gave him one of the fake cards our people are supplied with, thanked him again and made my way out. When I turned out of Bridge Street towards my car, I saw the Austin some thirty yards behind it I stood at my car door, looking about me as if uncertain of my whereabouts. A man was approaching on the pavement and I went towards him.

"Excuse me, but can you tell me where Handley Street is?"

"Handley Street," he said. "Handley Street." He shook his head. "Can't say I've heard of it. You're sure it's round this way?"

"That's what I was told."

"Sorry I can't help you. Tell you what, though. Ask at the post office. That's just at the end of Bridge Street there."

He moved off. I looked round again and let myself become aware of the Austin. I went towards it. But I didn't get a chance to speak to the driver. The engine must have been running, for the car was suddenly moving off. It shot past me with an utter disregard of what might have been coming on its offside, and in less than no time it was out of sight round the bend.

But I'd had a view of the driver: indeed, that car had been so near as it passed me that I could almost have touched him if the window had been down. He was a dark-haired man of about fifty; big, broad-shouldered and fleshy faced. There was something of the ex-cop about him. That was why I drove my car on, reversed at a side street and then headed west for City Detection.

Bill Fraser was in his office.

"Sorry we couldn't do more about that little job for you," he told me.

"Glad in a way that you couldn't," I said. "Someone was on the job again this morning, but in another car."

I gave him an edited version of what had happened. He said he was getting quite interested.

"You think the driver suspected you?"

"Don't think so. I've never acted as if I was the least bit suspicious. And I think the act I put on this morning was pretty good. No, Bill. What I think is that he didn't want me to get a good view of him. If he's had orders to carry on tailing me and I'd happened to have a good look at him this morning, and then some time later saw him again, that's when I might have begun being suspicious."

"Just wait a minute," he said, "and I'll get busy on the Austin."

When he came back he suggested adjourning for a cup of coffee. With luck we might know more about the car by the time we'd taken that break. Over coffee I described that driver again.

"A chance in a hundred," he said. "You and I only know the big agencies and I can't place him in any of them. What about leaving it to me to ask around?"

That seemed a good idea. We switched from shop to the inevitable politics and half an hour had gone by the time we were back in his office. He gave a wry smile at the message left on his desk and handed the paper to me.

"The same company but a different car," I said. "Someone's certainly getting interested."

"Changing your mind about letting us do a probe?"

"Don't think so," I said. "I'd rather give whoever it is a little more rope. Between ourselves it might be prejudicial to the job I'm on if it was known I was wise. On the whole I like it this way."

"You should know," he told me. "The trouble is you've got me interested."

"A week or so and I may be able to tell you more. Meanwhile, if you do pick up anything, let me know."

*

There was no sign of the Austin when I took my car back to the garage, but I went out the back way, just in case, and on to the club by bus. Later I went to a cinema and then had a sudden idea. I wondered what had happened to Tibball's old restaurant and made up my mind to have dinner there, just to see what the place was now like.

At the back of my mind, of course, was the thought that something might happen there to throw some kind of light on the queer things that seemed to be happening. But nothing did. It was as dull an evening as I've ever had. The name of the restaurant hadn't been changed, nor, I could ironically tell myself, had the menu. And I had also that hollow kind of feeling that comes to one who inadvisedly goes in search of a lost past. Four years is a long time when you're my age. When I left the restaurant it was as if that evening there with Jewle had never happened.

It was just before nine o'clock when I got back to the flat, and it was only just past the hour when the telephone bell rang.

"Hallo?" I said warily.

"Mr. Travers? This is Carlotta Dawson. Could you possibly come and see us?"

"You mean now?"

"If you can."

"I definitely can," I said. "Can you give me an idea what it's about?"

"I'd rather tell you personally. . . . Sure you don't mind?"

"Be with you as soon as I can grab a taxi," I told her.

She'd sounded a bit perturbed: for one, that is, who had struck me as quiet and singularly self-possessed. For the life of me I couldn't make even a guess at why she should want to see me in person at that time of night. If I'd been given a hundred guesses I doubt if I'd have hit on the answer.

The Harvey Dawsons mightn't have moved since the moment I'd last seen them. I shook hands and this time I did accept a drink. Carlotta Dawson started the ball.

"I know what you're going to say, Mr. Travers, that Harvey's been reading too many whodunits, but you've got to believe us."

I had to smile.

"Just a moment. Why this attack? I don't even know what it's all about!"

"Of course," she said. "You tell Mr. Travers about it, Harvey."

"We're being followed," he said, just like that.

I stared.

"You mean you suspect there's someone following you round?"

"That's just what I do mean," he told me. "I thought so yesterday, but I didn't say anything to Carlotta. It seemed so doggone crazy. Then this morning we were doing the round of the stores and I saw the same man again."

"He'd followed us all the way from Kensington to Oxford Street," she said. "Harvey managed to point him out to me."

"What was he like?"

"All I know is he was clean-shaven and about forty," she said. "Fairly tall, but not so tall as Harvey, and rather thin."

"It's mighty nice of you not to put us down as a couple of hop-heads," he told me. "But what's his racket?"

"It's just incredible," she said. "Nobody could possibly know anything about why we're over here. And we chose this hotel deliberately because a friend back home told us we'd never see any Americans here."

It was mysterious enough, as I told her. And yet there might be an answer. Not the full answer perhaps, but more than a hint.

"Since I saw you last I've been doing quite a lot of research into that robbery and the people concerned in it, and I think I know almost as much as the police knew. But did you know, Mrs. Dawson, that the man Tibball who was killed had a daughter?"

"A daughter?" Dawson said. "You think she was one of the gang?"

It wasn't exactly that, as I told them, even if the police had an idea that Tibball's daughter Gloria had helped Conward to fake an alibi for a snatch job. The important thing, or so it now seemed, was this: Tibball was dead but Conward was about to be released, and the people with whom he'd almost certainly be expected to make contact—if contact hadn't already been made—were Gloria and her husband.

"You mean it's them who might be having us watched?"

"That's all I can think of," I said. "How they got wise to your being over here is another question, but maybe we'll find an answer to that."

"It's horrible!" That was Carlotta Dawson. "I wish now we'd never thought about the whole thing. Let's drop it, dear. We can pay Mr. Travers anything he likes for what he's done for us so far."

"Now, baby, don't take it like that. I'm in this thing and I'm going to stay in it. People aren't going to follow me around without something happening."

I'd never guessed he could be so bellicose. His wife was looking as if at any moment she might be giving way to tears. What I felt it my duty to say didn't check the bellicosity even if it did halt the tears.

"You may *have* to abandon the idea," I told them. "If Conward hid the jewellery that night and he's been in touch with his friends, the Harbans, then they've probably recovered the jewellery already and, when he comes out, all he'll have to do is rejoin them and take his share."

"Mr. Travers is right," she said. "I think we should give the whole idea up."

"Oh no," he told her promptly. "Mr. Travers won't mind if I say he's wrong. If Conward's going to take us to whoever has the jewellery—"

"Just a moment," I cut in. "I've seen your point, but let's suppose Conward is followed and he leads us to the Harbans. What can you do? If, that is, the jewellery's already been sold. What can you prove?"

The shake of the head was a bit wry.

"You have a point there. All the same I reckon we ought to take the chance."

"Right," I said, and smiled. "As a whodunit reader you know the detective always has a card up his sleeve and this is mine. I don't think the jewels have been sold."

"You don't?"

"I'll go further," I said. "Gloria Tibball, as her father's heir, would expect half the proceeds when those jewels were disposed of. I don't think they have been disposed of. I think Conward's doing a double-cross. When he comes out he'll pick up that jewellery and skip the country."

"But why are you so sure?" That was Carlotta again.

"Because Conward hadn't time to dispose of the jewellery before he was nabbed. Everything I've learned about the case shows he was skipping the country till it was safe to come back and collect it. Also, the Harbans have their contacts and they know the jewellery hasn't been disposed of. Also, since prisoners can be written to in jail, the Harbans have almost certainly tried to worm out of Conward where the jewels are. He hasn't told them: ostensibly because there's no honour among thieves, and they're expecting a double-cross."

"You have another point there," Dawson told me.

"I've an even better one," I told him. "It's the Harbans who're having you followed. It can't be anyone else."

"But how—"

"I know. How do they know you're over here and what you're over here for. That doesn't matter. It was something all to the good that you should have been followed. If they don't know you spotted whoever it was, then they've made a false step. They've told us something we'd never have guessed. And now I'll tell you something you didn't know. I've been followed, too." Sensation in court. I told them as much as I thought they ought to know.

"So you see?" I said, as I rose to go. "That jewellery's still waiting to be picked up and we're not starting off so badly informed as we were at the start. There's a kind of treble twist and we're the only ones who know it. Conward's double-crossing the Harbans; they're getting ready to double-cross him and we're hoping to step in between the two parties. That being so, do you still want to give up, Mrs. Dawson?"

"No!" For one usually so quiet, there was almost something vindictive in the word.

"That's my baby," Harvey told her, and smiled.

7. DEVELOPMENTS

THE first thing I realised when I woke in the morning was that three days had gone by of the ten with which I'd started. In exactly a week's time Conward would be loose. Then would come the show-down. I'd done a whole lot of optimistic talking that had been backed by precious little fact. Whereas at the beginning I'd been merely exploring the case and allowing in my own mind about seven days for exploration, after which I'd take the case or refuse it, now I seemed somehow, especially after my talk with the Harvey Dawsons the previous night, to have committed myself entirely. Something extraordinary would have to happen to give me an excuse to back out.

But did I wish to back out? Frankly, I didn't. And yet I'd never had a case that I'd liked less. It was a kind of Dr. Fell dislike, but that didn't alter the fact that I was far from happy about the whole thing. However, I could tell myself that there were still three clear days to my self-imposed zero hour, and quite a lot might happen in that short time. Three days, and then I might be telling the Harvey Dawsons that I couldn't take the case after all. Or I might be deciding to go the whole way, in which case I'd be arranging to have Conward followed, which would be quite a job in itself.

I had breakfast, glanced through my two newspapers and settled down to a crossword. It was when I'd broken off to wonder if my friend in the Austin was parked somewhere handy with yet another car, and waiting for me to emerge from the flat, that the telephone went. It was just after nine o'clock. Who should be on the line but Bertha Munney. She knew I'd be still in town.

If I'd intended to go away I'd have notified the office.

"Someone rang and wanted you personally," she said. "He's going to ring me again in five minutes to hear if I managed to get you."

"What was his name?"

"He wouldn't give one."

"Well, what did he sound like?"

"A funny sort of voice," she said. "As if he was talking between his teeth. A common voice in a way and rather like a Londoner."

"Thanks, Bertha. Give him my number if he rings you back."

I hadn't a notion who the caller could be and I had to wait best part of ten minutes before I had a chance to find out.

"Hallo. Travers here."

"Good morning," the voice said. "Sorry to trouble you, Mr. Travers, but I wondered if you'd be prepared to undertake a job for me."

"I happen to be on holiday, but the Agency might undertake a job. That's what we're in business for. The managing-director—"

"I know all that," he told me. "I want to employ you personally, independent of your Agency."

Bertha had been dead right about the voice. Either the caller had some throat complaint or he was using the old device of a handkerchief gripped between his teeth.

"What is your name and where can I see you?"

"The name doesn't matter—not yet. The thing is whether you're prepared to do the job."

"What *is* the job?"

"The private investigation of a certain company in Vancouver, Canada. It would require you going there. All expenses paid and five hundred pounds for the job. It shouldn't take more than a fortnight."

"Sounds attractive," I said. "But why should you think that I'm specially qualified for such a job?"

"You were recommended. Sorry I can't tell you who by."

"And what do you pay me if I give you the name of a firm in Canada who'll do the job twice as quickly and at about a third of the cost?"

"It has to be confidential."

"They'd be confidential."

"I know about you and I don't know about them. Money doesn't matter and nothing would be saved by cutting down the time."

"Well, let's get down to brass tacks," I said. "You're going to pay me a lot of money to do a highly confidential job: so confidential that you won't even entrust it to one of the most reliable firms in the country—my own. So that means you trust me."

"I do."

"Right," I said. "Then tell me your name and where and when I can meet you to go into things more fully."

"Sorry. The job's far too confidential for that. You'd just pick up instructions at a place to be agreed on, and the plane ticket and a retainer."

I was allowing myself to get annoyed. The whole thing was such a palpable fraud.

"Allow me to make a suggestion," I said. "Your name isn't by any chance Harban?"

There was a silence as if the receiver had suddenly been cupped. Then I could just hear the faint sound of another voice, and then the line really went dead. The caller had hung up.

Was he Harban? I had no real proof but the guess seemed to have been shrewd or the caller would never have hung up.

And then all at once I was furiously angry. The whole thing had been so transparent, and the anger was not so much because

I'd been thought of as an utter fool as that the caller had been so sure that I was a bigger fool than himself.

I told myself that he had to be Harban. Who else would want me out of England for a fortnight? I suppose I ought to have taken it as a compliment that I should have been so definitely assured of my importance. As for that high-toned talk of expenses paid and a five hundred pound fee, I wondered what kind of knavery I'd have been up against if I'd accepted that blind assignment. Probably I'd have arrived in Vancouver to find a non-existent company and then been bilked of expenses home and the balance of the fee.

The whole thing had made me so angry that even when I'd simmered down I couldn't force my thoughts into any sort of logical coherence. It was trying to do so that set me thinking again of that far-back evening with Jewle, and then trying to hear again the sound of Harban's voice. But I'd heard only the professional voice: the suave deference which the better-class patron would look for as a standard. What Harban's voice would be like when the black coat was off him and he was in his domestic circle I couldn't possibly guess, though I couldn't be far wrong in taking it for the voice I'd just heard, disguised as it had to be. That was one of the things that made me decide to act on the assumption that the caller had been Harban.

I lighted my pipe again, sat back in the easy chair with my long legs well out, and tried to do some really careful thinking. Apparently, by Harban's calculations, I was a danger to his plans. Because the Dawsons were employing me? Because of something special that I knew? Something that the man on my tail had reported that I knew? And if so, what was it? And where had the information been unearthed? I could think of only three places: the Dawsons' hotel, Bridge Street, and Elmhurst, and it was the last that seemed the most likely.

But nagging away behind those questions was another one: the most important of all. How could Harban—and his wife—know that the Dawsons were in England? Once they were known to be over here it was fairly easy for Harban to guess why. Considering the facts, the arrival of Carlotta Dawson just before the time of Conward's release could scarcely be a coincidence, and yet, how on earth could the Harbans have discovered what the Dawsons swore had been known only to themselves? Had the Harbans been warned through a friend in America? Could the Dawsons have been seen and recognised over here? I didn't know. What I did know was that it was stupid to go on guessing.

One thing did seem obvious. My name and appearance—as I'd hinted to Jewle—must have been known to the Harbans from as long ago as that night we'd spent at the restaurant and gymnasium. And since the Dawsons had been under surveillance, then I'd been spotted, and after that the rest was easy. And about the Dawsons and myself. Ought I to tell them about that call I'd just received? I thought not. For one thing it could only perturb them, and for another it might give them the idea that I was putting myself on a pedestal. Travers, the latter-day, sea-green incorruptible. The man who couldn't be bribed by a free trip and five hundred pounds.

Thinking of that phone call made me hot under the collar again. The whole thing had been so blatant and so crude. Harban was—he had to be—a remarkably shrewd individual, and he surely couldn't have expected to fool me with anything so patent. But, wait a moment, I said to myself. Why shouldn't I have been expected to recognise the crudity of that proposal? In other words, had it been a proposal at all? Had it been merely a subtle threat?

All at once I was tired of questions. I drew in my legs and hoisted myself up from the chair, and I made up my mind to get away from the telephone and the whole business. I'd get away from the present and back into the past, but definitely not at the flat. So I went to the garage for the car. As far as I could judge there was nobody on my tail.

It was half-past ten when I reached Colindale. I'd used the *Telegraph* files before and knew the procedure, and in less than no time I had the relevant files for the Conward trial. I took a solid hour going over the reports of that trial and made a good few notes. Everything was now more real and even vivid. It was a good thing, I could tell myself, that I knew all the witnesses for the prosecution except Speer himself. Kate Howard, as the one who'd identified Conward, seemed to have made a special impression on the court.

When I came out of the building I looked about me but there was no sign of a parked car or a loiterer. I wondered what I should do with the rest of my day, and then I suddenly decided to go to Elmhurst again and lunch at the Lion. After all, Elmhurst was the likeliest place where the man on my tail had reported that I'd probably unearthed a something which had alarmed his employers, the Harbans. It was a very long shot, as I knew, but maybe I could go all the way back along the discovery trail at Elmhurst and try to find out just what it was that I was credited with having stumbled on.

I drove quite slowly for me. I had to, for though I'd determined to leave all thought about the case till I was at Elmhurst, I couldn't stop the thoughts circling round and round in my brain. And one of the thoughts that all at once came to me was so startling that I drew the car to a halt on the straight stretch of country road and began to think it out. It was this.

To the Dawsons I'd spoken of a triple twist. Three sets of people were about to twist or double-cross each other. But what if there was a fourth twist? What if I was the one who was being twisted!

It was more than a possibility. The Harbans would naturally think that Carlotta Speer knew all her father's business. She would know about the theft of extremely valuable jewellery that night. Whether or not Conward knew it didn't matter. Conward could be put wise when he came out and if or when he recovered the jewellery from where he'd cached it. So as zero hour was at last in sight, this is what the Harbans may have done: got into touch with Carlotta in America and said something like this:

"We're putting our cards on the table. By such and such a time we'll have the jewellery and we realise that if it's broken up and disposed of, we shan't get anything approaching its value. Very well, then: we're proposing to let you have the jewellery back and at well below its value, though at a bigger price than a fence would give for it. If you agree, then be in London by such and such a date and we'll get into touch at the appropriate time and fix everything up."

That, I triumphantly told myself, was the explanation of everything, and all that was needed to clinch it was a new assessment of the characters of Dawson and his wife. He'd be the one who'd be mad for the scheme. Frankly, I hadn't liked the man. He'd struck me as brash and what she'd seen in him beyond financial security I couldn't fathom. She was a woman of considerable culture: his ran about as far as Mickey Spillane. He'd be the one who'd agreed to the scheme and she'd just tagged along. But he couldn't be sure of her. It was she who'd suggested dropping the whole thing after the discovery that they'd been followed.

What he was really doing was, of course, perfecting a scheme to double-cross the Harbans-Conward set-up. I'd been brought in with the hope that I'd recover the jewellery and hand it over, after which the Harbans and Conward couldn't do a thing. I was the pawn in the game: the operative pawn who'd bring checkmate. Not that I could be completely double-crossed. In spite of my guarantee of secrecy if I took the case, I could easily become the worm that simply had to turn. Or, and this made a cold sweat break over me, had the Dawsons in mind some special twist that could make me appear a partner in the double-crossing? Would I find myself in such a position that I not only had to keep my mouth shut but be fobbed off with a token fee instead of a fat reward?

What, then, should be my policy? Surely to string along with the Dawsons for the last days of my allotted seven, and then give the expected decision. That that decision would be to refuse the assignment I had at that moment not the slightest doubt. Indeed, as I drove on, more rapidly now, towards Elmhurst, I was feeling quite an elation. I actually treated myself to half a bottle of quite good wine at lunch.

My first call was at the railway station. According to the full reports of Conward's trial he'd reached Liverpool at two o'clock on the Saturday afternoon. Conward's counsel had tried to throw up a smoke screen about that. Why hadn't Conward been arrested as soon as he walked past the barrier? The answer, which seemed to make no more than a certain amount of sense, had been that the police were anxious to see if he made any contacts. But what if the supposedly guilty Conward had slipped through their fingers? The reply was that he hadn't.

Station Road was one of the spokes of the market-place hub and cut back from it towards the east. The station was about three hundred yards from the centre of the town, and along the wall in which was the main entrance were the usual boards on which were pasted the time-tables. Assuming that Conward had made his way somewhere along the same direct line to Liverpool, I wanted to note the times and the stopping places. What I ascertained wasn't any help. A train that reached Liverpool at two o'clock on a Saturday afternoon could have been the one that left Elmhurst Junction at ten-thirty, after which it became an express. But the train timings might have been changed during the last four years and I checked that up at the booking office. To my surprise they hadn't changed.

Nevertheless that couldn't surely have been the train Conward had taken. He must have picked up another train further along the line: a train that also drew in at Liverpool at two o'clock. In other words, I'd have to acquire an old railway guide and check on trains, or, if I should decide it was sufficiently important, ring Enquiries at Lime Street and ask what trains beside the express were due in on that particular Saturday at two o'clock. A better short cut would be, of course, to put the question to Fusson, but I discarded that notion at once. The less Fusson knew or suspected, the better for general purposes. Besides, I was running short of prevarications.

The afternoon was beginning to wear away and the sky had some ominous clouds. The weather report had mentioned thunderstorms in the late afternoon and it looked as if we were due for one, so I hurried away on the rest of my schedule. What I'd proposed was to visit all the places I'd been to in Elmhurst and to try to recall from what had happened in each place anything which might have a bearing on that vital something which it had been assumed by the man who'd been tailing me, or by the Harbans from his report, was likely to be dangerous to their handling of the major scheme. The visit to Purdon and the *Recorder* office seemed to have no importance. Compared with what had appeared in the national Press, the local paper had printed precious little, and in any case I didn't want to recall myself to Purdon, whose first reaction, however suave my excuses, might be to report the call to Fusson.

So I drove to the scene of the accident. I didn't want to return to the centre of the town, so I navigated by guess and by God and I actually hit Ypres Road. I was on the left-hand side and I halted the car just short of the gate of Littlecroft. I'd never lingered in front of Speer's old house before and so it wasn't there that I could have been supposed to discover anything, but something that afternoon made me stop there for a minute, and in the light of the additional information I'd that morning acquired I tried to project myself back to the night of the robbery.

In less than no time I was at the old game of question and answer, if only because I've always found that the only way to insert one's self clean into the heart of a problem. Become aware of something and then query it. If it stands up to questioning, pursue the same line of thought till a possible snag appears, and then try to unravel it. Abandon, if necessary, the whole thing and try a new approach and tackle each idea in the same way. Be your own inquisitor, in fact, before you find yourself up against a real one.

These then were the questions I had to ask myself. What made Tibball personally undertake that robbery? Jewle knew him for a crook and the associate of crooks, though he couldn't then prove it in a court of law, but Tibball had never previously taken such a risk. He had people like Conward to do the jobs for him—that Kilburn wages snatch, for instance. Admittedly the rewards for that night's work were going to be high, but surely Tibball could have found a reliable man to accompany Conward? Or was it that, the job being so lucrative a prospect, he wanted to keep the whole thing in the family? I couldn't worry out any other reason, and that's how I had to leave it. Conward himself hadn't helped. At his trial he'd been absolutely mute.

Then there was the fact that Tibball himself had done the knocking out of Speer and the actual robbery. There might be a reason for that, as I saw. At the gateway, Conward would be driving the car and he'd have had to stay at the wheel, and that shouldn't have had to be for more than a very few minutes.

Thanks to Brittle, everything necessary had been known about the house and household, and the job should have been over in less than no time. Why, then, had it taken longer than had been thought?

And it had taken longer. Conward had become impatient and had left the car and made his way to the french windows of the study where the unlucky kick against the pail had led to his ultimate undoing. But it seemed to me there'd been something remarkably insouciant about the whole thing. Conward was a cocksure, conceited type: I'd guessed that the first time I'd seen him, but why on earth had he been so careless as to look up towards the window and so risk a sight of himself? Kate Howard was, of course, an unexpected factor, and the looking-up might have been involuntary. So maybe I was wrong in finding anything unusual. And the fact remained that as soon as Kate Howard called out,

Conward slipped into the study, warned Tibball, and the two scuttled round the house as fast as their legs could take them. In a matter of seconds that powerful car had shot off along Ypres Road as if the devil himself had been driving.

I still wasn't too happy about the events of that night but the clouds were more ominous and, as I've said, it wasn't in the neighbourhood of Littlecroft that anyone could have imagined I'd had some dangerous ideas, so I moved the car on to the scene of the accident. I drew the car up near the telegraph pole and began some more thinking, and almost at once I saw something of which I hadn't been aware before.

What I'm sure I've said is this—that Ypres Road was almost the last side road on leaving the town towards the north, and *almost* is the operative word. A little further on was the last side road, and running parallel to Ypres Road. As far as I could judge it wasn't made up, and only a few little houses and bungalows had been built. One or two looked new but some had certainly been there—chiefly those furthest from the main road—at the time of the accident. So why shouldn't Conward have taken that road on leaving the car? Presumably he set off north but the lights of the oncoming motor coach were already a visible blur in the fog.

As I was trying to work out that new idea, the storm broke. It didn't trouble to rain: the heavens opened and let the water out and almost at once it was tearing along the gutters of the road and I could scarcely see beyond the bonnet of my car. It was so dark that I switched on my headlights. And I don't mind saying that I wasn't at all happy. For a few minutes the lightning flashed and the thunder was so near and so deafening that more than once I thought that something quite close at hand must have been struck. Then at last the actual storm moved away north-east, though the rain was almost as hard as ever.

But at least I could think while I waited for the rain to be less heavy. About that road, for instance, which Conward might have slipped into till the coach had passed. Had there been an unfinished house or bungalow there in which he could have stayed till everything was quiet on the main road? Could he have concealed the jewellery there while he was waiting? It seemed a feasible idea, and before long that might be the answer, for if Conward made for Elmhurst on his release, then somewhere along that road might be just the one spot he was making for.

But for the rain I'd have driven along that road if only to get the feel of it and to find out if it was a dead end or turned ultimately into Ypres Road. But Ypres Road would have been the last place where Conward wanted to be seen, so the chances were that he'd done what the police had guessed he had—gone back to the main road and cautiously along it till he'd been able to get a lift.

I looked at my watch. Time had seemed to drag, and yet somehow the afternoon had slipped away and it was almost half-past five. I told myself that whether the rain had ceased or not, I'd begin the journey back at the half-hour. The rain didn't slacken till I was a good twenty miles on the road for home and then it began to peter out. In London there hadn't been so much as a drop.

On the whole it had been an interesting day, but somehow I hated the idea of staying in the flat and getting myself involved in endless questions. There comes a time in quite a lot of cases when you're no longer your own master, and the questions take possession of you and circle round and round and you can't even sleep, so I had a clean-up and went along to the grass-widower's refuge—the club. I didn't leave it till nearly nine o'clock. No one telephoned me and a tough crossword kept my brain employed, and then at soon after ten I got into bed with a stiff whisky inside me, and in less than no time I actually fell asleep.

I didn't even wake up till the alarm sounded at half-past six and when I got up I felt clear in the head and on top of the world. The sun was shining and I knew before I'd made my mind up to it that after breakfast I'd be going round to the garage and heading once more for Elmhurst.

8. Discovery?

I was in no particular hurry to move off that morning on the quest for whatever it was that had made me a dangerous person in the eyes of the Harbans, and it was lucky that I was still in the flat just after nine o'clock, for Bill Fraser rang me. He wanted to know if anyone had been on my tail since I'd last seen him.

"Not that I could discover," I told him. "Looks to me as if he's been called off."

"A pity," he said. "We've found out who he is."

"Fine," I said. "And who is he?"

"His name's Scant—Percy Scant. Runs a one-man agency in a one-room office just off Chancery Lane. Advertises in some of the Sunday rags: the through-the-keyhole-or-what-the-butler-saw type. Did you ever hear of a chap called Tibball?"

That hit me clean in the wind. I clammed up.

"Tibball? The name seems familiar."

"Got killed in a car smash when he was doing a job out in the country," he said. "One of the behind-the-scenes big-shots. Ran a restaurant and a gym in Soho. Mayworth Street."

"I remember him now."

"Well, Scant used to be an instructor in that gym. I don't think he had a record but he's said to be pretty tough. I think he'd double-cross anybody if he was offered enough, so what about trying him out and seeing who his employers were?"

"A bit risky," I said. "I can't tell you all the circumstances, Bill, but I still think it'd be better to give him more rope. Later on I might be glad to throw him to you."

That was how we left it. The news had been surprising: just one more piece of the jig-saw fitting comfortably in. The Harbans had wanted me followed so they'd looked up an old friend. Everything still nicely kept in the family.

There was no sign of Scant when I fetched my car. Once clear of the suburbs I kept an eye well out, but nothing, I was sure, was following me. When I was near Elmhurst I didn't go through the town. By now I had the topography in my mind, and even if I hit a wrong road I could always get myself oriented again, so I turned sharp right and came out at the station, and after that it was easy to make my way along Ypres Road to the scene of the accident.

But I didn't stop there, because I'd had an idea long before I'd reached the main road again. The person most nearly connected with the events of that night was Kate Howard, and therefore it was out of Scant's report on my visit to her that the Harbans had deduced that I'd learned something which might queer their pitch. Mind you, try as I might I could think of nothing Kate Howard had told me which hadn't been published in the Press, but nevertheless I thought it might be a good idea to pay another visit to Puckenford.

I drove past the little thatched cottage, reversed the car at the entrance to a farm, and then drew the car in at Kate Howard's gate. She and I must have hit it off together for she gave me a beaming smile when she saw who it was that had knocked. I was ushered into the living-room again. It was as spotlessly clean and as snug as ever: there was even a cat asleep on the rug.

"This time you're going to have a cup of tea," she told me. "I'll make it at once. The kettle is on."

I looked about me while she was bustling around in the tiny kitchen. Two Windsor chairs had a lovely patina. A pair of Georgian gun-metal candlesticks on the mantel-shelf shone like gold. The two Staffordshire figures of a sailor and his lass had never a chip. The white-faced grandfather clock might have been bought anywhere for under ten pounds, but I'd never seen one with a polish so high that its oak looked almost like mahogany.

"I've been admiring your things," I said as she came in with the tray. "Did you have to start furnishing when you came here, or were your things in store?"

"We had them all at Littlecroft," she told me. "We had two big rooms to ourselves upstairs."

Another moment and we were having another laugh. The only man's cup, as she called it, was one of the old-fashioned moustache cups, and if ever a moustache wasn't in need of protection it was that toothbrush one of mine. The tea was good and so were the little home-made buns.

"I've been thinking such a lot about Miss Carlotta since you were here that it made me quite miserable," she told me. "That's why it's so nice to have a good laugh."

"And you haven't thought of anything that might help me?" She frowned.

"Well, there was something, but I didn't know. I did think of ringing, and then I thought it couldn't be anything."

"That was very naughty of you," I told her archly. "It doesn't matter what it is, if you think it has any bearing whatever on what we were talking about, ring me any evening after nine o'clock. And be sure to reverse the charges. That's an order, young lady. And now tell me what it was that you didn't ring me about."

"Well, it was on the Thursday before all the trouble. Mr. Speer came home about two o'clock and he told me he'd had lunch and he was going to work in the study and he didn't want to be disturbed. Gladys was out because it was her afternoon off, so at about four o'clock I took a tea-tray to the study and just as I got to the door I heard voices—Mr. Speer's and another man's— so I didn't know what to do. At any rate, I thought I could fetch another cup if I was wanted to, so I tapped at the door and tried the handle, but the door was locked. Then Mr. Speer came to the door. He didn't open it. He just said 'Who's there?' and I said it was me bringing his tea. He didn't say anything for a minute and then he said I was to bring it in half an hour and I did, and then whoever it was had gone."

"Did Mr. Speer make any comment?"

"Not a word. He was working at his table and he said to put the tray down."

"Had that kind of thing ever happened before?"

"Not like that. But I knew he did have visitors sometimes when I was out, because there'd be cigarette ends in the ash trays and he'd given up smoking because of his chest."

"You didn't hear any actual words that afternoon?"

"I didn't," she said. "But they must have been talking loudly about something or I'd never have heard anything at all. It's a close-fitting door and there was a thick curtain inside against the draughts. Mr. Speer hated draughts."

"Mr. Speer's man Brittle came down occasionally, I understand?"

"Oh, he did. But he always came to the front door. This one, whoever he was, must have gone straight round to the back. I'm sure I'd have heard him if he'd rung. I've got wonderful hearing."

I told her that what she'd said might be of considerable help, which was another reason why she should ring me if she thought of anything else. A few minutes later I left.

"Why don't you come to town yourself for a day?" I told her at the door. "Kick your heels up for once."

"My dancing shoes were worn out long ago," she told me with a twinkle. "Still, perhaps one of these days I really will have a day up in London."

As we shook hands she reminded me once again that when I wrote to Carlotta I was to be sure to mention her and say she'd love to have a letter. And that was about all. She was still at her door and she waved as I moved the car off. A lovable soul, I thought to myself. I even thought it might be nice to lure her to town when Bernice got back and to make her have lunch with us. As for the half-hour I'd spent at Puckenford, I didn't dream of thinking it a waste of time, even if all she had had to tell me seemed to have no bearing on the case.

I drew the car close in, near wheels on the grass verge, and tried to pick up the thread of thought at where I'd left it at the tail-end of the thunderstorm of the previous afternoon. That road down which Conward might have made his way that night, was called Underdown Road. A notice just below the name said it was UNADOPTED, which meant that its surfacing and upkeep was still the responsibility of the owners of property. On the whole, the surface wasn't bad if one avoided the larger potholes.

Ideas didn't come, so I moved the car into Underdown Road. It was quite pleasant, but for the fact that there were no trees, for gardens were still colourful with autumn flowers and the small houses and bungalows stood well back on their lawns. If Conward had sheltered in one of them that night till the main road was clear, then I might have to pay a visit to the Rural District Council to find out which properties were either being built on that night or were unoccupied.

Not that I liked the idea. If the jewellery had been buried, for instance, in the garden of a house still unfinished, how could Conward assume that the spot wouldn't be disturbed when the owners or tenants began to make the garden up? If he concealed it in the house itself, how could he expect to recover it? Unfortunately I found an answer to both questions. Conward was expecting to be out of the country only so long as there was a danger in returning. He might never come under suspicion at all, in which case he could return almost at once, and, since the house would still be unfinished, he could expect to find the jewellery where he'd planted it. And that was a chilling thought. Conward had never left the country, and somewhere in one of those houses or gardens the jewellery might still be, and even he could never recover it.

As if washing my hands of Underdown Road I moved the car more quickly on. I took the only turn, to the right, and once more I was at the upper end of Ypres Road. I suppose it was involuntarily that I stopped the car and, as I did so, I had a happier thought. Conward *did* expect to recover the jewellery! Wherever he had hidden it, he knew he could find it, for if not what was all the fuss about?

As I now saw things, the Harbans had got into touch with Conward. Conward could write letters from jail and a two-way use of code could bamboozle both the prison censor and the Deputy Governor. Either Harban himself or Gloria could have seen Conward on visiting days, and for the purpose of getting news about the jewellery. But Conward had feared a double-cross and had merely said that the jewellery was in a safe place and could await his release.

And then, clean out of the blue, I had an idea that almost staggered me. How the police had missed it I didn't know, but it was this. What Conward did before leaving the wrecked car was to empty Tibball's pockets and remove every possible thing that might identify him. I didn't know if he'd had time to flood the carburettor, but when he put a lighted paper to the engine there'd have been sufficient oil to start the fire, and the fact remained that the fire was well alight when he left the car.

You see it? That car should have burnt itself out, by which time Tibball should have been only a charred and unidentifiable body. It might have taken days to discover who he was, if it was ever discovered at all. So what had Conward immediately to worry about? Why risk getting a ride? Why not go into the town, pass the night there and then take the morning train for Liverpool?

If anything was foolproof, that idea certainly was—or so I thought when I'd first worked it out. And then I began to test it and found only one problem. If Conward thought himself safe from suspicion, why did he go to Liverpool *without* the jewellery? I took me quite a time to find the satisfying answer. Conward and Tibball had expected to find a parcel of diamonds and the travelling case had been specially made accordingly. But what they found was a collection of jewellery, the total amount being pretty bulky, and there looked no way of getting past the Customs.

And another thing. Conward would be harassed with doubts. Could he be so sure that, working in the comparative dark, he'd taken every single thing that could possibly identify Tibball? I tried to worm myself into his mind. What I'd have decided on was what everything I'd so far discovered in the case told me he must have done himself: decided to put the jewellery in a safe place and use that ticket to America till he knew just what was known by the police.

It's no use finding a theory and not working it out, so I thought of Conward carrying his bag along Underdown Road that night and coming past the spot where I sat. Everything would still be quiet, before the arrival of the police, at Littlecroft, and in any case there might be a certain amount of fog at that end of Ypres Road. Would he be making for any particular hotel? He could be in one long before ten o'clock and my guess was that he'd cased the town and knew it pretty well before the job was done. Would he have gone direct to the station in the hope of finding a late train? That was another chilling thought, and I felt a relief when it could be rejected. Conward couldn't have done anything about that jewellery when in a train, and surely the fact that he'd arrived at Liverpool at two o'clock the following afternoon showed that the train he'd actually taken was the morning one from Elmhurst Junction.

So it was up to me to discover where he had passed the night. I moved slowly on and almost at once had to make a decision. Left or right? I went right, and pretty soon I knew where I was—at Alton Road which I'd taken once before: a road which kept right and tapered off till it turned into the main road about a hundred and fifty yards north of the market square. A furniture van was ahead of me as I neared the end and if my car hadn't been virtually crawling some fifty yards behind that van I'd never have seen what I did. Projecting from the opposite wall was a notice—

COMMERCIAL HOTEL
GARAGE

I moved the car a few yards on till I could see through the opened doors to the hotel yard. The hotel then was at the corner of the main road and Alton Road, and the entrance would be in the main road. That western end of Alton Road was a second-class shopping centre: an overspill, as it were, of the last shops that straggled north from the town centre. A greengrocer's shop was almost within touching distance across the pavement from where I sat and just beyond it was what looked like a combination of newsagent, tobacconist and fancy store.

I looked at my watch. It was after midday, so I drove the car into the hotel yard. A man in his shirt-sleeves was washing it down with a hose.

"Can I leave my car here while I have lunch?"

"Certainly, sir, Just draw it up against that wall. You needn't go round, sir," he told me when I'd parked the car. "You can go through this door here."

I went along a passage that took me past the kitchen and then through to the small entrance hall. Its glazed doors had coloured lozenges but I could see through to the main road and its traffic. As I turned back a man came from a side passage. He was about forty, florid in face and with a scar along one cheek. I guessed he was the manager.

"Pardon me, but can I have lunch here?"

"Certainly, sir. First lunch at half-past twelve."

He had a colourless but not unpleasant voice.

"You're the manager?"

"Yes, sir. The proprietor, actually. Comes to the same thing."

He smiled, and I smiled.

"The cloak-room's just through here, sir. And the bar, if you'd like a drink before lunch."

I had a bit of a polish and went through to the bar. It was comfortable and airy. I'd had not too good an opinion of commercial hotels, but this one, though not so large as the Lion, or so showy, looked as well-conducted. There were about a dozen people in the bar, and I took my pint of bitter to an easy chair by the window. I listened to scraps of conversation and I learned that the barman was called Joe. He was a big, fattish man of about fifty with an amiable moon face. He'd have made an excellent Bottom the Weaver—not that the bar seemed to regard him as any sort of a fool. He was just a friendly part of a friendly room and he did his job well.

The gong went. Joe told me how to get to the dining-room. It wasn't very large and it was pretty full by one o'clock.

The steak-and-kidney pudding was as good as I'd had in a long time and there was an excellent plum tart. I gave the waitress a good tip.

"What's the proprietor's name?" I asked her.

"Carver, sir."

"Do me a favour," I said. "Ask Mr. Carver if he can see me for a minute."

She was back in about three minutes. Mr. Carver would see me in the office. She showed me the way.

It was a smallish room with the usual desk, files, telephone and odd chairs. I gave him one of my business cards. He looked at it and then at me.

"Just something I'm hoping you might help me about," I told him. "Mind if I close the door? It's rather confidential."

I told him that my firm was trying to trace a man who was known to have spent a night at the hotel some four years since. He was wanted as evidence in the matter of witnessing a will. A lot of money was at stake.

"Afraid I can't help you," he said. "I've only been here for a year. My father died and I took over. After the war I managed a place down in Brighton and I never used to come here except occasionally on a holiday."

"You'll excuse my being a bit secretive," I told him, "but we know the man we want actually slept here on a certain night early in November four years ago. I can't tell you how we know except that it happened to be a night when there was a bit of excitement here. There was a robbery and a car got burnt and a man killed."

"I've heard about that," he said. "Caused quite a stir. And you say this man was staying here that very night?"

"Yes. Something that was let fall told us that he must have been here that night. Do you think any of your staff would remember? He was a youngish man and he almost certainly arrived late. Not far short of ten o'clock."

"There's no one here," he said. "My wife took over as housekeeper and there's a new cook. Always changing staff in a place like this. It's a regular headache."

"Nobody at all who was here that night?"

"Only Joe," he said. "And he wouldn't know much about residents, unless he took a drink up after closing time."

"What about the hotel register?"

"I might find that—if it'd help."

It took him quite a time to find the requisite book. It had been well kept. There were the names of guests, the numbers of their rooms and how many nights they'd been staying. That particular night six rooms had been occupied. I took down the names. Their addresses weren't sufficiently detailed.

"Do you know any of these personally?" I asked Carver. "I notice, by the way, that there's one married couple and five single men."

"Most that we get here are passing through. This was originally thought of as a commercial travellers' hotel. Used to be quite a lot of them before they started having their own cars and doing in a day what used to take best part of a week. This one, for instance—Stockwold. He still puts up here and I know him well, but there was a time when he used to make this his centre for three or four days."

"You think I could get into touch with him?"

"I don't see why not," he said. "You could find out where he is from his firm: McMorrows, the big seed and fertiliser people at Peterborough."

I made a note. Then I asked him if I might have a word with the barman.

"He'll be off duty in another half-hour," he said, "and then he has his dinner in the kitchen. Tell you what: I'll have it sent to the saloon bar and you can talk to him there, and you won't be disturbed."

I thanked him. I said I'd be only too glad to pay for his own or anybody else's time.

"Glad to be of help," he told me. "If you like to give Joe a tip that'll be nobody's business."

Joe and I had quite a chat in the smelly quietude of that saloon bar. I gave him the same story and as soon as I mentioned a certain night, there was no stopping him. Not that I wanted to.

He gave me a complete account as remembered by Elmhurst and seen through its eyes.

"Quite a lot of customers in that night," he said, "not that we aren't always pretty full. Though I say it, this is as popular a bar as any in the town. The beer's good for one thing. But about what I've been telling you, sir. The real sensation was when Fred Borrow came in—he's the chemist just across the road. Lives in the first house as you turn into Ypres Road, if you know where that is. We'd already heard about this car accident and a man being killed, and when Fred came in he reckoned the police knew who the man was. He'd seen the fire from his house and had gone there and had heard the police talking about it. Later on it all came out in the papers."

"Any strangers in here at that time?"

He smiled.

"Bless my soul, sir, it's no use asking me that. Seven thousand people here, you know, and I don't know the quarter of 'em."

"Any of the residents in for a drink?"

He frowned as he tried to think back.

"A Mr. Stockwold was here that night," I said, trying to jog his memory.

"Ah!" he beamed. "I remember now, sir. He wasn't in here. A rare one for a game of solo, Mr. Stockwold is. The first thing he does round about dinner time is to try to make up a four, and that night there was a four in the upstairs lounge. I remember taking a tray of drinks up after we'd closed and having a dekko for a minute or two."

I heard a whole lot more from Joe and had to listen with an ersatz interest though nothing further seemed pertinent. Finally I thanked him, gave him a ten-shilling note, reported briefly back to Carver and went out to my car. I drove clear of the town and then stopped the car and did some quick thinking. Somehow I was certain that Conward had slept that night at the Commercial Hotel.

To prove it to myself I had to work from the wrong way round. I'd wondered why Conward had decided to go on to Liverpool and to hide the jewellery when he'd taken every precaution to conceal the identity of Tibball. But *if* Conward had been in that bar near closing time that night—and he'd probably have been anxious to hear what was known—and *if* he'd heard that the police knew the identity of the dead man, then there was no need for me to ask myself any more questions.

9. A New Mystery

When I reached the flat it was too late to ring that Peterborough firm of seed merchants and I was annoyed with myself for not having called them up from somewhere along the road. In the morning I'd have to wait till after nine o'clock, and as I'd then have an eighty mile drive—if Stockwold were available—it looked as if a whole day would be gone from the few that were left. And now that I was at last on a really warm scent, I grudged every minute that kept me from following it up.

I'd expected the Dawsons to ring me that night, but they didn't, and it would have been an early bird who rang me the next morning, because I was on my way not long after nine. Getting through North London was a slow business, but I made good time after that and it was still well short of midday when I parked my car among a score of others in front of the long range of the McMorrow buildings. The clerk to whom I was ultimately directed happened to be the one who'd talked with me on the telephone that morning and he showed me the way to Stockwold's office.

It wasn't much larger than a private cubby-hole. Stockwold himself was a man of about fifty: shortish, running to fat and with a reddish purple face that wouldn't have been a bad advertisement for a firm of brewers. The clerk had told me that Stockwold was their star traveller and I could well believe it.

"Mr. Travers? Glad to see you, sir."

He was beaming. The welcoming hand might have been for a long-lost friend.

"Glad to see you," I said, and gave him a business card. He looked a bit nonplussed for a moment.

"Your sins haven't caught up with you," I told him. "It just happens that your name was given me as likely to supply some information."

I was looking about for room to sit.

"A bit crowded in here," he told me. "Tell you what, sir. They're open, so why shouldn't we slip across to the George?"

We went to the George. On the way I told him what it was all about. We were entering the saloon bar by the time I'd finished. He said he'd have a whisky and didn't demur when I suggested a double. I had a pint of bitter. The room was almost empty and we found a table well away from the bar. He'd apparently swallowed my story, hook, line and sinker.

"To tell you the honest-to-God truth, sir, I don't remember much about that evening. I read about it in the papers later on, but I was upstairs from after dinner till best part of eleven o'clock. I like a game of solo and I'd managed to get a four."

He put his glass down and I thought he was listening for something.

"Just a minute, sir. I don't know that I can't help you. Someone who might have come in late, you said?"

"That's right. And probably young. Say in the early thirties."

"It's coming back," he said. "I got this solo four as I was telling you, but one of them was there with his wife and he wanted to stop at soon after ten. You know that upstairs lounge, sir? . . . You don't. Not that it matters much. But you know the layout of the upstairs and how all the bedrooms open out on the passage that goes right round to the stairs. Well, I had my usual Number 6, the room I've had for donkey's years, and we were playing, as I said, and I think it was about half-past nine or just after when I heard Jessie—she used to be one of the chambermaids—say something to somebody outside.

"To cut a long story short, just after ten o'clock the wife of the man who was playing hinted it was time for bed. She'd been sitting in front of the fire knitting, and when the last hand was played they went off and I thought it was a bit early to break the game up. Then I remembered about Jessie and how she might have been bringing someone up, so I told the other two to wait and nipped off downstairs and had a look at the register, and, sure enough, there'd been someone booked in."

"Here's a copy from the actual register," I said. "The last name on the list for that day was a H. J. Mills, said to be from Birmingham, and staying the one night. In Room 7."

"That's right," he said. "The next room to mine. What I thought was, you see, that he might make a four and we could carry on for a bit, so I tapped at his door and I heard him say, 'Who's that?' and when I tried to open the door it was locked, so I guessed he was in bed and the light out and everything, so all I did was apologise—called out it was the wrong room, see?—and that's how it was."

"Did you see him at breakfast?"

"I didn't," he said. "I used to be away pretty early in the mornings. But I did say something to Jessie about him." He gave me a wink. "Always used to have a joke with Jessie, so I asked her what he'd had for dinner that made him on the trot. I'd heard him get up in the night, see? Might have been once or it might have been twice, I can't remember, but she did tell me he'd been caught by the fog on his way to Birmingham. Oh yes, and that he'd got toothache. He asked where the nearest dentist was. And that's about all. To tell you the truth I'd forgotten about the whole thing till you reminded me."

A pint was enough for me but I fetched him a refill.

"Here's how," he said. "Know this toast? May the skin of your backside never cover a banjo. Not bad, is it?"

I said it was pretty good and I'd have to remember it.

"I've got a string of 'em," he told me. "Goes down well with the customers. But about what we were talking about. I thought of something else while you were at the bar. I'm practically sure Jessie told me he was a youngish sort of chap. You think he'd be the one you want?"

I said I was practically sure he was. Then he wanted to know what my next step would be and I had to concoct something on the spur of the moment. I think he'd have been there, absorbing refills till closing time, if I hadn't asked him to recommend a good place for lunch. He said I couldn't do better than where I was.

"What about Joe, the barman?" he asked me, when we were at last on our feet. "He's about the only one left from the days when the old man was there. Joe might remember something."

"I did have a word with Joe," I told him. "It was he who suggested seeing you. I don't know if you remember, but Joe brought up a tray of drinks that night just before you finished the game."

He smiled.

"That's right. I was in the chair. The lady had a harlot's joy. You know, a port and lemon."

He laughed as he held out his hand. He cut me off when I began thanking him.

"Always glad to be of help. Which reminds me"—I think he must have winked, though I didn't catch it, "the waitress is Mabel. Tell her I sent you and she'll look after you all right."

I went with him to the door. We shook hands a second time and he told me he might be seeing me.

"And thanks for the drinks."

"It strikes me I'm lucky you didn't sell me a ton of fertiliser," I told him.

He laughed. He turned back.

"You could do with a ton?"

"I could," I said. "Provided you sold me a garden. I happen to live in a flat."

"I might do that," he said, and from the way he smiled as he nodded his head, I'm pretty sure he meant it.

He waved a cheery hand. I watched him for a moment before I went in search of the dining-room.

I suppose that if that meal had been the worst I'd eaten for years I wouldn't have grumbled much. It had been a morning beyond all expectations. Had it come to a bet. I'd have laid pretty heavy odds on the H. J. Mills of the hotel register and Frank Conward as one and the same person.

I even thought I could follow Conward from the time he left the burning car till almost the next morning. I didn't think he was over-grieved at Tibball's death. His kind would have had a couple of other thoughts: relief at his own escape and the fact that that jewellery could be entirely his own. Whereas he'd been prepared to act on the square with Tibball—in fact, it might have been highly dangerous to do otherwise—the loyalty didn't extend to Tibball's relatives.

Once that car was alight and he was away in the fog, he'd have been rather cock-a-hoop. If he'd been casing the town prior to the robbery, then he'd have been making straight for that hotel. There was no real danger, of course, to himself. By the time the police discovered who the charred body had been, he himself would have returned from America with the proceeds of the jewellery sale. Or maybe he'd been wondering if it mightn't be better to stay there altogether.

But Conward wasn't foolhardy. That accident must have been too near and the stakes too high for that, so if he had a muffler he put it round his mouth, and if he hadn't he'd turned his coat collar up round his ears before he entered the hotel. At that hour of night there'd have been nobody at the desk. When he rang, the proprietor might have appeared, or Jessie, and he told his tale, signed the register and was taken to his room.

But he'd be restless up there and probably in need of a drink, and he'd be wondering, too, if there was any news as yet about a burned-out car, so he put on his hat and coat again and went down to the bar. Then came that shock when the chemist came in with the latest news. Something had gone badly wrong. If the police really knew the dead man was Tibball, and since that woman at the house might have seen his own face, then the hue and cry might be on almost at once.

It was a scared man, then, who went back to the bedroom. That jewellery had to be disposed of, and his own getaway had to be planned, so when the hotel was quiet and everyone asleep he did hide that jewellery, and he made up his mind to go on to Liverpool in the morning. How that latter was done didn't matter. It was the main problem that was left, and the answer to that ought to lie in the hotel itself.

I paid my bill and prepared to leave. As I went past the bar I thought I heard Stockwold's voice, and there he was talking to an elderly man who had the look of a farmer. When he caught sight of me he broke off his conversation.

"I thought you'd gone back to your office," I said.

"Just had a few things to finish," he told me. "What about one for the road? There's just time."

"Not for me," I said. "I've got to be off."

"They give you a good lunch?"

"Quite good."

"I don't always bother about it myself. Drop in here for a sandwich and then have a good meal at night. Nothing else I can do for you?"

"Now I think of it, there is," I said. "I'm pretty sure my man was the one you told me about, but what about a word with Jessie? He might have asked her about trains, for instance, and then I might pick up his trail from the railway station."

"I've read about people like you," he told me, "but I never thought I'd meet it in what you might call real life. You mean to say you think you can trace him after all this time?"

I smiled.

"The job's easy, compared with some. And there's no telling what he may have told Jessie."

"Yes, Jessie," he said, and frowned. "I think she got married about three years ago. I remember asking about her not so long ago and someone told me she was living in one of the new council houses as you come into the town. But what about Joe? Why don't you ask him? He'd be bound to know."

"I think I will," I said, and held out my hand. "Thanks again."

This time I did catch the wink.

"I'll still have the name and address at Christmas," he told me, "and still be drinking whisky. Any proprietary brand'll do."

"Good," I said. "I'll make a note of it."

It was about forty miles across country to Elmhurst and I made it before four o'clock. I left my car in the main road and went into the hotel by the back door. There seemed to be no one about, but before I could ring a waitress appeared.

"Tea, sir?"

"Later, yes," I said. "I'd rather like to speak to Joe if he happens to be about."

"He's in the kitchen," she told me. "I'll send him along to you. Just wait a minute, sir."

Joe must have remembered the tip I'd given him. He smiled at the sight of me and flicked a finger.

"Came to thank you, Joe, for one thing," I said. "I've just been seeing Mr. Stockwold and he gave me quite a lot of information. And he advised me to see someone named Jessie. Used to be chambermaid here."

"Jessie Porter." He smiled. "Used to be Jessie Green. Married a man who works on the railway. Saw her only the other day." He thought her house was one of the first as you came into the town on the London Road. Another ten minutes and I'd asked for it and found it. And she was at home.

She was a thin-faced but quite good-looking woman of about thirty. When I mentioned Joe, she smiled, and asked me in. The little sitting-room was hideous, but I think she was quite proud of it, from the pair of pink vases with pinker roses on the mantelshelf to the fumed oak furniture and the flowered green carpet. From the prim way she sat I gathered she didn't know quite what to make of me, but she was quick-witted enough to follow what I told her and she couldn't help laughing when I brought in Stockwold.

"He was a scream," she told me. "Always one for a joke. But I don't see what else I can tell you."

"Well, what about going over everything that happened that night from the time you saw this Mr. Mills?"

She frowned for a moment or two.

"Well, as far as I remember, I was going to the side door of the bar to fetch old Mr. Carver's gin. He always had one about that time, and then I saw this Mr. Mills come in. He said could he have a room and I said he could and did he want anything to eat, and he said he'd had it; and then he told me about his car and the fog and how he should have gone on to Birmingham and how he had toothache and did I know a dentist where he could go in the morning."

"He had his face wrapped up?"

"I don't know. I think he had his coat collar turned up so as to keep his face warm."

"What age would you say he was?"

"I don't know. Somewhere about thirty, far as I remember."

"Good. And what then?"

"Well, I showed him where to sign the book and then I went to take his bag, but he took it himself, so I showed him his room and he said it was quite nice. Oh, and he asked me about trains in the morning, and I said there was always a time-table in the lounge."

"What about the morning?"

"I didn't see him. I always did the lounge first—that'd be before breakfast—and I didn't get round to the bedrooms till about half-past nine, and he was gone by then. He'd left me a tip, though. Oh, and I remember something. He'd been out for a newspaper because there was one in his room."

"If I remember rightly there's a shop just across the road."

"That's right. As you come out the back way, in Alton Street."

"Do you know if he had breakfast?"

"He had it brought up. I remember now. We always used to get to talking in the kitchen about the residents and all that, and I remember Mary—she was the head waitress then—she told me she'd taken up his breakfast, and how he wanted nothing but porridge on account of his toothache. Porridge and coffee."

"Do you remember what his bag was like? Was it new, for instance?"

She said she hadn't really seen it but from the way he'd carried it she'd thought it was fairly heavy. And that was about all I thought I could ask her, except about his bill, and Mary, it appeared, had been asked to bring that up with his breakfast. After that, all there was to do was to thank her and make a suitable exit.

I was out of the town so I didn't go back to the hotel but drove on. It was almost five o'clock and it had been a long day. But a lucky one. I was as sure of Conward now as that my hands were on the driving wheel. And there was still one more day of my allotted seven. In the morning, I told myself, I'd pay yet another visit to Elmhurst and on Operation Jewellery.

That was what I thought but things didn't turn out that way. It was half-past seven when I got to the flat so I thought I'd have a night at home. I rang down for a service meal and after it I thought I'd catch up with some reading and keep my mind off the case for fear it should upset my sleep. Then at about ten-past nine the telephone went. I guessed it'd be the Dawsons, but it wasn't. I smiled when I recognised the voice.

"Is that Mr. Travers?"

"It is," I said. "And isn't that Mrs. Howard?"

"Yes," she said. "And, oh dear! I've had such a time trying to get you. Mrs. Uttley's very good about using the phone, but I really thought I'd have to give it up."

"The great thing is you've got me."

"Yes," she said. "There was something I thought of after you left me the other morning and I wondered if I ought to tell you about it, and then I thought I would." I seemed to catch a sigh. "Oh, dear! I'm in a muddle already."

"Never mind the muddle," I said. "Just go on talking."

"Well, it was something I didn't want to talk about over the telephone. You never know who might be listening, so I thought I'd do what you said I ought to do."

"You mean have a day in town?"

"Yes," she said. "I suppose I oughtn't to, but I thought I would."

"Fine," I said. "What train are you coming in by?"

"The one that leaves at half-past nine," she said. "I can get the bus from here and have plenty of time."

"Good," I said. "I'll be at Euston and meet you with the car. We can have some coffee and you can tell me all about it, and then you can carry on with your day in town. How will that do?"

"It's very nice of you, and you really oughtn't to go to all that trouble."

"Not a bit of it. It'll give me an enormous pleasure. I'll be at the barrier when you come through."

I thought she'd rung off but she hadn't.

"Excuse me asking, but I suppose you haven't heard from Miss Carlotta again?"

"Expecting to—"

That was what was on the tip of my tongue. But I didn't say it. I still don't know what it was that made me say what I did. Maybe it was a combination of a whole lot of things: the lovable soul that she was, how much she'd always thought of Carlotta Speer and the thrill I knew she'd have when I gave her the news. And I did speak almost in the act of thinking.

"I've got a great surprise for you. Who do you think is now in England?"

"Not Carlotta?"

"Yes. And her husband. I'll let them know you're coming to town and perhaps they'll be at the station to see you."

"That'd be wonderful! I feel so happy—well, I feel I'd like a good cry."

"Well, have it now and have a nice smiling face in the morning," I told her. "See you at the barrier."

I was still smiling as I hung up. Then I frowned. I ought to tell the Dawsons, and I wondered how they'd take it. However much Kate Howard thought of Carlotta Speer, the fact remained that Carlotta hadn't kept up correspondence. Then I took a deep breath and decided to get it over. I had her on the line almost at once.

"Travers here, Mrs. Dawson."

"Oh! How are you Mr. Travers? What have you been doing?"

"Still making enquiries. Haven't unearthed anything worth reporting."

"Are you still being—you know?"

I gathered she meant being followed.

"I don't think so. And you?"

"Harvey isn't sure. If we are, it's a different man. An older man. We did think of changing the hotel but Harvey thought that would be stupid."

"A change of hotel might make a difference if you could do it without leaving a trail."

"Wait a minute and I'll tell him."

In less than a minute I was being told that Harvey had decided to stay put. He was getting a kick out of it all.

"Oh, and I was to tell you, or remind you, that you're supposed to give us your decision tomorrow about taking our case."

"I haven't forgotten," I told her. "But in the meanwhile I've got a surprise for you. Someone who's very fond of you is coming to town tomorrow morning to give me some information about that very case, and I thought it would give her pleasure to tell her you were over here."

"Someone who's very fond of me," she said slowly. "Whoever can that be?"

"Kate Howard. Your old housekeeper. I'm meeting her at Euston at about half-past ten. I was pretty sure you'd like to see her and I know she'd love to see you."

"Just a moment," she said again. "I'll ask Harvey what we were supposed to be doing."

"You there?" she said in a moment or two. "Harvey says you could send her on here or bring her. We might have lunch or something."

"That'll be fine," I said. "I'll see she gets there. It'll probably be soon after eleven."

"It was very nice of you," she told me. "It'll be wonderful seeing her again after all this time. How is she?"

"Very well. And very spry. She told me you'd written to her about your father, and she's been expecting another letter."

"Yes," she said. "I wrote to her at Puckenford and I believe she answered. You know how it is. You can't help forgetting things."

"Well, till tomorrow then," I said. "Allow me to thank you beforehand for the pleasure I know you'll be giving her. And I'll let you know my decision about that other matter some time tomorrow."

All's well that ends well, I could tell myself. But that proposed visit to Elmhurst would have to be put off till the afternoon. And even that might depend on what information it was that Kate Howard would be bringing me. It was no use wondering what it was. It might be as useless as what she'd told me about Speer's visitor, or it might be something really important. And, come to think of it, I might put her in a taxi after we'd had coffee and our chat, and still be at Elmhurst in time for a late lunch.

Probably a pious background of good deeds accomplished made me sleep as well as I did. I woke in the morning with the feeling of a pleasurable day ahead, and the time went slowly till I got the car out and was on the way to Euston. I was a quarter of an hour early, so I verified the time of the train and the platform.

I was waiting at the barrier well before the train came in, and as soon as I caught sight of it I was giving my horn-rims a polish and craning up to get the first sight of Kate Howard. The passengers began to come through and there were quite a lot of them. Five minutes and the platform was empty and there'd been no sign of her. There was a queer emptiness in my stomach.

The barriers were being closed except for the passage of luggage and mail.

"Pardon me, but could you tell me the next train due in from Elmhurst Junction?" I asked an elderly porter.

He looked up at the clock.

"A slow at eleven-twenty, sir. Platform twelve."

I didn't know what to do. Kate Howard had obviously missed the train. But I certainly ought to give the news to the Dawsons.

I found an empty telephone booth and rang. It was Carlotta who answered. She didn't seem too perturbed.

"She probably missed the train."

"But the next one's not in till almost an hour. What about your plans?"

"Just a minute."

She didn't cup the receiver too well. I heard her giving her husband the news and heard the sound of his voice from somewhere across the room. I didn't hear anything else for a few seconds.

"Are you there? . . . Well, Harvey says it won't make any difference. We weren't going out in any case."

"Right," I said. "Thought I'd better let you know. If she turns up on the next train I'll put her in a taxi and send her straight along."

"That's very nice of you. We'll both be here."

But Kate Howard wasn't on that later train. The hundred to one chance might be that I'd somehow missed her and that, as she had my address, she might have gone to the flat. So I shot off as fast as the car could go in the traffic. The porter on duty knew of no one enquiring for me. I went up to the landing and looked along it. I even went into the flat, but it had an enormous emptiness.

A minute or two and I was ringing the Dawsons again. Carlotta was as puzzled as I. Harvey spoke to me, too. His idea was that she'd changed her mind for some reason or other. Or maybe she'd been taken ill.

"I don't like it," I said. "I think I'll run out to Puckenford straight away and try and find out what's happened."

"You do that," he said. "We're a bit upset, too. And let us know what you've found out."

10. The Mystery Deepens

I FELT a tremendous uneasiness. Lunch was the last thing I thought about and if the best meal in Elmhurst had been put in front of me I doubt if I'd have touched it. I didn't take a side road to avoid the centre of the town but drove straight through and on to Puckenford, and I stopped for a moment or two at the downhill turn to the village. Just by that turn, on the Elmhurst side, was an open-fronted shelter for people waiting for a bus.

Ahead on the main road, and about a hundred yards away, was a house, and two or three others straggled away towards the north, but Puckenford as a whole was at least a quarter of a mile from where I sat. There was the little thatched cottage and then one house and then a farm as a kind of preliminary, and after that the road went uphill out of the dip and round to the left, with houses along it and one little central group round what must have been a green, and still further beyond was the tower of a church set in the hazy green of trees. I'd had that view before me twice before, but perhaps my senses hadn't then been sharpened by anxiety and also I'd never seen it in the mellow sun of a September afternoon. I had a queer feeling as if it were all unreal.

I didn't need to start the engine down that slope of the road to the village, and I put on the brake at the cottage gate. I went along the path to the front door and it was the first time I'd noticed some dwarf chrysanthemums among the asters and dahlias in the beds beneath the windows. The sound of the knocker seemed to reverberate inside the house as if it had some new and utter emptiness.

I went round the cindered path to the back door. Through the kitchen window I could just see the white of the sink, but that part of the cottage was still in shadow. By the door was a cast-iron boot-scraper, and a white, empty saucer. As I listened, ear to the door, there was a sudden mewing sound and a cat came literally leaping from some old currant bushes, and in a moment was nibbing itself against my leg. It purred loudly as I stooped and stroked it. It was the same black cat with the white pads that I'd seen asleep on the sitting-room rug. It followed me, still mewing, back to the front gate.

I walked the hundred yards or so to the brick and tiled cottage whose front door opened almost on the grass path. A youngish woman answered my knock. The tiny girl clutching her skirt looked at me with wide, goggling eyes.

"Pardon me, but could you tell me where I can find a Mrs. Uttley?"

She smiled and stepped forward through the door and pointed. "At the farm, there. The big gate's just past that big tree."

I thanked her and went on towards the farm, another hundred yards down the slope. I went past the farm entrance where I'd twice reversed my car and on to the green gate set in a holly hedge. I went along a weedy gravelled drive to the front door. The creeper that covered the house front was already beginning to change colour.

A middle-aged woman came to the door. She was short and stout. Her eyes were friendly and there was a smile in the enquiring look.

"Pardon me, but are you Mrs. Uttley?"

"I am," she said, still smiling.

"My name's Travers, Mrs. Uttley—"

"But I've heard Kate Howard talk about you! Do come in." Then she stopped and I could guess why.

"But wasn't it you she was going to see today?"

"Yes," I said. "I expect you heard her telephoning to me last night. I should have met her, as you probably know, at Euston this morning at twenty-past ten, but she didn't arrive. And she wasn't on the next train either."

She looked aghast.

"But whatever could have happened to her?"

"She has no relatives in town?"

"None that she ever spoke of to me. All I've ever heard her speak of was a niece in Coventry."

Her eyes opened wider.

"Could anything have happened to her before she left? A stroke or something?"

"I can't say. I do know that she put her cat out, and gave it a saucer of milk."

She was looking more and more perturbed.

"Perhaps we ought to have a look. I know where she keeps her key."

"You've known Mrs. Howard for a long time?" I asked her as we began walking up the hill.

"As long as I can remember," she said. "And her late husband, too. He was a Puckenford man."

"Well, I've only known her a few days but I liked her as soon as I knew her."

"Yes," she said. "Everybody likes Kate."

The cat came bounding towards us as we went through the cottage gate.

"Poor Tiny," she said. "He isn't used to being kept out all day."

The back-door key was under the scraper.

"You take it," she told me. "I feel almost afraid to go in."

I unlocked the door and went in. I went through to the little sitting-room. A door which I opened revealed the stairs. I went up. There were two small bedrooms. One had its bed made up and the other was being used as a kind of box-room. Mrs. Uttley was entering the back door when I came through again to the kitchen.

"She's not here," I said.

"There's nothing in the shed either."

We wondered what it was best to do and then she had an idea.

"I wonder if Mrs. Collins would know anything? She's in the house just down the road."

The cat had already installed itself on the sitting-room rug. Mrs. Uttley found milk and poured a saucerful. We left the cat there, locked the door again and went back down the hill.

Mrs. Collins came to the door again at my knock. She looked surprised to see the pair of us.

"Sorry to trouble you, Freda," Mrs. Uttley said, "but we're worried about Kate. She should have met this gentleman in London today but she didn't turn up, and we've just been to the house and she wasn't there."

"But she went somewhere this morning. I saw her go, and I thought how lucky she was getting a lift."

She told us about it. She'd happened to be looking through her pantry window at about ten minutes to nine and she saw Kate Howard come out of her gate and begin walking up the hill.

"She's going shopping in Elmhurst, I said to myself, and then this car draws up and in a minute she's getting in it and off they go. I saw it go Elmhurst way."

"What colour was the car?"

"I can't say," she told me. "All I know was it was dark. Might have been black."

"You didn't see it parked down the road at any time?"

"I couldn't have," she said. "There isn't a window that looks that way."

I asked her to let us have a look through the pantry window. From it there was a good view as far as the turn to the main road.

"Well, she certainly set out for London," I said. "But wasn't ten to nine a bit early for the bus?"

The two began speaking together. Kate Howard was a stickler for punctuality, it appeared.

"She'd never miss that bus," Mrs. Collins said. "She'd rather be a quarter of an hour early than a second late. But I don't think there's any reason to worry. Kate could always look after herself. What I think is she must have got in the wrong train."

"I expect you're right," I told her.

The small daughter had appeared and I nearly tripped over her as I turned. Her mother snatched her quickly up. I found a shilling and put it into the fat little hand.

"Say thank you, Marilyn."

She was too shy to say a word. Her mother couldn't even get her to wave a goodbye from the door. Mrs. Uttley and I found ourselves walking down the hill towards the farm.

"Do you think she might have got in the wrong train?"

"I don't know," I said. "I don't know what to think. All I know is that I don't like that business of the car and the lift."

"Yes, but whoever would dream of hurting anyone like Kate! You hear of young girls being attacked, but surely not anyone like Kate. And who was to know she was going to town? I mean if the car was there on purpose."

"I know," I said. "It all sounds stupid. But did she tell you what train she was coming home by?"

"Yes," she said. "We'd worked it all out together. The five-past five, it was, which gets in at six. Kate said she'd have had enough of London by that time."

"I think I'll be there when it comes in. Just in case."

"But what a long wait you'll have! It can't be much after half-past four. Won't you come in and have some tea?"

I said that was good of her and perhaps I would. It was a long while since breakfast and I was beginning to feel hungry. So we had tea together: her husband was at market and mightn't be home till after six.

"What will you do if Kate doesn't get off that train?" she asked me.

"I'll telephone you from the station. And perhaps you might look in again at the cottage later tonight and telephone me. If nothing has happened by then I think I ought to notify the Elmhurst police."

She gave a little shudder.

"I do hope it doesn't come to that. I can't bear to think of it."

Then her eyes suddenly opened wide.

"But what about that Miss Speer, as was, and her husband she was going to see?"

I shook my head.

"She didn't know where they were staying. I was going to put her in a taxi and send her there. She might have hunted all London and never found out where they were."

It was after five o'clock. I said I'd see Mrs. Collins again and try to find out what clothes Kate Howard had been wearing that morning: then I could make enquiries at the station.

"I think that's more of a woman's job," she told me. "Perhaps I'd better ask her. Besides, I know Kate's wardrobe and I don't think she'd have had time to get anything new."

We had another idea before we made a move. Mrs. Uttley rang Elmhurst Hospital but no Kate Howard had been admitted.

And there'd been no car casualties that day at all. So we walked up the hill again and I only had three or four minutes to wait.

"She was wearing her black hat—that's a round felt hat about this size, with mauve petunias, and she had on her best black with a little mauve scarf. The handbag must have been her best one and that's black with her initials on in silver. I'm sure she'd have taken that because Miss Speer gave it to her."

We confirmed the arrangements for telephoning, and then I thanked her warmly and went on to my car. I had half an hour to spare for enquiries at Elmhurst Station, but I could find no one who could remember Kate Howard. Then the train came in dead on time. I waited just by the exit but there was no Kate Howard. I found a telephone kiosk and rang Mrs. Uttley.

The bracket clock on the living-room mantel-shelf was striking eight o'clock as I let myself in at the flat. I rang down for a meal and was out of my bath by the time it came up. George, the hall-porter, came in.

"This came for you, sir, and I knew you weren't in, so I kept it." It was the cable from America. In the rush of the day's events I'd forgotten everything about it.

SUBJECT ARRIVED WENSBURG LONG ISLAND NINETEEN FIFTY THREE STOP DIED AUGUST LAST YEAR STOP ESTATE EIGHT THOUSAND DOLLARS APPROX. STOP DAUGHTER CARLOTTA MARRIED HARVEY DAWSON HOTEL OWNER NOW RETIRED NINETEEN FIFTY FIVE STOP YOUR TIME ALLOTMENT INADEQUATE STOP DO YOU WANT FURTHER INVES-TIGATION STOP

THORONESS.

That cable told me nothing that I didn't already know, except that the late Louis Speer's estate had been small. As for further investigations, there was no need of them, and as I had time to kill and another air-mail letter, I wrote to THORONESS accordingly. By way of palliative I said that Harvey Dawson and his wife were now in London and that I could get any further information direct from them. The account to be sent to me at my private address, yours sincerely Ludovic Travers, and that was that. I gave the letter to George to post straight away.

Just before nine o'clock Mrs. Uttley rang.

"I thought you'd like to know I've just got back from the cottage. Everything's as we left it, except that I've brought Tiny here."

"No news from this end either," I told her. "But do something else for me. Go up to the cottage again first thing in the morning and give me a ring as near eight o'clock as you can. If still nothing's happened, I'll be coming straight to Elmhurst."

Not long after I'd hung up, the telephone went again. This time it was Harvey Dawson.

"Glad you're in, Mr. Travers. We've been trying to reach you most of the evening. Any news about that Mrs. Howard?"

"Hardly any," I told him. "I'd rather not talk about it over the phone. Might I come to the hotel?"

"Sure," he said. "Sure. You do that, Mr. Travers. Carlotta's worried about all this. She thought a lot of Mrs. Howard."

I thought a lot, too—but about the Dawsons. I wondered if that hunch of mine had been right: that they were in England for the purpose of making some kind of deal with Conward and the Harbans, and that I'd been intended as some sort of cat's-paw. In the taxi that took me to the hotel I finally made up my mind. Mind you, I anticipated that the Dawsons would have something of a shock when I announced my intentions, however apologetically I did it. For one thing, there wouldn't be too much time for them to replace me. One thing above all I had to do, if only as a measure of self-protection, and that was to leave the Dawsons that night with an awful lot of thinking on their hands.

Harvey Dawson let me in. Carlotta was there, too, and she tackled me straight away.

"Is there really no news about Kate?"

"None," I told her. "I've been down there practically ever since I rang you this morning. All I know is that she left her cottage. After that—nothing."

"But what could have happened to her? You don't think she could have lost her memory?"

"Sounds as good a reason to me as any," Harvey said, and went over to the table where the bottles and glasses were.

"I think a drink'd do us all good. Carlotta, honey?"

"Just whisky. Not too strong."

"And you, Mr. Travers?"

"Not just now," I said. "But you go ahead."

Carlotta tried the whisky.

"I needed that," she said. "I don't know when I've been so worried. And what's to be done now?"

"If she hasn't turned up by the morning, I shall go to the police."

Harvey gave a start.

"The police!"

"It's the only right thing to do, dear," his wife said. "Besides, Mr. Travers knows best."

"I meant, of course, the police at Elmhurst," I explained. "Which reminds me. If anything really serious has happened to her, you two people will almost certainly be interviewed."

"Interviewed? But why? I mean, we've had nothing whatever to do with whatever's happened to Kate. Why should they have to interview us?"

"Let me explain," I told her. "I had to make preliminary enquiries at Elmhurst before I decided whether or not to take your case. Among other people, I had to see the local police and I had to concoct a reason. The one I gave was that nearest the truth: that your father had been too unwell to clear up entirely his affairs before he left England, and when he died you wondered if insurance had ever been paid on what was taken from the safe that night. . . .

"Just a minute, Mr. Dawson. Let me finish. In connection with those preliminary enquiries I had, naturally, to see Mrs. Howard as the only available person who'd been in the house on that occasion. It's no use pretending to be frank and above-board with the police and not living up to it. Very well, then. I now report the strange disappearance of Mrs. Howard. The police already know I've been interested in her, so I'll be questioned. The longer she's missing, the wider they'll cast their net. Now do you see?"

"Surely you've left something out," she told me quietly. "Or am I wrong? I mean, don't the police think from what you told them that I may still be back home?"

"True enough," I said. "So long as they continue to think so. But let's suppose the worst. Suppose something really serious has happened to her."

"You don't mean—" She baulked at the word.

"I do mean it. I'm taking this very seriously and I don't rule out murder. And if it is murder, then I have to talk." Harvey had gone across to the side table to make himself another drink.

"Talk?" he said. "But you can't tell them anything about us? Everything was confidential."

"Oh no," I told him quietly. "Just think back a bit, both of you, to the night when you made me a certain proposition. This is what I said about things being confidential:' If you tell me you've committed a murder, then I won't take your case but I'll keep my mouth shut. If you tell me you're going to commit a murder, then I still won't take your case and I definitely *won't* keep my mouth shut.' Those were my words. Murder expressly mentioned, Mr. Dawson, because over here murder's something different."

He was still shaking his head. I began getting up from the chair as if to show there was no more to be said.

"Mr. Travers did say that, dear."

"He's gotten us all wrong," he told her. "He's the only one who's talking about murder."

"It was my duty to warn you," I said. "Murder's something the police never let go of. I'll have to tell everything I know, and when I say everything, I mean just that. Those are the implicit terms on which I do business."

"But aren't we getting too far ahead?" Carlotta put in quietly. "Who *could* have harmed Kate Howard? And nobody but us three even knew she was coming to town."

"Friends of hers at Puckenford knew it—not that they really matter. Also, there might be those people we talked about once before—the Harbans. Don't forget they're mixed up in this too. They had a man following me. And they might have begun to think Mrs. Howard knew too much."

"But how could they have known she was coming to town?"

"Don't know," I said. "Maybe it was all a coincidence."

"I agree with my wife," Harvey said. "We're too far ahead. But I'm a business man, Mr. Travers, and I'd rather talk about that proposition of ours, as you called it. I take it this business of Kate Howard isn't going to interfere with that?"

"I'm afraid it is," I said. "I'm sorry, but I can't accept the assignment."

Even Carlotta gaped.

"But why? We were counting on you."

"Sorry, but I shall be too busy. If Mrs. Howard turns up safe and sound, that might make a difference. If not, all my time will be spent in finding out what's happened."

There was a heavy silence in the room. After all the talk it seemed to last for minutes till Harvey Dawson broke it.

"If your mind's made up—"

"It is," I said. "Sorry, but that's the way I have to see it."

"Well, I'm a very disappointed man." He began feeling in his pocket and brought out his wallet. "Maybe we shall now drop the whole thing. Honey, get Mr. Travers some paper so he can write a receipt."

"If it's for the ten pounds I tentatively mentioned, then I can't accept it," I told him. Ten pounds wasn't worth any hold he might have over me. "Sorry again, but I don't feel I've earned it."

"Five pounds then. Name your own price."

"No. I'd rather not take anything. No ill feelings, but that's how I feel."

He sat looking at the notes in his hand, then slowly put them back in the wallet. He got to his feet.

"Well, we can part good friends, so what about that drink?"

I smiled.

"I'm beginning to think I ought to have brought a gramophone record. The answer's still no. And thank you just the same. But what I will do is let you know anything that turns up about Mrs. Howard. And I'll do my best to warn you beforehand if the police think of interviewing you: if the worse comes to the worst."

"That's real kind of you," he told me as I moved towards the door. Carlotta went out with me to the corridor.

"I do hope you're all wrong about Kate," she told me. "I'm beginning to feel guilty, somehow."

"Don't let yourself feel like that," I told her. "If anyone's guilty, it's I. I ought never to have dragged her into all this."

"Oh, and another thing I ought to tell you. I remembered it as soon as I'd hung up the other night. If you remember, I told you I'd written to Kate at Puckenford, and that was stupid of me. I didn't know she was at Puckenford. Where I wrote to was my old home and I put a 'Please forward' on the envelope."

"I never even noticed it," I said. "Anyone could have made the same mistake."

I held out my hand.

"Goodbye, then, Mrs. Dawson."

"No," she said. "Not goodbye." She gave that quiet smile of hers. "Let's say *arrivederci*."

"*Arrivederci*, then," I told her.

What I didn't tell her was that that one phrase made a big hole into all the Italian I knew.

11. WAITING

MRS. UTTLEY rang me as arranged, soon after eight o'clock the next morning. All she could report was that everything was the same.

"Then I'll ring the Elmhurst police," I told her, "and I'll be along as soon as I can. One thing, though, I'd like you to do. Whether or not I'm there when the police question you, don't mention Miss Speer and her husband. There's no need to have them bothered."

"I quite agree," she said.

"I saw them last night and naturally they know nothing at all," I went on. "Besides, I was the one she was really coming to see."

"I know," she said. "I'll remember. Only mention about her coming up to see you."

"Exactly. And, of course, having a day in town. I was the one who put her up to that, as you know."

I waited till half-past eight, hoping that Fusson might then be in his office, but he wasn't. The man on duty took my name and told me the inspector usually arrived at about nine. I asked him to let Fusson know that I'd called up and that I'd be along in about an hour and a half's time on a matter of extreme urgency. He repeated it all as he slowly wrote it down.

In a few minutes I had the car out. I was getting to know that road like the palm of my hand and I think if they'd cut a tree down during the night I'd have spotted the gap. Maybe it might be better if I shifted my headquarters to Elmhurst itself now the Harvey Dawson business was all over. I could give myself a complacent nod as I remembered the previous night at the Dawson's hotel. I'd extricated myself pretty deftly and I'd left behind me plenty to think about.

Of course I knew all the time that some of those thoughts were sheer humbug. Though I might have dissociated myself from the Harvey Dawsons, I wasn't going to deprive myself of a chance to recover that jewellery. A million to one chance? Maybe, yes; but such things do come off or they wouldn't be chances at all. And that led to a little day-dreaming. If I did bring off that miracle, then I'd hold on to the jewellery till I squeezed out of the Harvey Dawsons the names of the original owners. "We can always discuss ethics," Carlotta had said, and I wondered if she'd be so amenable once she knew the jewellery was in my hands. But she wouldn't be able to help herself. Mind you, I was daydreaming, as I said. I was ignoring the fact that her father had never divulged the name of the original owners.

And there was something else I was ignoring: the fact that she and her husband were probably in on a deal with Conward and the Harbans, and that whereas I'd been congratulating myself on having suavely bowed myself out, the combine might be congratulating itself on having got rid of me. So I shouldn't be alone when zero hour came and the jewellery was picked up. Not that that daunted me. Travers, the modern Galahad: Travers with the strength of ten because his heart was pure. I chuckled to myself as I drove on.

But I wasn't chuckling as I neared Elmhurst: Kate Howard was too closely in my mind. Fusson spotted it as soon as I walked into his room.

"Hallo, sir. What's on your mind? You're looking as if you had all the troubles in the world."

"Don't know about that," I said, "but I'm pretty worried. It's about Mrs. Howard—Kate Howard. You remember her?"

He smiled.

"I certainly do. A very nice woman."

The way I put it was this, so that all my cards should appear to be on the table. I'd seen her, as he knew, and I'd liked her enormously. I'd had a cup of tea with her and in less than no time we'd been like old friends. I'd asked her if she ever came to London and she said only rarely, so I said if ever she did come she was to ring me and I'd pick her up at Euston and take her round. I'd thought she could have lunch with me and my wife. And so to her ringing me, my meeting her at Euston and all the rest of it, including Mrs. Uttley and Mrs. Collins.

"Queer, sir, as you say. But why didn't you drop in here last night?"

"Because till Mrs. Uttley rang me last night there was still a chance she might have turned up. Taken the wrong train or something and found herself landed at God-knows-where. Then this morning when Mrs. Uttley rang me again, I knew I had to let you know at once."

"I see," he said, and leaned back in his chair. "Looks as if I'd better get out to Puckenford and hear it all at first hand. It may come to getting a description; clothes she was wearing and all that, and getting some publicity to work."

He gave himself a nod as if he had had an idea.

"Your car outside?"

I said it was.

"We'll go out there in mine. Park yours in the yard. I'll be with you in a minute."

I guessed he wanted me out of the way while he did some telephoning. And probably to his Chief Constable. Not that it mattered. I parked the car back of the station and I had to wait about ten minutes before he came out.

He had a car with plenty of power, and once we were through the town we moved pretty fast, but that didn't stop him from wanting to hear all over again just why I was so interested.

"I thought I'd made it clear," I told him. "Before I'd actually seen Mrs. Howard, all I knew about her was what I'd gathered from the papers—that she was an elderly woman with a great deal of pluck. When I met her I found out she was very much more. She was a fine type. She had natural dignity and naturally good manners, and a sense of humour. In fact, I liked her enormously."

"I see. And then you kidded her up to town."

"I don't know that I'd put it like that," I said. "I asked her if she ever went to town: said she ought to kick up her heels a bit more. It would have given me great pleasure, as well as my wife, to take such a nice person to lunch, for instance. What's more, she evidently thought so, too."

"I've got you, sir," he told me. "She *is* a nice person."

We were almost at the Puckenford turn. In the distance I could see an approaching bus. Fusson had seen it, too. He slowed the car into the turn and got out. I got out as well.

"Might do worse than see if the bus driver knows anything," he told me. "Or the conductor."

As soon as the bus stopped he was beckoning the conductor over. The two had met before. The conductor flicked a finger to his cap.

"Morning, Bert," Fusson said. "You been working this shift all the week?"

"That's right, Inspector."

"Do you know a Mrs. Howard? Lives in the thatched cottage there."

"Know her well," Bert said. "When you've been doing this route for best part of ten years like I have, you know everyone in Copley and Harton Magna and Puckenford and damn near everyone in Elmhurst too."

"Did you see anything of her when you drew in here at nine yesterday morning?"

Bert shook his grizzled head.

"Never hardly get anyone here at nine. Them as work at Elmhurst go in by the eight-thirty. Them as don't bike, that is, and save the fare. It's further back at Copley we pick up a load."

"Anyone here at all?"

"Yes," he said. "The Jacksons what live next to the grocer's. They were meeting their daughter, who was coming in on the train." He grinned. "All the joys and sorrows: they tell me the whole damn lot. If I told you all the things I hear from time to time you'd blush."

"I doubt it," Fusson told him dryly. "Right-ho, then, Bert. Won't keep you any longer."

The bus moved on. We went to our car.

"One advantage of living out here in the long grass is that everyone knows everyone else," he told me with the same dry smile. "Sometimes I've wondered if you city slickers don't think us a bit slow."

"That's rather funny," I told him amusedly. "Don't ever tell my wife I'm a city slicker or I'll never live it down."

"Well, you can tell mine I'm a hick sheriff, or whatever they call it, and that'll compensate. Where do we go first?"

"Have a look at the cottage and then on to Mrs. Uttley."

We went round to the back door of the cottage but the key had gone, so we went on to the farm. Fusson and Mrs. Uttley thought they'd seen each other somewhere before, though they couldn't remember where.

We sat in the same room where I'd had tea. I spoke only when I was spoken to: I didn't want Fusson to think I was putting words into her mouth. I wasn't even apparently listening, though my ears turned very red when I was given a first-class testimonial. Kate Howard, Mrs. Uttley said, had liked me very much and had alluded to me as one of the most unassuming gentlemen she had ever met; which just shows what ordinary courtesy can do. Then Fusson took down a description of the missing woman.

"You might as well wait here, Mr. Travers," he said. "I'd better see if that Mrs. Collins can add anything and then I'll be going along to the Jacksons, so I'll call for you here if Mrs. Uttley doesn't mind."

"He isn't trying to get rid of you?" Mrs. Uttley asked me as soon as he'd gone. "Not after all you've done?"

I assured her he wasn't. All he wanted was to see everything through his own eyes and not at second-hand. Then she asked what about a cup of tea. The kettle ought to be on the boil.

We drank our tea and sat there like two conspirators. It was curious how she trusted me and hadn't yet quite accepted Fusson. And then Fusson came back sooner than we'd thought, and he, too, accepted a cup of tea. Mrs. Uttley asked him what he could do to find Kate Howard.

"Hard to say," he told her. "Try to find out if anyone else saw that black car. That's about all we can do, for the moment." But she didn't ask him what I knew was on the tip of her tongue when we'd been talking alone. The fear had been there: the secret knowledge that she might never see Kate Howard again. And Fusson didn't want to talk, so as soon as he'd drunk his tea we moved off again: this time up the hill. It was really only a gentle rise. Looking across the tiny valley from the bus stop had given an illusion of height.

The general store-cum-post office was on the near corner of the little green and the Jacksons' house next door. The man was out but the wife and her newly arrived daughter were at home.

Mrs. Jackson said that she and her husband had got to the bus stop at about two or three minutes to nine. They'd seen nothing of the missing woman, either there or at the railway station.

Fusson stressed that missing woman business and the absolute necessity of identifying that black car.

"There's a meeting of the Women's Institute this afternoon," Mrs. Jackson said. "If you like I can mention it there."

Fusson didn't say anything till he'd driven round the green and we were going down the hill.

"Before the day's out," he then told me, "there won't be a soul in the village who doesn't know as much as we do. We might have some luck. You never know."

At the main road we turned right. Someone at the cottage a hundred yards along might have seen something. He evidently didn't hope for much. There wasn't a window, as he pointed out, that looked towards the bus stop. I waited in the car and it wasn't more than a couple of minutes before he was back. He merely shook his head.

He drove on about a quarter of a mile to a side turn to reverse the car. There wasn't much to talk about till we got back to Elmhurst. He did say that he'd get busy on finding out what private cars had been going Puckenford way from Elmhurst at about the right time the previous morning. Someone might have passed the car and noticed the woman in it. If only one could get the actual make of the car, that'd be something.

"It's about your lunch-time," he said. "Like to be dropped at the Lion?"

"You'll join me?"

"I doubt not," he said. "Looks like sandwiches for me for the next few hours. You in a hurry to get back to town? If not, you might like to meet my Chief. He's a nice chap, name of Yelding. Drop in at about half-past two."

*

A rather peculiar thing happened at that lunch, and to tell you about it I have to jump a bit ahead. When I went into Fusson's room at half-past two and met his Chief Constable, I knew I'd seen him before, and where. He'd been lunching at the Lion. He'd come in just after me and had sat at the other end of the room. I wondered if it had been arranged by Fusson that his Chief should have a good look at me beforehand. There had also been a certain off-handedness about Fusson's invitation that had struck me as suspicious. And, of course, I'm someone who's easily identifiable. You can't hide a lean six-foot-three behind the back of a chair.

Yelding did look a nice fellow. He looked about fifty, and if I'd worn the old tweed coat he had on my wife would have acquired it at the first opportunity and given it to a rag-and-bone man. He was smiling as he held out his hand.

"Your name's quite familiar, Mr. Travers, but this is the first time I've had the pleasure of meeting you. Make yourself at home. This is just a sort of unofficial conference."

He was much more solemn when we began talking about that curious disappearance. It emerged that he was regarding it with the utmost gravity: in fact, if no progress was made in a matter of hours, he'd feel it his duty to ask for help from Scotland Yard.

All that had taken, perhaps, about ten minutes, and as soon as he'd mentioned the Yard he leaned forward on Fusson's desk, fingers together, and his face suddenly had that friendly smile again. This is it, I told myself. Now I'll know why I'm really here.

"About why you should have wanted to make contact at all with Mrs. Howard," he began. "Don't take this as in any way personal, but you seem to have given two different reasons. There was one—so Fusson has told me—which you mentioned at the *Recorder* office."

He allowed the smile to become even more friendly and more broad.

"That, I understand, was just so that everyone shouldn't know your business. But what about the reason you gave the Inspector here?" He put on a frown. "Wasn't it something about an American client and finding exactly what had been taken from the late Mr. Speer's safe so as to make an insurance claim?"

"That was it, sir," Fusson said, and didn't even glance my way.

"Seems a bit late in the day. Just between ourselves, Mr. Travers, that couldn't have been another natural wish to keep your own business to yourself?"

I smiled, too.

"What am I supposed to be—indignant?"

"You're not that type," he said. "But can we take that as absolutely genuine?"

I had to do some quick thinking. Travers of the thousand-and-one-nights was running a bit short of fairy tales. What I said was rather neat, or so I thought.

"Well, I've no intention of flouncing out of this room if you don't accept it as such."

He shook his head. He looked a bit flummoxed, then he was sitting back again, everything pleasantly official. My client, he understood, was the daughter of the late Louis Speer, and that brought us back to the events of a certain night four years ago. He gave the whole thing a very definite logic. Mrs. Howard, the star witness to something that happened four years ago. My client, after four years, worrying herself about a claim for insurance that might already have been met. Mustn't there be some sort of connecting link?

"And don't forget, sir, that Conward's due out in a couple of days' time."

That was Fusson. I put in a quick word.

"And that Conward and Tibball were part of an organisation. Tibball's daughter was suspected of all sorts of things. Her husband, Harban, hadn't a record, but that doesn't say he wasn't just as dangerous."

"Ah!" Yelding said, and leaned forward again. "Now we're getting to it. You think Mrs. Howard's abduction—let's call it that—has something to do with all that?"

"Don't take me wrong," I said, "but from what I've thought in the last twenty-four hours it seems almost obvious. Get your hands on the Harbans and hear what they've got to say."

"They were responsible for the abduction?"

"In my judgment, yes." And, as he looked like making a query—"Don't ask me why. Maybe more was taken from Speer's safe than he admitted at the time. Maybe something was taken that might be damaging evidence against the Harbans themselves. I don't know. I only put it forward as a theory."

We talked round and about and got no further. It must have been getting on for four o'clock when the session ended. I put in a final word. Scheherazade—Travers, feeling in form again.

"I don't want to get in anyone's hair but I feel very concerned about Mrs. Howard's disappearance, and if you people want to make use of me at any time, you've only to ask. In fact I think I'll put up somewhere in the town till something definite happens. I don't feel like running backwards and forwards."

Yelding looked at Fusson.

"I think we'd be very grateful," Fusson said. "You never know when something might crop up and Mr. Travers might have an answer. When do you think you'll come, sir?"

"Probably around tea-time tomorrow. I'm on holiday, as you know, but I've one or two things to clear up. And that reminds me. The client and that insurance claim business. I've let her know that I'm not taking it on."

Yelding and I shook hands. Fusson went with me to my car. "What'd you think of the Chief?"

"A very nice fellow," I said. I might have added that he'd had a pretty good appetite at lunch, but it doesn't do to be too clever. "A pity, though, that you people seem a bit suspicious of me."

"Not at all, sir," he told me heartily. "You ought to know how it is. If you don't start right you might as well not start at all."

"How true you are!" I held out a hand. "Be seeing you some time tomorrow."

I let out a breath as I drove off. I don't like skating on ice as thin as that, and I also had the uneasy idea that I still hadn't been given an absolutely clean bill of health.

I pulled up at a road-house on the way and had tea. It was well after six o'clock when I got to the flat. There were letters on the mat—one of them from Bernice—and another one with an expensive-looking envelope. On the flap at the back in embossed type was THE SOMERTON HOTEL. I opened that letter and read it at once. I didn't even take off my hat.

Dear Mr. Travers,

I've been trying for the last few days, as you've doubtless known, to give up a certain matter, but I couldn't convince my husband. Last night, as you heard, I really thought he had been prepared to take my advice and because of that business about poor Kate Howard.

Then this morning something really fortunate happened. He had a cable about a business deal we thought had fallen through. It's a big thing for him and so he decided to take a plane at once and he was lucky enough to get a seat. By the time you get this he may be on his way. I'm very relieved. I do realise now he's going that the whole idea was hare-brained from the beginning.

I shall be staying on in England for about ten days, but naturally I don't want to go on living here so I'm going to ring an old friend or two and I may be going to Dorset or Sussex or even both. I still hope you are wrong about Kate. She is such a dear soul that I just can't think that anything can have happened to her. All the same I do confess that during the rest of my stay in England I shall be almost afraid to open a newspaper.

May I thank you on behalf of my husband and myself for what you have done.

Yours sincerely,

Carlotta Dawson.

Hotel paper. Various things that betrayed the unprofessional typist. Signature bold and determined. I took off my hat, dropped into a chair and read the letter again. I shut my eyes and leaned back.

Could it be that there was no racket? No collusion with Conward and the Harbans to take over that jewellery at a price? Since Harvey had considered the new fish more important to fry, it certainly had that look. And yet I didn't know. If Carlotta were flying home with him, that would be different. And why should Harvey be needed? He'd had his kick out of various happenings in any case, and Carlotta would be more than capable of handling things from then on. From what I'd seen of her there was a pretty good brain in the cinquecento head of hers. And, after all, the jewellery was her concern and not his.

Then suddenly I was reading something else into that letter. She knew that it must have been the Harbans—the very ones with whom she'd have to negotiate—who'd abducted and maybe killed Kate Howard. And she was scared of the whole thing. That was why she was hiding herself with friends till it was time to go back to the States. At all costs she had to avoid becoming involved in murder. Or perhaps it was only a lying low till she knew if it really *was* murder. But whatever it was, I doubted if I'd ever run across Carlotta again. And the trouble was, I didn't know whether to be glad or sorry.

Still, for the first time for days my evening was free, so I went to the club, had dinner and looked at all the weeklies, and it was almost bedtime when I got back. I treated myself to a nightcap, went to bed and slept like a log. In the morning there was no hurry about getting to Elmhurst so when I'd done a crossword I answered Bernice's letter. After that I packed my bag, and I was just placing it handy by the door when the telephone went.

"That you, Travers? Jewle here."

"Hal-*lo*!" I said. "Nice to hear you again. How're things?"

"Can't tell, really," he said. "We had a call about that Elmhurst business earlier this morning and I'm running along for a look-see. I hear you're going that way, too."

"Yes," I said, and waited.

"Then why not go along in my car?"

"I might stay for a day or two, and not having my own might be awkward. What time are you going?"

"Well, soon. I'd rather have liked a word with you about things first."

"Why not?" I said. "It's getting on for lunch-time. Bring your car here and we'll have lunch brought up."

"Good," he said. "A half-hour or so and I'll be along."

12. COMMERCIAL HOTEL

IT TURNED out that all Jewle wanted was a first-hand account of the Kate Howard mystery, or so I thought. It took me quite a time to go over everything with him and we'd taken in a bottle of beer apiece and most of a lunch by the time I'd finished. Then he gave a quizzical sort of smile as he put a question.

"What did you think of Fusson?"

"Quite a nice fellow," I said. "The sort who does his job without fear or favour."

"Tell me"—the smile was still there—"was there any truth in the yarn about insurance that you put across?"

"You mean he doesn't believe me?" I asked virtuously.

"I got that impression," he said. "To tell you the truth, it doesn't sound all that convincing to me either."

I had to laugh. He'd said it in such a disarming way.

"I owe Fusson nothing," I said. "You're different, so here's the absolute truth, everything that started the ball rolling down at Elmhurst. I was definitely offered the job of finding out what was in Speer's safe that night. It appears that when he was practically on his death-bed last year he began telling his daughter about a valuable collection of jewellery that had been in the safe and how it belonged to an old family who were selling it to him surreptitiously and wanting him to make replicas. He wouldn't reveal the name of the family and he died before he could tell her any more, but she did know that he'd impoverished himself by paying an agreed sum to the owners, since the jewellery wasn't insured.

"Now, as you know, I'm on holiday, so I thought I'd just take a general look at the case before accepting on behalf of the Agency. I found out very little and, what with that and this Kate Howard business breaking, I decided not to go on with things. Harvey Dawson—he's the husband of the woman you knew as Carlotta Speer—has now returned to America. All I'm interested in is finding out what's happened to Kate Howard. And you can take all that as gospel. I wasn't prepared to tell Fusson my business, but now I have told you."

"And very interesting, too. Like to add just what you did find out?"

I told him about that brand-new bag of Conward's and how, if he remembered it, it had been specially designed to smuggle into America a parcel of diamonds which he and Tibball had expected to find in the safe. But the bag couldn't hide what they did find—a valuable collection of jewellery—and, since that collection had never been found, Conward must have hidden it somewhere, expecting, of course, to pick it up when it was safe to return from America.

"It's beginning to fit in," he told me. "But what about Kate Howard?"

I put forward a theory of a double-cross: Conward refusing to tell his old friend Gloria Harban, and her husband, where the jewellery was, since he might then never see it or the Harbans again. Conward, due out, and obviously going to recover the jewellery and so double-crossing the Harbans. They out to keep an eye on him, snatch it and work their own double-cross.

"As for Kate Howard, someone suspected she knew too much," I said. "That's the only way I can account for what's happened."

He frowned in thought for a good long minute.

"Sounds a pretty good theory to me. Mind if I ask a couple of questions? If Kate Howard had to be removed for the reasons you suppose, then it could only be because she knew—or someone thought she knew—where that jewellery was hidden."

"I agree."

"Then doesn't it follow that the jewellery was hidden somewhere near Speer's house?"

"How could it have been?" I said. "The getaway was too quick for that. To tell the truth, I'm up a gum-tree. That she did know something seems a certainty, but don't ask me what."

"Fair enough, but one other question. Assuming the Harbans are after the jewellery, how did they know there *was* jewellery?" That caught me clean in the wind. Then almost as quickly I had the answer.

"They still don't know," I said. "Tibball's information must have been unusually accurate and what he and the gang expected to find was a parcel of diamonds. Let's go back to the actual night. Tibball could have knocked Speer out, taken his keys from his pocket, opened the safe and been gone in a matter of a minute or two. But he was startled to find not a parcel of diamonds but a collection of jewels. He was so long over the job that Conward actually left the car to see what was keeping him.

"Very well then. There's the getaway and the accident. Conward takes the jewellery, sets fire to the car and slips away. Since he can't hide the jewellery in the bag he dumps it somewhere. But he gets caught almost at once, and after that he doesn't see fit to enlighten the Harbans through letters or visits about what was really found in the safe. He may even have said Speer was right in claiming that only oddments worth about three hundred pounds were in there. But the Harbans didn't believe him. They're going to be on his tail when he comes out of jail. They think he dumped a parcel of diamonds. The whole thing's the old story of everyone double-crossing everyone else."

"Sounds logical," Jewle said. "The only thing is, if you take it in conjunction with this Kate Howard business, that it cuts right across our idea of Conward getting a lift on the road. It may sound steep, but it's beginning to look to me as if he doubled back to Elmhurst. Might be worth looking into; not that it matters. My immediate job's the Kate Howard affair. Mind if I use your phone? No need for you to go."

He rang Det.-Sgt. Matthews at the Yard and told him to get busy at once on unearthing the Harbans.

"Look up the Tibball-Conward files," he said. "You'll find everything there."

He thanked me for the lunch and said he'd be pushing off. I said I'd be right behind him.

"Where shall I find you if I want you?" he asked me. "At the Lion?"

"I'm not sure," I said. "I had a couple of lunches at the Lion and neither was worth writing home about. Then I had one at the Commercial Hotel and it was good. Struck me as being a clean little place, too. And less expensive. And I can always change if I don't like it."

"Right," he said. "I may be looking you up. You staying there long?"

"Only as long as I can help in the Kate Howard business," I told him as we went to the lift. And I was telling myself that by then Conward ought to have paid his own brief visit to the Commercial Hotel.

I saw Jewle off and fetched my own car. I was pleased he and I had had that talk and that he now knew the facts. There had been certain omissions, of course, but only those that might be concerned with the whereabouts of the jewellery. Nothing concerning Kate Howard had been concealed: that was far too vital a matter. If I kept from Jewle the fact that she had been coming to London to give me what she thought might be valuable information, that was scarcely concealment. She had *not* told me anything, and therefore I'd have been still as ignorant as Jewle himself.

Mind you, I didn't expect that I'd be called in by either Jewle or Fusson. I was no more than a witness who'd already been pumped virtually dry. Jewle might drop in at the hotel for a drink and slip in some question or other, but that would be the full extent of anything wanted from me. As for my helping to unravel the mystery of Kate Howard, that was out of the question. The police could do the job a thousand times better than I. I smiled at that. A million times would be more like it. Beyond what I'd told Jewle, I knew nothing at all and, even if I knew what to do, I hadn't the means to do it.

I turned the car into Alton Street and parked it in the hotel garage. It was a garage big enough to take a dozen cars: half of it with a sliding door and the other half open in front. My car was in the open part, not that I wanted to save money. It was just that the weather was warm and, provided the car had overhead cover, that was good enough for me.

I'd rung Carver about a room and had mentioned that I wasn't sure how long I'd be staying. It might be for only two or three days or it might be for a week. He'd said it didn't matter. The hotel was far from full and it wasn't likely that my room would be wanted. We had a bit of talk about that after I'd signed the register. The hotel had only ten bedrooms, so there wasn't exactly a fortune to be made out of residents. The bar and the dining-room were his safeguards against bankruptcy. That, of course, was meant as a joke. I guessed he wasn't doing too badly. Not all who plead poverty are financially insecure.

A chambermaid called Annie took my bag up to bedroom 3. I hadn't mentioned any special room but the one I had seemed remarkably handy. In view of what was to happen, you ought to know, as well as I came to know, the lay-out of that second storey. The hotel, as you've already gathered, was shaped like an "L" standing on its head: that is, with its long side in Alton Street and the shorter one on the main road. There were two sets of stairs: one leading up from near the kitchen to the rooms occupied by the Carvers and the staff, and the other going up to a landing. At the head of those stairs was bedroom 10, and then the bedrooms went along the passage and turned a little way along the angle. Further along came the other set of stairs, with a notice FOR STAFF ONLY, and then the staff rooms.

Suppose now that you came up the main stairs to the landing. You could turn back to Rooms 10, 9 and 8, or go on to Room 1, but the bedrooms would always be on your left hand. On the right of the passage was the lounge: a very big room as you'll have gathered, since all the bedrooms really enclosed it. It had two doors. One was opposite Room 7. That was, of course, in the long side of the room. The other door was exactly opposite my room—Room 3. That door was handy for the staff stairs and the kitchen. It was through it that drinks would be brought and it was through it that the waitress on duty was to bring my tea.

For a single room mine was almost commodious. The bed felt comfortable, and when I turned on the hot-water tap the water began running really hot in a very few seconds. The one window overlooked the main road. The bathroom was at the head of the staff stairs—maybe a relic of the time when water had had to be carried up—and there was another one between Rooms 8 and 9. The lavatory was between Rooms 6 and 7. Everything was handy enough and I'd only to take a couple of steps across the passage to be in the lounge.

I must have taken a fairish time unpacking my bag and having a wash, for the waitress—Hetty—tapped at the bedroom door and said my tea was in the lounge. I came out at once because I wanted a word with her. You can't tell the number of actual residents from a hotel register, unless you check those leaving, and I hadn't had time for that. But first I asked her name. Friendliness like that makes for good service.

"Many people staying here, Hetty?"

"Only four, sir," she told me, "and one of them's leaving in the morning. Of course, you don't know if anyone'll be booking in tonight."

"You often get people arriving late?"

"Well, fairly often," she said. "It depends on the trains. Travellers, mostly." Commercial travellers, I gathered she meant. "They generally stay two nights, sometimes three."

I went into the lounge and it looked even larger than I'd expected. It had radiators for central heating and there was a fireplace at the far end. My tea-tray had been put on a low table at that far end, near one of the windows that overlooked the yard and facing the side door. I was the only one in the room.

I like my tea early and on such a fine day it wasn't surprising to find oneself alone. But I did have a good chance to look round that room.

It was a curious mixture of the old-fashioned and the modern. I'd guessed from the furnishings of my bedroom that Carver must have spent quite a lot of money since taking over the hotel, but though that lounge had been considerably modernised there was something left of the old. Over the mantel-shelf, for instance, was a huge stuffed pike in a glass case, and on the shelf was a hideous marble clock with the usual pair of bronze figures. The framed engravings on the walls were spotted with age and ancient damp and ranged from the trial of Mary Queen of Scots to Napoleon at Waterloo. Old Carver had probably bought a job-lot at an auction when he himself had taken over from his father. And there was one other survival that so intrigued me that I got up to have a look at it. It was a stuffed dog—a Sealyham—and it stood on a table in the corner on the left-hand side of the fireplace. It was in a glass case with a wooden back and sides, and a little plaque on the front said:

CHUMMY
(1936-1950)

It was a friendly-looking little dog and must have belonged to old Carver. As for the rest of the room, there was a corresponding table on the other side of the fireplace, and on it the read and reread magazines left by various guests, and the usual glossy publications of the big motoring concerns. There were plenty of easy chairs, in both leather and fabric; three writing tables along the yard wall, each with a stationery stand and each with modern overhead lighting. There was a large cretonne-covered chesterfield and plenty of low tables. The floor was entirely carpeted in dark red. The walls were buff. On a table in the centre of the room was a larger low table with a huge bowl of dahlias.

It was an airy room, both comfortable—in spite of its size—and colourful on that September afternoon, and, in the winter, with central heating and a fire, it would be just as comfortable, and even snug. I could see myself in one of those deep chairs, legs well out towards the fire, pipe going and a book in my hand. And then all at once I was trying to see it on a winter night: that night almost four years back—the cold, foggy night of the robbery.

There had been a woman knitting—or was it darning?—in front of the fire and, well within range of it, on a table probably brought across, Stockwold and the three men had been playing solo. Joe had brought a round of drinks up the staff stairs, through the door opposite my room, and across to the table. Conward had been in Room 7, just across the passage through the door I was facing. And Conward had left that room at least once during the night. Where had he gone? To the lavatory? To a bathroom?

There's a Shakespearian quotation which is often popping into my mind: that soliloquy of Brutus in which he contemplates the time between the first suggestion of some deadly idea and the moment of action. I thought of it then, and I don't know why, unless it was that I too was realising just why I was in that lounge in that hotel. I was there for two reasons. The time for philosophising and theorising was over. I was there to try to work out where Conward might have hidden that jewellery. I had few hopes of that, but Conward himself could lead me to it. If my assumptions were correct—and I was too far committed to have doubts—then, as soon as he'd thrown any likely followers off his trail, Conward would show up at the hotel.

And straight away I had the chill of an alarming thought. Maybe that collection of jewellery had been hidden in so obvious and handy a place—like Poe's famous purloined letter—that Conward would need only to enter the hotel—for a meal, for instance—and be gone in a matter of minutes. And how could I keep an eye on him all the time? Maybe I mightn't even recognise him! And that meant that I'd have to do the impossible; find the jewellery before Conward could get his hands on it.

I looked round that lounge. A collection of jewellery might be fairly bulky. It couldn't be hidden, for example, inside that pike or that little dog. Damage to either would have been discovered long ago. And the chimney was out of the question since there'd been a fire. I had a look at the stuffed pike and it definitely had never been touched. I had a look at the dog. The case top lifted off—for cleaning the glass—and again everything was normal. Besides, that little dog could hardly have had a collection of jewellery inside it. That would have meant ripping its stuffing clean out.

I'd just replaced the top of the case when Hetty came in and I had to make some excuse.

"May I take your tray, sir?"

"Do, please," I said. "Just looking at Chummy here. Someone seems to have thought a lot of him."

"Oh, they did," she told me. "He was old Mr. Carver's dog. I wasn't here then, of course, but they say he taught it all sorts of tricks. Used to have it in the bar sometimes to amuse the customers."

Just as she was leaving with the tray, two elderly people came in and ordered tea. We got into conversation. They were a Mr. and Mrs. Browning who'd arrived two days before and were staying on for a week. He, it appeared, was an Elmhurst man who'd spent the last thirty years in South Africa and was now looking for a small property in which to spend his remaining years. He'd known old Carver well and we had quite a chat about him and Elmhurst. They were nice people, the Brownings. I learned from them that the remaining two guests were both travellers and we shouldn't see them till dinner-time. One represented a hosiery firm and what the other one was Browning didn't know. He'd only arrived that morning and he hadn't done more than pass the time of day. The hosiery man was called Peters and he was leaving the next morning. That put me up to date and I shouldn't need to do any surreptitious searching of the hotel register.

With the Brownings safe in the lounge I had a look at bathrooms. That near the landing was bathroom-lavatory and I looked without much hope in the cistern. I looked in the cistern of the other lavatory and then I realised how hopeless it all was. Conward might have gone anywhere that night. Stockwold hadn't mentioned the duration of the sounds he had heard or the interval between them, so there was all the ground floor and even the yard outside. Conward could easily have let himself out by the back door. He could have got to it by either staircase.

I went downstairs myself and out by the back door. I took my first good look at the yard. Along the wall to my immediate right was a large dustbin. Across the concreted yard were storage and other sheds, and through the open door of one I could see a stack of coal. Then came a short stretch of wall, its top covered with broken glass, beyond which would be another property. Then came the garage and, finally, the tall twin doors through which I'd driven in from Alton Street. They were open and I went through and stood looking about me. I caught sight of that stationer's shop and wondered if they'd have an evening paper. It was nearer six o'clock than five and I thought they would.

I crossed the road and went into the shop. It was a twin affair: tobacco and papers on one side and fancy goods on the other. A couple of women were at the fancy goods counter. The middle-aged man who was sorting newspapers at the other counter merely glanced up from his job as I entered.

"An evening paper?"

"Yes, sir. Which will you have?"

I said a *Standard* and he gave me one from the pile.

"Think I'll also have a paperback or two. Mind if I look round?"

"Do, sir."

He wetted his thumb and went on with the sorting. There were two whole shelves of paper-backs and I found a couple which I either hadn't read or which might bear re-reading. Then I saw something else hanging from a hook—a card on which were tubes of what called itself "Holdfast". It was excellent, it appeared, for anything that needed sticking, including broken china.

Two boys had come into the shop to collect their bundles of evening papers for delivery. I waited till they'd gone. I asked the proprietor if he kept "Stickwell".

"No, sir. Only 'Holdfast'. Pretty good stuff, so they tell me."

"Did you ever keep 'Stickwell'?"

"Yes," he said. "But it's been off the market the last two years. Never hear of it now. I think the firm went out of business."

I paid him for the two books and told him he needn't wrap them up.

"A funny thing about that 'Stickwell'," I said. "A friend of mine was staying at the hotel across the road nearly four years ago and I saw some of this 'Stickwell' in his house. He said it was good and told me where he bought it—in this very shop."

"Well, now. would you believe it!"

"You may remember him," I said. "At least you remember the robbery on that November night. There was a car accident and a man was killed."

"Remember it well. A foggy night. Some places you could hardly see your hand in front of your face. I know. I had to go out in it."

"Well, if I remember it rightly myself, it was the next morning when this friend of mine came in here to buy a paper. He had pretty bad toothache, so he told me. That bring anything back?"

"Pretty early was it?"

"I think as soon as you opened."

"Ah!" he said. "Now I've got you. It was just after seven and I was still sorting out the delivery. He bought a paper and I couldn't help noticing his cheek was all swollen. And do you know what he bought besides a tube of 'Stickwell'? A Guy Fawkes mask for his boy. It was after the Day, but we still had 'em in the window. I remember he had one with a moustache."

His face lighted up again.

"I remember something else. He was going straight to London, where he lived, and then on to the South of France or some place, like that, and I remember saying how lucky he was. At any rate he bought a pair of sun glasses—the plastic, imitation kind—something like yours, sir, only not so good." He chuckled. "Funny how you remember things."

I bought a tube of "Holdfast", if only to keep within the pattern of that brief chat. As I left the shop I looked up at the hotel windows. From Bedroom 7 Conward would have noticed that shop as soon as it was light. It ought to have been a lucky break and it would have been if the police hadn't known about that ticket for America.

The lower part of his face had been covered from the moment he'd entered the hotel. When he allowed it to be seen he'd have been wearing a moustache and dark glasses, with something still in his cheek to simulate a swollen jaw. I wondered what he'd be looking like the next time he came to Elmhurst. Or should I have said *if.*

13. ZERO HOUR

THERE were about twenty people to dinner that night. The hotel prices were much cheaper than those at the Lion and the food, in my experience, every bit as good. The Brownings and I had coffee in the lounge. Peters, the traveller in hosiery, came up later and spent the evening at one of the writing tables. The fourth resident didn't appear at all.

I chatted with the Brownings and read one of the paperbacks. The Brownings rose to go well before ten. They said they were early birds, but I sat on for another half-hour. I did some more reading in bed. Everything seemed quiet below and by eleven o'clock I'd heard the last sound of steps on the staff stairs. I waited another half-hour and put on my dark dressing-gown and went quietly out to the corridor. A dim light was on at the passage angle.

I went to the staff stairs. They were narrower and uncarpeted, and I had to move with care and by the light of my little torch. Ten steps brought me to a landing; eight more and I was in a kind of hall beyond which a passage turned to join the one which led straight from the back door to the hotel front. I looked at that back door. A key was in its lock and it was loosely bolted at top and bottom. I went on to the main passage and the main stairs, and up to my room again.

I slept uncommonly well. I hadn't been awake more than ten minutes when Hetty came in with early morning tea. My two newspapers were on the tray.

I had wondered the previous night why Jewle had not looked me up, and when I ran an eye over the front page of one of the papers I knew why. Jewle had had a busy time. The hue and cry was on for Kate Howard. Everything was there: a full description of the missing woman and the events, as far as they were known, of the disappearance morning. Nothing further seemed to have been discovered about the car. My name, of course, wasn't mentioned. It was simply said that she was going to town to meet a friend and that that friend had notified the police that she'd never arrived.

For a day or two I'd had an idea at the back of my mind and after breakfast I thought I'd do some telephoning. I might perhaps have got my information through Bill Fraser and now I was glad I'd kept it in reserve, so I went round by Alton Street to the post office and rang the Agency.

"Travers here, Bertha."

"Oh!" she said, surprised. "How are you, sir? Enjoying your holiday?"

"Having quite an interesting time. But listen, Bertha. I want you to do something highly confidential. Strictly between you and me. Take a letter, will you?"

She said she was ready.

"No heading, no date. Envelope addressed to Inspector Jewle, New Scotland Yard."

"Didn't I see his name this morning?" she cut in. "About a missing woman?"

"That's right," I said, "but forget it. Now the actual letter, which is not to be on office paper. You're to write it yourself, and the envelope, in a disguised hand and sign it 'Interested'. You got that?"

"Letter and envelope, disguised hand, Interested."

"The letter is, 'Dear Sir, I saw in the paper this morning about that missing woman and how the police want to trace a dark saloon car. You might make enquiries at a Drive-Yourself place called Linfolds of Selby Street'"—I spelt both names out—"'and you might pick up something there. Interested.' If you've got that will you read it back?"

Everything was correct. She asked if any words were to be wrongly spelt and I said no. But what she was to do was to post that letter during her lunch hour at somewhere in the neighbour-hood of Portland Place.

It wasn't too good a morning. The sky was overcast and there was too much wind, and by the time I was back at the hotel it had begun to rain. I looked at the hotel register but nobody new had booked in. Peters had booked out. I ordered coffee in the lounge, just to pass the time, and once more I had the room to myself, so I read my papers and did two crosswords. At midday I went down to the bar. It wasn't very full. Joe seemed pleased to see me and I asked him to have a drink with me. I stayed there till the gong went for lunch. More customers had come in but neither Jewle nor Fusson put in an appearance.

The Brownings came in late and it turned out they'd been inspecting a property and had made up their minds to buy it. Again I had the lounge to myself and it wasn't too comfortable there, though not so cold as to ask for a fire. I tried to do some thinking but the only decision at which I arrived was that it would be a waste of time to try to search that hotel for a likely place in which that jewellery might have been hidden. Ultimately I had a nap and it was after four o'clock when I woke.

Tea, a little reading, and then the Brownings came in. I heard all about their house and what they were already proposing to do with it. More reading and then it was time for the bar to be open. No Fusson, no Jewle, and so to dinner. Another married couple, name of Rathbone, address Manchester, had booked in, Room 8. The Brownings had Room 9. The man I hadn't yet seen—Holland from Peterborough—had Room 10.

General conversation with the Brownings and Rathbones over coffee in the lounge, after which I did some more reading. Holland turned up and did some writing, then he joined the circle round where the fire would have been and I heard him say he was leaving in the morning. At nine o'clock I went down to the bar. The room was pretty full. Jewle and Fusson were still ignoring me, though maybe Jewle was still in town. I did some more reading in bed and, in spite of the afternoon nap, had a good night's rest. When I woke I straight away remembered that it was Zero Day. To-day the gates of Wandsworth would be closing behind Conward.

Before breakfast I went across to the paper shop. My own papers were still covering the Kate Howard disappearance, and Jewle had now harked back to her part in the robbery. I wanted to see if the more popular Press had its own angles.

I had a hearty reception from the proprietor.

"Hallo, sir. How do you like Elmhurst?"

"Quite a nice little place," I said. "Restful, at any rate."

"It's that all right," he said. "In the news, though. Have you read about that Puckenford woman who's disappeared?"

He showed me a couple of papers. One of them had half its front page given up to the story. A photograph of Kate Howard, dating from the time of the robbery, was flanked by one of Speer's house. I bought both papers. When I came to look through them at leisure there was nothing new for me in either. The only significant thing was how wide Jewle was already beginning to cast the net.

There was no rain that day but it was muggy and overcast.

I found it both restless and boring. I didn't want to leave the hotel even for a walk, since either Fusson or Jewle might drop in. And I kept looking at the hotel register whenever I got the chance, though no new residents were to arrive. Not that I was expecting Conward so soon. He'd have to hide his tracks, for one thing, and he wouldn't dare go near any old haunts.

So it was a boring day, as I said: chats in the lounge, visits to the bar, meals and reading, and all of it like someone who expects a guest and listens all the time for the ring of a bell or steps outside a door. I wasn't sorry when I finally laid my book and glasses aside, turned out the reading light and settled down to sleep.

I slept badly and was awake long before Hetty brought the tea.

"A lovely morning, sir," she said as she drew the blinds.

It looked a lovely morning. The sun was shining and I ought to have felt full of beans, but somehow I didn't. It was the day when Conward might arrive and all the difficulties were suddenly weighing on my mind. Would I recognise him if he came? How could I possibly keep an eye on him if I did? How could I follow him if I knew when he left? I shrugged my shoulders. It seemed pretty hopeless and all the optimisms of previous days were suddenly gone.

After breakfast I'd hardly the heart to tackle the crosswords. There'd been nothing new in the papers, so if Jewle had got results from that clue I'd sent him he was keeping it well up his sleeve. And so to another trying day. The Brownings were at their new house and put in an appearance only at lunch, and the Rathbones, nice quiet people though they were, were so pedestrian that we'd long since exhausted any likely topics for talk. In the bar still no Fusson or Jewle. I wondered how Matthews had been getting on with his job of unearthing the Harbans or whether Jewle had traced them through my old friend Percy Scant and the Drive-Yourself garage.

I consigned both Fusson and Jewle to the devil and took a long walk out into the country beyond the railway station and it was tea time when I got back. I looked at the hotel register and found no new bookings. After dinner I joined the circle round the fireplace, if only to kill time. At nine o'clock I went to the bar and had another look at the register as I went through. There was a booking. P. W. French of Southend was in Room 7.

I looked in the dining-room but there was nobody there. I thought of going upstairs and trying to keep an eye on Room 7 but knew it would be too difficult, for the door would be round the passage angle. I went through to the bar instead and all the talk seemed to be about the Kate Howard affair. At a quarter to ten I had another quick look at the register. Another resident had booked in! This time it was a H. Louden of Crewe—Room 6.

I went upstairs and looked in the lounge. The two couples were still chatting away, and I said I was turning in early and bade them good night. In my room I rang for the chambermaid but it was Hetty who came. It was Annie's night off.

"Hetty, I wonder if I might have an extra pillow?"

She told me I should have asked before, instead of putting up with just the one. When she brought it I asked if there were any more guests.

"Two," she said. "They both came in late."

"Nice to have someone new to talk to," I told her. "What were they like?"

"Well, the first one was a youngish man with a moustache. Rather pale-looking but quite nice. The other looked like a traveller. Clean shaven and rather thin and much older. I expect you'll see them in the morning."

When she'd gone I slipped the bottoms of my dark-red pyjamas over my trousers and took off my jacket, collar and tie and put on the dressing-gown. I turned out my light and left my door just the merest crack ajar, and I stood there and listened. I heard the two couples go to their rooms and the fainter sound of running water and the flushing of the lavatory. Then there was quiet except for faint noises from downstairs. I peeped out to the corridor. The dim light from the tiny overhead bulb at the passage angle barely showed up the door of Number 5. I gently undid the door to the lounge and left it, too, slightly ajar. I might have to skip through quickly if I happened to be seen.

I turned my watch under my wrist. It was getting on for half-past ten. I heard Hetty's voice as she came up the staff stairs and then I heard Joe's. A few minutes and someone else came up. A few moments more and I heard the Carvers. Another minute or two and the light above the staff stairs was switched off. Everything was quiet and it was a quietness that dragged heavily on. I opened my door to listen more closely but there was never a sound. The minutes went by and soon it was well past eleven o'clock.

Another minute and I heard the faintest sound round the passage angle. I didn't hear the click but suddenly the light went off above the angle and I could see nothing. I slipped silently along and looked round. They say that the senses are compensatory: that a man suddenly stricken with blindness will soon acquire an acuteness of hearing. That may or may not be true, but what I do know is that though I'm blind as a bat without my glasses, I can see far better than most people in the dark. Maybe that was why I saw, or thought I saw, a dark shape that disappeared through the door into the lounge.

I slipped back at once. With infinite care I pushed open the lounge door across from my room till I could move through, and I stood there. A pencil of light from a tiny torch was moving in the far left-hand corner. I heard a click as if something had been touched or moved. Then the light from the torch was hidden except for the faintest glow. I saw another movement across the room between me and the light of the torch. There was a dull sound like a thud. My heart was racing like a mad thing as I moved quickly forward. There was a sound like a groan and when I reached the corner I tripped over something soft. A foot seemed to brush me and a shape was moving away towards the door.

I got to my feet. My glasses hadn't fallen and as I got to my feet and made for the door I could just discern the shape of the man over whom I'd tripped. Across the corridor by the door of Room 6 my hand came by chance into contact with the light switch. I heard a sound on the stairs and saw the dark shape moving down. The faint light penetrated no more than a foot or two as I began the careful descent. My feet made no sound on those thickly carpeted stairs and I heard the sound of the bolts as someone opened the back door.

I felt my way along the passage wall and in a moment was through the open door and in the yard. I went slowly towards the garage; as I reached it I heard the lift of the bar that closed the doors to Alton Street.

"Hi! Where d'you think you're going?"

In the stillness of the night air the sound was like an explosion. I drew back instinctively to the shelter of the open garage. There was the sound of feet. I saw the shape making for the back door. There was the sound of metal on metal and then another shape.

I saw the flash of a torch just inside the door and then suddenly there was a tremendous silence again.

A moment or two and I made my way towards that back door. As I steadied myself by the wall I brushed against something—the ash-bin. I lifted the lid and felt inside. There was something round and hard and curiously hairy. I lifted it out. In a moment I knew what it was—that Sealyham dog! Its paws had been wrenched from the bottom of the case, but the body was intact. My heart seemed to stand still for a moment or two while I tried to think. Then I slipped back to the garage. I took my spare keys from the locker, undid the boot and put that dog in. I locked the boot again and looked round. An upstairs light was on, and as I looked, another went on downstairs.

I listened at the back door, then made my way to the staff stairs. I heard a sound by the front door and then men's voices.

I slipped up the stairs and into my room, turned on the light to find the top of my pyjamas, and then I undressed in the dark.

I got into bed.

In a matter of seconds I heard voices again. There was Carver's voice outside my door, and then the sounds seemed to be in the lounge. Then came a woman's voice and she, too, went into the lounge. The voices became louder. I got out of bed, put on the dressing-gown, tousled my hair and went into the lounge myself. I'd have been blinking in any case without my glasses.

"Anything wrong?" I asked sleepily.

"A hell of a lot wrong," Carver said.

I rubbed my eyes, hooked my glasses on and went forward. Browning came through the door.

"Anything happening?"

He looked down and I looked down. Mrs. Carver was on her knees supporting the head of a man. It was the man I'd tripped over. That little moustache of his was, by a miracle, still firmly on his upper lip, but I knew at once that he was Conward.

Everyone seemed to begin talking at once—the Carvers, who were in their night clothes, two men who looked like police off duty, and then Browning asking again, as I'd done, if anything was the matter.

"But Chummy!" That was Mrs. Carver, wailing to one of the coppers. "Why should anyone want to interfere with Chummy?"

"Did you hear anything, sir?" one of the men was asking me.

"I heard a noise just now and wondered what it was."

"We'd better get him to his room," Carver said. "One of you lend me a hand."

"We'll do that, sir," one of the men said. Conward went out, head flopping and body sagging. Mrs. Carver brought up the rear of the cortege.

"What's it all about?" Browning asked mildly.

"Don't know myself yet," Carver told him. "Looks like Mr. French in Number 7 heard something and came to investigate and got knocked out."

"Sounds like a burglar," Browning said. "What was that about the dog?"

"See for yourself." He waved a hand. "Wrenched out of the case. Did you or your wife hear anything?"

"Not till just now. Don't think the Rathbones are awake. I'll go and see."

"Seems a queer business to me," I said to Carver when Browning had gone. "Anything been taken, do you know?"

"Haven't had time to make a check. Joe's having a look downstairs. What beats me is anyone wanting to interfere with that dog."

"The police came pretty quick, didn't they?"

"It was they who gave the alarm," he told me. "They gave me a tip a day or two ago about a hotel thief expected this way, and every night I had to give a description of any arrivals. Apparently—"

Browning was coming in again, and one of the plain-clothes men with him.

"What d'you think of this, sir?"

This was a fibre suit-case.

"Tapped at his door and nobody answered so I tried it and it wasn't locked. No one there. Only this."

In the case were four bricks wrapped in newspaper, and a lump of concrete. Carver went to investigate.

"A chap called Louden," Browning told me. "In Number 6, or should have been. Looks as if he's the one who did the job."

"How's the other man? The one who was knocked out?"

"Just coming round. He's got a nasty bruise on the head. One of the police is in there with him."

I managed to yawn at the right time: maybe because Browning had yawned first.

"Don't know about you," I said, "but I think I'll get back to bed. Doesn't look as though we can do any good here."

"Don't expect we'll get much sleep for a minute or two down this end," he told me. "You're in 3, aren't you? Ought to be a bit quieter there."

"Right," I said. "I'll turn in again. If you see Carver, say he's only to knock at my door if he wants me."

When I was in bed I tried to go over the happenings of that amazing half-hour. Something, somewhere, was very, very wrong. The body of that small dog could never have held a collection of jewellery and still kept its perfect shape. And who was the man who'd knocked Conward out? Was it Harban? Or Scant? I didn't know. What I did know—and I couldn't stop knowing—was that that stuffed dog was in the boot of my car. Or was it?

I might have the keys but a boot could be forced. But I didn't think so. After that unexpected challenge by the man Fusson had on watch at the hotel back, "X" had done the only possible thing in nipping back to the hotel and dropping the dog en route. Once his pursuer had been lured inside, "X" could slip out again. But once he found the dog had gone, all he could assume was that his pursuer had somehow got hold of it. I'd been lucky. If the man on duty at the back hadn't let in the man at the front, I might never have been able to return to my room.

Then I realised something else, and it made me wince like a remembering of a morning after. Jewle hadn't been fooled. He'd known that I'd chosen the Commercial Hotel for a different reason from the one I'd so airily given him. Jewle had merely used me as a focusing point. Travers, the latter-day Machiavelli. I winced again as I thought of a possible interview with Jewle in the morning.

After early morning tea I went to the paper shop, but only so that in passing I could run a quick eye over the rear end of my car. There was no sign that the boot had been tampered with. Soon after eight o'clock I was beginning my breakfast, and I'd only just poured my first cup of coffee when Jewle walked in.

"Morning, stranger," I said, and not too ironically.

"I know," he said. "But I've been pretty busy."

"Coffee? Breakfast?"

"Had breakfast, thanks. Wouldn't mind another cup of coffee, though."

"You seem to have had a hectic night here," he went on as I fetched a cup from another table.

"Didn't disturb me much," I said. "I wish it had. Help yourself to sugar."

He stirred the coffee very slowly. Something was coming and I wondered if I'd be ready for it.

"Funny you should be here at all. Or was it just luck?"

"Luck?" I said. "Didn't we agree that Conward might have doubled back that night? If he did, wasn't this the handier hotel?"

"Yes," he said. "I worked it out that way, too. But we didn't take chances, except that we lost his trail in town and had to guess he'd be coming here. We had men on both the Lion and here. Funny business about that dog."

"Look. I'm not a suspect. Why fire sudden questions?"

He smiled.

"Sorry, but what about that jewellery? From what I've heard you couldn't have got very much inside that dog. And it's been here for years and nobody noticed any tampering with it."

"I've changed my ideas about all that," I told him. "What Conward might have originally thought was to make a slit in the dog's belly and slip in a piece of paper telling where he'd really hidden the jewellery. That was for Harban, say, in case things were too hot for him to return to England. Then he changed his mind. Thought he'd keep the stuff for himself."

"Doesn't sound too good to me," Jewle said. "Why all the roundabout stuff? If he originally wanted Harban to have the jewellery why not tell him where it was? Why start a sort of comic treasure hunt with clues?"

"Well, there we are," I said. "Nobody'll know the answers now except the one who took the dog. What's happened to Conward, by the way?"

"You spotted him?"

"Moustache and all. Did he talk?"

"Only the way we thought. Heard a noise, went to investigate, crack on the skull—just that kind of guff. When I asked him what he was doing at Elmhurst at all, he said it'd struck him as a nice little place when he saw it last and he thought he'd take a few days' rest. Afraid we shan't be able to hold him."

"Well, he's only a side-line," I said. "What about Kate Howard? Any news?"

"No. I did get a tip about a man but I can't pin anything on him. All we might have is the make and number of the car. But we're not sure enough to use it."

He finished the cold dregs of the coffee, refused another cup and rose to go.

"Where now?"

"Having a look round. Getting a description of the man who's missing from Bedroom 6. What about you?"

"Don't know," I said. "No real point in staying on here. You don't want me, do you?"

"Not for anything I can think of. Still, you might give me a ring when you're back in town. Or are you thinking of Monte Carlo?"

"That's an idea."

He waved a cheerful hand from the door. I let out a breath. Providence is said to watch over children and drunkards. Liars, I thought, aren't always neglected either.

14. Shock of Discovery

I PAID my bill, distributed baksheesh and took my bag to the car. I put it in the back seat and ran another quick eye over the boot. It was exactly ten o'clock when I started off.

But I didn't trust Jewle. I've known him and worked with him for more years than I like remembering, and we've always been the best of friends; but, for all that, if he thought I was pulling a fast one, I knew he'd have no scruples about pulling one himself. That was why I took the back way by the station and emerged well through the town. A mile or two on and when nothing was in sight on the road, I took a turning to the left. It was a winding country lane and at a convenient spot I pulled up the car and had a look at the boot. When I'd turned the key I hardly dared to look. But I needn't have worried. The dog was still there.

There was no room to turn so I drove on till I came to a village. I had a look at the map and found I could take more side roads and finally emerge a good twenty miles from Elmhurst. Later I kept left and came into London by Enfield. At Finsbury Park I rang the flats. George happened to be on duty.

"Travers here, George. Anyone been asking for me?"

"Not that I know of, sir."

"Right," I said. "I'll be along with the car in a few minutes so you might look out for me. I'd like you to run the car to the garage for me."

George was waiting when I drew the car up.

"Still no one asking for me?"

"No, sir."

I had the dog under my arm, well concealed by the raincoat.

"Good. When you get back, forget you saw me. If anyone does enquire, then I'm not at home."

I opened the flat door and had a peep inside. It still had that empty look. I shut the door, bolted it, chucked my hat towards the pegs and took that dog over to my desk and got out a glass. As soon as I looked along the belly I saw something. It looked as if at some time the skin had been slit and turned back and then replaced. And it had definitely been held in place by some kind of adhesive. "Stickwell!"

I took out my penknife, used the smaller, sharper blade and slit open the belly again, and at once the blade met something hard. I ripped the tear apart with my fingers and at once things began dropping out. Shiny things. Things that ranged from the size of a big hazel nut to the size of a pea. Dazzling things as the light caught them. Diamond after diamond, till I'd probed the last one out with the knife. I counted them. Exactly sixty-five.

I sat back in the chair like a man utterly bewildered. I listened instinctively for a sound at the door. I got up to see if the door was really bolted. I came back to the desk, still like a man in a dream. I went to the refrigerator and poured myself a glass of beer. I'd finished the bottle before I could really begin to think.

Everything was wrong. The story the Harvey Dawsons had told me was wrong. And, as I stirred those diamonds with a finger, I knew that the information Tibball had received through Brittle must also have been wrong. This was no parcel of diamonds. What I had in front of me was not a package worth up to ten thousand pounds, but a fortune in stones. Those two pear-shaped stones alone were worth a good ten thousand. What the whole lot were worth I couldn't begin to calculate.

I went to scoop them into my pocket and then stopped. What could I do with them? My own little safe was useless, so what about making a parcel and taking it to my bank? And then I had another idea. I turned that idea over and over and then made up my mind. Bernice is a hoarder. She keeps everything that may have a future use, and in one of the drawers of her desk I found a stout chocolate box. I'd put on gloves and when I found some cotton wool in the bathroom, I carefully packed those diamonds. Then I began concocting a letter. I looked at my watch. Bertha would soon be taking her lunch break.

I rang her.

"I'm back in town now, Bertha. When are you taking lunch?"

"At any time now."

"Right," I said. "Grab a taxi and come to my flat. Come straight upstairs. And not a word to a soul."

It was half an hour before she arrived. I'd found an odd sheet of paper.

"Remember that letter you wrote, signed 'Interested'? Think you can write another in the same style of writing?"

She was sure she could. I said we'd have two goes at it, just to make sure. This was the final effort.

Dear Sir,

    I hope that tip I gave you did you a bit of good. Will you keep what's inside this for me as I have an idea there ought to be a reward.

INTERESTED.

I put the letter inside the box and put on the lid. I cut string and knotted it to make it look more casual, found some brown paper and finally treated all the knots with sealing wax. Bertha wrote the address—

Inspector Jewle,
New Scotland Yard

In the top corner Bertha wrote PERSONAL. I slipped the little parcel into my coat pocket and then we went downstairs. At Charing Cross we got a taxi, and I slipped Bertha the money to pay. She was bound for the post office in Albemarle Street where she'd register that letter. The receipt was to be posted to me in a plain envelope. I went on to my club. Bertha was to ring me there as soon as the post office had taken over the parcel.

I didn't feel like lunch till I knew everything was safe and somehow I didn't feel hungry after she'd rung. When the meal was over I went to the Reading Room where the silence rule would be broken only by the heavy breathing of an elderly member or two or perhaps a gentle snore. On a sheet of club paper I began putting down questions which had to be answered, and the amazing thing was that I got no further than the first. What I wrote was—Why did the Dawsons deliberately deceive me?

But did they? Now I came to think things out, it was clear that there'd been no deception. That valuable collection of jewellery had consisted apparently of diamonds in various settings, but could not Speer have decided that the stones, as such, would be more saleable out of the settings, particularly as those settings would be old-fashioned? Maybe he had had each piece photographed and drawings made, and then he'd removed the stones and melted the settings down. In fact, that was what he must have done, and when he had mentioned jewellery to his daughter, the expression merely connoted for him the most valuable asset— the stones. Since the settings must have been melted down at Bridge Street, Brittle must have had his guesses about what had been done. The information passed to Tibball had been correct.

All of which showed, I told myself, how stupid it was to let oneself be stampeded into headlong conclusions. But wait a minute. The stones themselves. Wasn't there something wrong? Since that jewellery was an heirloom of some fine old family, then the stones were old. They couldn't be South African. But the stones I'd examined so closely were neither Brazilian nor Indian. I knew enough about diamonds for that. The colour was wrong and the cutting, and that almost imperceptible dullness that comes with age. The stones I'd sent to Jewle were comparatively modern. The odds were enormous on their being South African.

Which meant that Speer had lied to his daughter. But why? A man doesn't lie when making that kind of final confession. And therefore the Dawsons *had* lied. And again, why? What was the point of it? What was there either to conceal or to suggest? I thought and thought, and I couldn't find an answer, and it was only when I began thinking far back that I knew all at once where an answer might possibly be found. One man might give me, if not the answers, at least a clue and that man was Bernard Brittle. But Brittle, I'd been told, had a kind of religious mania and wasn't too sure in his wits. Another minute or two and even that didn't discourage me. It's a fool in a mighty bad way who hasn't even a lucid moment.

Half an hour later I was paying off a taxi at the beginning of Laverock Street, Clerkenwell. Lave-rock, the taxi-driver had pronounced it. I thought of it as Laverock. That's what the elderly people of my Suffolk boyhood used to call skylarks. Maybe skylarks had once sung in the fields around that pub I was passing—The Waggon and Horses—but there weren't any skylarks now. Laverock Street was drab even in the sun of that late afternoon: a street of pubs, shabby houses and little fly-blown shops, an eating-house or two and a pawnbroker's. I passed a little inset of a garden with grimy roses, turf worn in spots to bare earth and a seat or two under sooty trees, where no one was sitting but one old man.

I wondered what the taller building which I was approaching was, and then, by announcements on its side wall, I knew it must be a Salvation Army Citadel. Laverock Street was almost deserted that afternoon—it was early closing day—and I'd met nobody I'd thought of questioning about Brittle, but when I was just past the Citadel I heard voices and I looked back to see a couple of young-ish women in Army uniform coming out of the door, and behind them came a grey-haired man in the uniform of an officer. The three had a last word and then the women came my way and the man went the other. I turned back and overtook him.

"Pardon me, sir, but could you tell me where I could find a Mr. Brittle? Bernard Brittle?"

He was rosy-complexioned, blue-eyed and had what I can only call a happy face.

"Why, yes," he said, and ran a quick eye over me. "Perhaps I'd better show you. He's not a friend of yours?"

"No," I said, as we walked on the way I'd come. "He used to work for a diamond merchant and jeweller named Speer. Speer died last year in America, and the daughter, who was over here recently, asked me to look Brittle up and tell her what had happened to him."

I'd been trying to adjust my stride to his much quicker and shorter pace when he all at once stopped, and it was just past one of those small junk shops that seem to flourish everywhere in the suburbs.

"He may be in," he said, and went through an open side door. "One of our soldiers found him a room here. Perhaps you'd better wait."

He went up a short flight of bare stairs. I heard him knock at a door. A minute or two and he was coming down.

"I'm sorry, but he's out. He often takes long walks by himself when the weather's fine."

I thanked him for the trouble he'd taken. Then I hesitated.

"I wonder if you'd do me a favour and tell me about him. In confidence, of course. He was in trouble a year or two back, I believe, and served a short sentence."

"Yes," he said, and: "Are you going this way?"

We began walking on. He asked my name.

"Travers," I said. "L. Travers. You'll find me in the telephone directory."

He smiled.

"My name's Hooker. But tell me something, Mr. Travers. Are you what's known as a Christian?"

"Not perhaps in the way you mean it," I said. "But that doesn't alter the fact that I believe, and perhaps as strongly as you do, that the world would be an impossible place without Christianity."

He nodded. He smiled dryly.

"Almost thou persuadest me," he quoted quietly. "But about Brother Brittle. He's happy with us and we're happy to help him. That's why we're in Laverock Street. A very simple purpose really: to seek and to save the sick and the lost. Brother Brittle was lost and we had the good luck to find him. He's still sick in his mind but he isn't lost. He's proud of being a soldier: he wears the uniform as if he were a general. And he loves the open-air meetings and marching with the band."

"That's good to hear," I said. "But you mentioned something about his mind. Is he capable of a serious conversation? I promised Miss Speer I'd see him."

"Speer," he said, and slowed his step. "I've heard quite a lot about Speer. When I first knew Brother Brittle, of course. He told me a lot about his past, though I never heard him mention that Speer had a daughter. But about talking to him yourself. I hope you'll forgive me, but I wouldn't advise it. There're times when even I don't find him very coherent, and then again he begins talking about things which are best forgotten. I'd forgotten them myself till this afternoon." He laid a hand on my arm. "He's harmless, of course. You might even call him gentle."

We'd stopped at the corner of a side street. We must have walked a good half mile and I'd only a vague idea of where I was.

"Well, this is my way now." He smiled. "You're going on?"

"Yes," I said. "And it's going to puzzle me what I'm going to say to Miss Speer. Write, I should have said."

He looked away for a moment and then nodded to himself as if making a decision.

"I think I can trust you, Mr. Travers, but I wonder if you think it rude of me to advise you *not* to write. I can't say more, but it's like letting sleeping dogs lie. No," he said quickly, "that's hardly what I mean. It's just that it might make trouble."

He couldn't help seeing the look of bewilderment on my face.

"Don't ask me more," he said. "But I know a lot of things I had to hear from poor Brittle about his work and his employer. I can't say more than that. Except that Speer wasn't all his daughter thought he was."

He held out his hand and once more he was smiling. He shook mine warmly.

"Goodbye, Mr. Travers. God bless you."

I watched him for a moment or two as he moved along that road of drab, terraced houses: a shortish, sturdy man; sixty-five if a day, and walking with the stride and purpose of one not half his age. A good man: the kind of man I'd often heard in my boyhood described as good-living: one who poetised what he preached. I liked him: there was a sincerity about him.

And that's what made me suddenly begin thinking about that cryptic allusion to making trouble: trouble if Brittle talked too much in the company of the wrong people. Trouble for whom? Not Speer, for he was dead. But what about that other allusion—that Speer hadn't been all he seemed?

That's when I saw it. It hit me with such a shock of revelation that I stopped in my tracks. At last I had something that made sense. I'd found one clue to the crossword and at once clue after clue was fitting its space. But what could I prove? Speer was dead and Brittle might as well be dead. As I walked slowly on towards where I guessed the Underground must be, I was frowning to myself annoyedly. It was like having something on the tip of one's tongue: somewhere or other there *must* be proof.

And then, just as suddenly, I knew I had the answer. Jewle could get the proof. Once I put the hint in his mind he'd be forced to carry on. And the hint would come just when he was bewildered by receiving that parcel of diamonds. So that was why I didn't make for the Underground. I cut through to what seemed from the distance to be a main street and there I took a taxi to the Agency.

It would have been natural enough for me to have dropped in on Norris for a brief chat, even though I was taking a holiday, but, as it happened, he wasn't in.

"You might as well take your receipt, sir," Bertha said. "I was just going to post it."

I put it carefully in my wallet. One day that receipt might be worth a lot of money.

"This is all very mysterious," I told her, "but before long I might be able to tell you the story."

"Doesn't worry *me*," she said. "If I worried about half the things I listen to in this room I'd go cuckoo."

"That's fine," I said, "because I want you to write another of your soon-to-be-famous letters."

"From the same party?"

"And *to* the same party—which reminds me, they'll have your prints at the Yard by now."

Dear Sir,

I hope you got that little parcel I sent you, and mind you don't lose it because I've got the post office receipt. Now I have something else for you. The papers have had a lot about a man called Louis Speer who Mrs. Howard was housekeeper for. I used to know Speer, so this is my tip and I think you'll find it'll pay. Find out from Speer's bank if he had a large sum in cash in his possession during the week before that robbery at his house in Elmhurst. I think you'll be surprised.

INTERESTED.

Bertha wrote the address and sealed the envelope.

"Getting me quite interested myself," she said. "It's like one of the old serials they used to have at the movies years ago. Want me to post it somewhere?"

"Not this time," I said. "They may be watching the pillarboxes round that part of the town. All you do now is sit back and wait for next week's thrilling instalment. And do I owe you any money?"

I took the Underground to Baker Street—L. Travers, Ltd., late Sherlock Holmes—and posted the letter there. Then I went home, but not to stay. I didn't want to be there if Jewle should decide to drop in, so after a tidy-up I went back to the club. I dined and then played billiards with an old friend. It had been one of my proficiencies in my callow youth but I didn't make much of a show that night, though it passed the time and kept me from thinking about a score of other things. And it was well after ten o'clock when I got back to the flat. The man on duty told me that nobody had enquired for me. I felt a slight and wholly unreasonable hurt, but it didn't keep me from a good night's rest.

In the morning I dressed myself leisurely. October was in and it looked a bit colder, so I put on a slightly thicker suit. In the same leisurely way I propped a newspaper against the coffee pot and began glancing at the headlines over a service breakfast. At once a headline hit me clean in the eye.

MISSING WOMAN FOUND
MURDER SUSPECTED

I grabbed that paper and began to read. This is the substance of what it said, and there was a map which made things easy to follow.

You remember the side road, almost the first after leaving Elmhurst, which I'd taken in order to look in the boot of my car?

That was the country lane along which Kate Howard's body had been found, and I must have gone past it. It was in a ditch on the far side of a low hedge that ran alongside a field of sugar-beet. It mightn't have been found for years if the farmer hadn't decided to make a filling-in as a bridge to the lane in order that his lorry could pick up the stacked beet when drawn up close to the verge.

According to the report, she had been dead for some days and death had been due to a heavy blow on the skull. A handbag, its contents apparently untouched, had been found with her. That was about all, except that Chief-Inspector Jewle and Det.-Sgt. Matthews of Scotland Yard were said to be at Elmhurst.

I didn't feel like breakfast. It's hard to say just what I felt. You can't feel anger against an unknown person and all I could think of was the Kate Howard I'd known and how I'd never see her again. I kept seeing her in that little room of hers and I could hear her very laugh, and soon my nerves began to fray and I knew I'd have to go to Elmhurst. What I could do there I didn't know, but I began to have an idea of the things I might say. I mightn't be welcome, but that was no matter.

And there was one thing I could do at the same time—get rid of that damned dog that was hidden in the back of the top shelf of my wardrobe. Conward had slit the belly and inserted the stones, and then had discovered that the sides of the slits hadn't properly met. That was why he'd bought the "Stickwell" and had managed to stick the slit together at some time the next morning after Jessie had tidied the lounge. And he'd made such a good job of it that nothing had ever been noticed.

I didn't have to make so good a job, but I did my best with the "Holdfast". When I got to Elmhurst I circled round to that unadopted road and came out at the main road. When nothing was in sight I dropped that dog on the path and moved the car quickly off. All Elmhurst would know by now just what dog it was. As for the remnants of feet, they might be artistically stuck to what was left of them on the bottom of the case, and Mrs.

Carver would have her Chummy again. As for me, I went round by Ypres Road and came out short of the town, and from there I went on to the police station.

15. THE LONG ARM

FUSSON was slowly stirring a cup of tea. The ash-tray in front of him was full of butts. Jewle was smoking his pipe and both of them looked as cheerful as if the air outside had been November smog. They half got up as I came in, and then sat down again. Fusson indicated a chair and asked if I'd like a cup of tea. I said I would, if it wasn't any trouble, so he rang for another cup. Jewle had given me a nod and he now seemed aware of his own tea.

"I saw the news in the morning papers," I said, "so I thought I'd come along, just in case."

"You liked the old lady," Fusson said.

I said he knew that. That was why I was there. I thought I owed her something.

"You'd like to see her? She's looking quite peaceful."

"I don't think I would. I'd rather see her in my mind's eye the way she was. Any news beside what's in the papers?"

"Practically none," Jewle told me. "We're where we were before, except for a body. You any ideas?"

The cup of tea came in: a big cup that looked half milk.

"I've been thinking," I said. "A couple of things you don't know. They may make more sense to you than they did to me." I told them about the man in Speer's room on the afternoon before the robbery.

"Speer!" Fusson said, as if he didn't like the word. "No matter where you turn you get back to Speer. She wasn't killed four years ago—she was killed last week."

"You'd like my opinion on that? I'd condense it further. She was killed because Conward was due out of jail."

"Look," Jewle said mildly. "Let's stop making epigrams. What was that other thing you thought of?"

"This, that I didn't want to hurt her feelings when I couldn't see any use for what she told me about Speer's visitor, so I said it was helpful and would she ring me if she had any more ideas. It was just after that that I told her she ought to treat herself to a day in town. Then she did ring me, as you know, and about coming to town, and I had the idea there was something else she wanted to tell me but didn't like doing it over the telephone. That's all I can tell you."

"Gets back to the same old thing," Fusson said. "All you asked her about was that old robbery. But for that she'd be alive today and we wouldn't have a murder on our hands."

"True enough," Jewle said, "but writing epitaphs won't get us very far." He swivelled round in my direction. "What about that business at the Commercial? Someone steals a stuffed dog and no one's going to convince me that it was stuffed with a valuable collection of jewellery. Who did that job? Harban?"

"You bring out a bob," I said, "and I've got a pound note that says he did it. And where *are* the Harbans? Any news yet?"

"Yes," he said. "As soon as Gloria had got the old man's estate cleared up, they went to Canada. No prospects for her ladyship here after all that stink. What we're trying to find out from passenger lists and so on is when they came back. We hope it'll be a few weeks ago."

I finished the tepid cup of tea and lighted my pipe. Jewle's pipe was cold, but he shook his head when I offered my pouch. "Something I think we ought to tell Mr. Travers," he told Fusson. "Three heads are better than one—"

"Even if they're sheeps' heads."

"True enough." It was the first time he'd smiled. "But it's this, and perhaps you can throw some light on it. Remember I told you about a mysterious tip I had? Well, the same mysterious person—a woman by her writing and prints, by the way—sent us another tip late last night, and since the first one was pretty good, Matthews is following it up. That first one led us to a Percy Scant who runs a flea-bitten detective agency, a one-man show, and he took out a car from a Drive-Yourself place the morning Kate Howard disappeared. A black car. An Austin. Mrs. Collins has seen a photograph of it taken from the rear and she says it could be the one that offered Kate Howard a lift. Scant admits taking the car out, but says it was such a fine day he thought he'd treat himself to a trip to Whitstable, only when he got there he didn't think much of it so he came straight back. No lunch, no pals, no alibi, no nothing. Couldn't bolster it up with a thing, except the time and the mileage. The same mileage, as you'll see, as if he went to Puckenford."

"You had to let him go?"

"Nothing else for it. We know where to pick him up if we want him. But about that second tip. That said it'd pay us to find out from his bank if Speer had drawn out a large sum in cash during the week before that robbery. Matthews is on that now. as I said, he's ringing me here if he finds anything. And another thing in that context. Speer did draw out a pretty big sum in cash on the Tuesday *after* the robbery. From the bank here. He had the two branches for convenience."

I silently blessed the secrecy of banks and the local manager who hadn't mentioned my own enquiries.

"I don't see yet where it's all going to fit in," I told Jewle, "but without flogging an old horse, everything still goes back to Speer and that robbery. But about this woman who keeps feeding you tips. Could she be your old friend Gloria? And double-crossing her husband?"

"I didn't miss it." he said. "The trouble is we haven't got her."

"Hardly worth the trouble of looking," Fusson said. "It might be anywhere between where she was killed and London. We know it was something round—like a bit of lead piping. The medical report showed that. Cracked the poor old lady's skull like going through a nut."

I winced. The telephone went. Fusson reached for the receiver, listened, and handed it to Jewle. Jewle spoke in monosyllables, grunted once or twice and finished by saying he'd be along.

"Well, there we are," he told us. "I have an idea the tip was good. Speer drew out seven thousand pounds in cash on the Thursday morning before the robbery. In pound notes and fivers."

"But would that be unusual?" I asked him. "A man in his way of business would handle large sums, and cash transactions would dodge tax."

"Maybe," he said. "But don't forget that visitor he had at his house here that same afternoon. That may tie in. And I'd like to check up on all his cash transactions."

He was ready to leave. I thanked Fusson for the tea and he, too, smiled for the first time as I held out my hand.

"That's all right, sir. And thanks for coming along. Drop in any time you feel like it."

A nice fellow, Fusson. I left it at that and went out with Jewle to the car.

We didn't talk a lot on the way back, and then about anything but the case. It was as we got to the outer suburbs that I decided to insinuate some more ideas.

"Do you know, Jewle, I've been thinking about something you told me this morning—that man Scant. I didn't like to mention it before and because it seemed to be my own business, but I was pretty sure I was followed that day I went to see Kate Howard."

He swivelled round as if he'd been stung by a wasp.

"Did you get a look at him?"

"Quite a good look. His car happened to draw up behind me when I stopped, so I thought I'd have a look-see, but he shot his car on at once and I got a look at him as he passed. He was a big fleshy-faced man of about fifty. Looked like an ex-cop or army man."

"That's the one! That's Scant for a fiver."

"Certainly a bit of luck. And do you know what I'd do now? I'd have him in again. I'd spring what I've told you and make it sound as if you're about to make a charge. Keep talking about murder and how he's tailor-measured for the job. I don't want to tell you how to handle things, but it might be worth while trying a big bluff, that that car he hired is known to be the one that picked up Kate Howard. If he still clams up, then think up a holding charge, but my bet is he'll be sweating like a pig. If he didn't do the job himself, I'll bet you ten to one he tells you who hired him. He'd have to."

"Yes," said Jewle. "It mightn't be a bad idea."

He asked me to stop at the first police station we came to and he got out and rang the Yard. When he got back he told me Matthews would be bringing Scant in. I said I'd take him to the Yard to save time. It wouldn't be much out of my way.

As we were coming through Camden Town I said I had another idea. It was vague and I had to watch the traffic, but maybe I'd have it worked out by the time I dropped him. As a matter of fact I went down Whitehall and round into Northumberland Avenue so as to be heading for home.

"This idea of mine," I said. "Speer. We always get back to Speer, and that's what I've been turning over in my mind. You remember that evening we spent at Tibball's restaurant and the grouse you had? You were all steamed up about not being able to lay your hands on any of the big fences."

"That's right," he said, and gave a wry smile.

"And you mentioned a whisper that was going round about a Band of Hope or something like that. It might even have been a fence whose name was Hope, or some underworld password for him; isn't that what you thought?"

"I believe I did."

"Did? You mean you don't believe it now?"

"Not exactly that," he said. "What I mean is that I never heard any more about the whisper."

"Perhaps I can guess why," I told him. "But about the word hope. Speer's name was Spiro before he was naturalised. That convey anything to you?"

His mouth gaped slightly.

"Yes," he said slowly. "Forgotten most of my Latin but *Spero* means hope." Then he looked me clean in the eye. "You think Speer was a fence?"

"Work it out," I said. "Maybe his bank accounts will tell you something. And another thing. Speer got out of England as soon as he could. Speer wouldn't talk much because he was too ill. Tibball expected a haul from that safe but Speer swore there wasn't much in it. And ever since Speer dropped out, you've heard no more whispers."

"Yes," he said. "The more you think, the more you begin to see."

He held out his hand.

"Thanks for everything. Between ourselves, I think we're seeing some daylight."

"You'll let me know what happens? Particularly about that man Scant? I'll be at the flat all day."

"I certainly will. Scant may take a bit of finding, though." He waved a cheerful hand.

"Thanks again. Be seeing you."

I drove on and round Trafalgar Square, and I was feeling pretty good myself. The pigeons, usually a pest, seemed now to be fluttering happily, and I could smile at the children who fed them. Me, and Francis of Assisi. And the light was beautiful on the front of St. Martin's. There was even a rosy streak on the carpet of my study where the sun edged through the window.

Did you know that I own that small block of flats? Not through the sweat of my brow, but because I inherited it from my father. Not that it puts me on a par with the Rockefellers. I don't even manage it and you know what taxation is. Some day I'm going to write a really nice letter to the Chancellor of the Exchequer and point out that for years I've been one of his mainstays, so what about a knighthood? Any old knighthood. The Traverses never were particular.

I mention that because it was after two o'clock and lunch was over in the little downstairs restaurant, but they managed to grill me a chop and sent it up with some warmed-up vegetables and some cheese and coffee. After it I had a good look at the papers and then did the crosswords. I wrote to Bernice, who'd be home in a few more days, and I had to use an air-mail letter to be sure of catching her. That made me realise that my fortnight was nearly over. And that Jewle was pretty long in ringing me.

It was well after my usual tea-time. A tray came up and the evening papers I'd asked George to send with it. There was nothing new for me about the Kate Howard case, but they passed the time till almost six o'clock, and then Jewle did ring.

"Look," he said, "I don't want to bother you but would you like to come along for a minute?"

I've timed myself before and I can walk to the Yard in seven minutes. Matthews was in Jewle's room. It's always refreshing to see Matthews: he of the grin and the surreptitious wink: nearing forty now and his black hair with never a sign of grey.

"Something for you," Jewle said, and handed me a copy of Scant's statement. I polished my glasses and read it. It was roughly this, and the sting in the tail.

Scant had been rung up by a man who'd asked if he'd received a registered letter containing twenty pounds in notes. Scant said he had, and the man said he was the client. The commission was to follow me and report on every movement. Another twenty pounds would be in the post the next morning. The client would ring up at night to get verbal reports and he wanted Scant's private number. The reports were given, including my visit to Puckenford, and then Scant had to report that he'd been spotted. He was told to stand by in case he was wanted again.

At about half-past ten on the night preceding the disappearance of Kate Howard, the client rang. Scant was to hire a car and leave it at precisely half-past seven outside Finsbury Park Station and he was not to attempt to see who the client was. The car could be collected as near to the same spot as possible at eleven o'clock the same morning. Subject to those conditions, twenty pounds would be found in the front locker of the car.

Scant admitted he'd tried to see the client but there was a lot of traffic, even at that hour, and trouble about finding a vantage point, and by that time the car had gone. When it came back a boy came and told him the car was parked just round the corner, opposite a picture shop. The money was in the locker. And that's all that Scant knew.

J. What about the client's voice? Anything special about it?

S. It sounded sort of disguised. Just a bit of American about it, though.

J. And you've heard nothing from him since?

S. Nothing. Not a word.

"Well, what d'you think of it?" Jewle asked me.

"It's what you think of it," I told him. "Did it ring true?"

"Like gospel truth," Matthews said. "He was a pretty scared man. If he'd known the client's name he'd have blurted it out like a shot."

"He said something else after the statement," Jewle said, "but there wasn't any point in adding it—that he was pretty sure he'd recognise the voice if he heard it again. What do you think yourself about that American touch?"

"Only one thing to think. It's pretty far-fetched, but it might tie in with Harvey Dawson, Carlotta's husband, who wanted me for that job."

"And he's now back home, you said?"

I told him every word I remembered of that letter Carlotta had written me.

"Wait a minute," he said. "You didn't tell me *she* was over here? I thought it was only the husband."

I'd slipped up somewhere. I had to look startled.

"But I did!—or I thought I did. Surely it was implicit in what I told you?"

"Maybe I missed it. But the husband went home. And just after the Kate Howard business."

"Might be something in it," Matthews said.

"If he went back because of what we think he might have done, then he might take some finding," Jewle said. "But the wife. We might trace her from the hotel."

"Don't be in a hurry," I told him. "I've remembered something."

Too late I knew I'd landed myself in a worse muddle: a bad one this time. The look I put on had to be very sheepish.

"Sorry," I said, "but there was something I didn't tell you. I expect I thought it didn't tie in in any way, or I may have just forgotten it. I remember I meant to tell you if you'd dropped in on me when I was at Elmhurst."

That switched the blame partly to him.

"It's this. I told the Dawsons Kate Howard was coming to town and they were delighted and said I was to send her along to their hotel for lunch."

Jewle was giving me that disturbing look, clean in the eye. Matthews had his head on one side like a blackbird on a lawn.

"Yes?" Jewle said.

"Well, so naturally when Kate Howard didn't turn up at Euston I rang the Dawsons. Mrs. Dawson answered and spoke to her husband and he apparently said she'd be on the next train. But you see the point. If it had been he who killed Kate Howard, then he couldn't possibly have been in the hotel at, say, a quarter to eleven. Besides, you know Carlotta Dawson, so do you honestly think she's the kind of woman who'd let herself be even remotely mixed up in a murder?"

"No," he said grudgingly. "All the same, I'd like to have a talk with her."

"The Somerton Hotel. Why not ring them now?"

He did ring. It didn't take five minutes, but it was five minutes wasted. Mrs. Dawson hadn't left any forwarding address.

"Shouldn't be too hard to run her down," Matthews said. "She must have left a trail."

Jewle clicked his tongue annoyedly.

"I know. And it might take a day or two."

"Mind if I suggest something?" I said. "A few hours—say till after breakfast tomorrow—shouldn't make all that difference. Will you let me see what I can do about Carlotta Dawson? I have an idea I might be able to lay my hands on her."

Jewle rubbed his chin.

"It's unorthodox. You really think you can? You sure we can't do it better?"

"Don't think so or I wouldn't have suggested it. I can't tell you how, but I think I've got a good chance."

"Right then," he said. "And let us know the moment you have any news."

I told him I'd be on the phone within five minutes of locating her.

"One thing has to be understood. You people are to do nothing about it at all. Too many cooks might scare the rabbit."

"It's all yours," he said. "A warrant card be any use to you?"

I told him I'd been just about to ask for one.

Let me deny at once any claims to superior powers of deduction. Jewle would probably put two and two together and make them four far oftener than I, but in this case he hadn't found an answer for the very simple reason that he hadn't been given the figures until a few hours before. Since my talk with that old

Salvation Army officer I'd had plenty of time in which to think and deduce, and that's why I had an idea I could find Carlotta Dawson more quickly than Jewle. This is how it worked out.

The assumption simply had to be that the Dawsons *were* implicated: if not, then there was no point in finding Carlotta. If they were, then that letter which she'd written to me was a calculated attempt to throw me off the scent. And, since that letter in essence tried to make me believe that her husband was off at once to America and she herself off to stay with English friends, then both statements were untrue. Dawson had *not* left England, and she was *not* in Dorset or Sussex.

One thing the letter would not have lied about and that was the times, and because, until Carlotta left the hotel, I might have wanted to get into touch with her there. Assume then that Harvey Dawson did leave the hotel in the early evening, ostensibly to take his night plane for New York, and that Carlotta left the next day. Her movements didn't matter but I was sure she would leave as soon as possible so that I couldn't question her about the letter. So, as I saw it, what Harvey did was to go to another hotel where the next day Carlotta would join him.

Why all that scheming? Why make me think that Harvey had gone home and that she had quite abandoned any idea of recovering the jewellery? To that there seemed two answers, and each was good enough.

Speer, the ex-fence, must have told Carlotta something: that valuables *had* been in that safe, and that Conward had been pulled in before he could dispose of them. That left me with the original theory of collusion: that Carlotta would buy the jewellery—no matter what it was—from Conward and Harban.

The alternative was this. Harvey Dawson, reader of whodunits, who'd been getting a kick out of things, had made up his mind to have a personal try for that jewellery. It was he who had knocked out Conward and taken the dog. I liked that idea the better of the two, and because he was like the man of Hetty's description—if he'd shaved off moustache and beard.

That left only one question to answer. I'd broken off with the Dawsons, so why should they have anything to fear from me? I'd made myself out to be a regular Bayard, so why should they think I'd have a crack at the jewellery myself? The answer was that they suspected me of nothing. Why they had to get away from the Somerton Hotel was because of the death of Kate Howard: murder is perhaps the better word, since they, like me, must have suspected it. The last thing they wanted, whatever their activities, was to be interviewed by the police.

So much for all the theory. What, then, did I think had actually happened? Simply this. Harvey had left the Somerton and had doubled back to, say, one of the big termini where he could have had his disguising hair removed. Then he had gone on to the hotel at which he had booked a room or rooms for himself and his wife. At the hotel he had said his wife would be along the next day. And the next day she joined him.

And finally, you might put in yourself, how could that find Carlotta more quickly than Jewle could find her? I'd have to find the taxis that took the pair to the hotel, wherever it was and when, and that might take days. But I didn't think so. There was more than a chance that I knew of a short cut. Which gets us back to where all this philosophising began. Jewle knew as much as I did, as far as concerned the essentials. The trouble was that he hadn't had time to think of all the answers.

16. SOME OF THE ANSWERS

I WENT straight to the Somerton Hotel and asked to see the manager. My old warrant card which Jewle had dug up made for co-operation. Various people were questioned. Harvey Dawson, accompanied by his wife, had left at about five o'clock and both the chambermaid and the waiter at their table knew he was taking the night plane to New York. Mrs. Dawson told both the chambermaid and the hall porter, who fetched a taxi for her, that she was going to Dorset before rejoining her husband in America. She left the following morning at about ten-thirty. The hall porter knew nothing about the taxi except that it was a taxi.

"Is there a record kept of residents' telephone calls?" I asked the manager.

"Certainly," he said. "They all go through our own exchange, otherwise we'd have no check."

"Then would you be so good as to let me have any numbers Mrs. Dawson called on the morning she left?"

It turned out that she had made one call. I used the hotel exchange and rang Enquiries, and in a few moments they identified the number—The Sheridan House Hotel, Regent's Park.

It was as simple as that. The long shot had come off. As for that new hotel, the manager's hotel guide told me it was a fairly expensive one. It might have been awkward if it had been a caravanserai with a few hundred rooms. The Sheridan House had only thirty-five.

I thanked the manager, told him to keep everything under his hat, and left. The hall porter got me a taxi and I went to the Sheridan House Hotel. It was as secluded as could be for London and it obviously had class. A uniformed commissionaire stood just inside the handsome swing doors. I beckoned him outside and asked if there was any other way to the manager's office except across the main hall. It was not till he'd seen my warrant card that he took me round to the back, through a door that skirted the kitchens and on to the office. I slipped him half-a-crown and told him to keep his mouth shut.

The manager was highly perturbed and the last thing he wanted was scandal. I said if there were any, it'd be his fault, not mine.

"All I want is the room number of two possible residents—man and wife. The man probably booked a room a few days ago and arrived in the evening. His wife arrived about noon the following day. He's tallish, thin, probably clean-shaven and looks about forty-five. If he still has a beard and moustache he'll look fifty. The wife is younger: about thirty, and looks like an Italian: black hair and dark complexion."

I warned him that his enquiries would have to be better than discreet. If the couple had the least idea that their whereabouts were known he might find himself in trouble. It was about a quarter of an hour before he came back. There *was* a couple in suite 7—two rooms and bathroom between—who fitted perfectly except for one thing. The woman had fair hair. The name was Pryke; registered as British.

He'd given me a queer look. I must have had an even queerer one on my face. Everything had suddenly gone wrong.

"Looks as if he's got another woman there instead of his wife," I said.

"We can't do anything about that," he said. "Besides, I understand they're leaving tomorrow."

I don't know why that last bit of news should have made a whole lot of things suddenly coalesce, but it did. Everything was as plain as sky-writing, and I could have kicked myself for not having seen it before.

"Right," I said. "Just carry on as usual. If you happen to see the couple, just be as you've always been, but don't go out of your way to see them. Provided that's done, everything will be handled with discretion."

"And if they leave tomorrow?"

"That'll be our business," I told him. "Just forget I've ever been here. Everything's going to be taken care of and no one will know a thing."

I went out the way I'd come, walked a few yards and caught a bus. If I'd walked, it'd have been with head in air, and the ride gave me time to think in peace. I got off at Leicester Square and walked on to the flat. I asked for a dinner to be sent up and then went upstairs.

Just before it came, the telephone went. It was Jewle.

"Glad you're in. Been trying to get you for the last half-hour. Fusson rang us with some news. That dog's been found!"

"Where?"

He told me. Why it should have been found there, almost opposite the spot where Tibball had been killed, he didn't know. Probably someone had found it somewhere else and when the news got out had thought he'd better get rid of it. At any rate, it had been taken to the Carvers and they'd rung Fusson.

"Anything special about it?"

"Oh, yes," he said. "The underside had been cut open and then stuck together again. I'd say something was taken out but it couldn't have been much. Any news from you? Or is it too early?"

"Yes," I said. "For one thing, Harvey Dawson didn't leave England. All that letter business was eyewash. I'll tell you about it in the morning, but both husband and wife are still in town. Suite 7 on the first floor of The Sheridan House Hotel, Regent's Park—"

"Just a moment. Let me get it down."

Naturally he was asking what was behind it all. I said I couldn't tell him the whole story, but if he wanted to interview the couple he'd have to hurry. They'd probably be booking out in the morning.

"Listen," he said. "You'll have to straighten a thing or two out. I think you're right about that Speer business, but it's going to affect everything. His daughter, for instance. Did she know the old man was a crook?"

"She probably didn't. In fact, I'm pretty sure she didn't."

"There we are," he said. "Everything's changed since I told you I wanted to interview the Dawsons."

"Everything's changing every minute," I told him. "If you hadn't rung me a bit prematurely I'd have been still on the job and making enquiries. And I'm already getting somewhere: well, far enough to tell you this—that you've got to have the Dawsons pulled in for questioning by nine o'clock in the morning. And I think you ought to do something else. Have Percy Scant brought in at the same time. And Hetty, the waitress at the Commercial Hotel. Fusson can bring her with him from Elmhurst."

"Why not run along here for a minute?"

"Because my dinner's just come in and it's getting cold. And I've earned it. But what I will do is be along in the morning. Half-past eight suit you?"

"Well, yes—if you're sure you can't drop in tonight."

"I'm going to be busy," I told him unblushingly. "But you'll do what I suggested about Scant and Fusson and the waitress?"

He said he certainly would.

"Just one last thing," I said. "Have a warrant ready for a search of that suite. And you might warn a policewoman to standby." He wanted to get a word in but I cut him off. "Everything'll be explained in the morning. There'll be plenty of time. See you at half-past eight."

I took my time over the meal and I went to bed early, and I had no fears whatever about an uneasy night's rest. Only one thing worried me: what I could do about those diamonds when Jewle, as he would have to do, told me about their mysterious arrival at the Yard. But it wasn't much of a problem. I actually woke up with the answer.

I got to the Yard ten minutes early. There were signs of preparation in the neighbourhood of Jewle's room; a policewoman and three plain-clothes men standing by. Matthews and Jewle were inside.

"Glad you're early," Jewle said. "Fusson isn't here yet but he's due at any minute. Now what about putting us more in the picture?"

I hung up my coat. It had been a bit nippy for early October.

"I don't want to sound flippant," I told them, "but I'd like to make a bet. Just a gentleman's agreement. You bet me that the next couple of hours won't see the absolute end, except before a judge and jury, of the whole of this case, the Kate Howard business and everything. I bet you that it will. If you lose, you allow me to keep back any pieces of information I think fit, provided they don't prejudice the result. Agreed?"

"You win either way, sir," Matthews said with his usual grin. "You'd probably keep them back in any case."

"Oh, no. I'll play absolutely fair. So what about it, Jewle? The bet's on?"

"Sounds too good to be true," he said. "You honestly think you've got the answers?"

"All we need," I said.

"All right. Then it's on."

"You won't regret it," I told him. "You go to the hotel yourself, because, if you hadn't thought of doing so, I think you should change your mind. As soon as you walk into the suite you'll have the answers yourself. I think you ought to go. It may make a difference."

"Well, no particular reason why I shouldn't. But you still haven't put us in the picture. Do we ask these Dawsons very politely to come here and help us with some information? Or what?"

"As soon as you see them you'll know what to say. The only thing is, get them here, even if you have to drag 'em here. And look out for the double doors of that suite in case anyone thinks of bolting. And pick up their passports. When they're here, put 'em in a waiting-room: one with a peep-hole if possible. I think Fusson ought to run a private eye over them. And Hetty. Then, if Scant can hear them talking, he might justify his claim to recognise the voice of the one who hired him."

"Matthews can fix all that up." He looked at his watch, tapped his breast pocket, probably to be sure the search warrant was there, and got to his feet.

"Well, here goes, and I hope to God it'll be as good as you say. Sure you wouldn't like to tell me anything else?"

"You've got more than enough," I told him. "I wish I were as certain of a front seat in heaven as I am of winning that bet."

"Good luck, sir," Matthews said and I echoed it. Jewle gave us a nod and went out.

Matthews' head went on one side as he listened. When the sounds ceased outside the door he gave me another of his grins.

"What about giving me a private tip, sir, now they're on their way?"

"Oh no you don't," I said. "You go and fix things up like the big man told you. And you might send Fusson up here when he comes."

Fusson came up about five minutes later and a couple of cups of coffee with him. Matthew's must have had a chat with him: he seemed on such good terms with himself. He almost crushed my hand when he shook it.

"I hear that you've got the case sewn up," he said. "Hetty's here, by the way. I take it she's to identify that chap who skipped from the hotel: the one who took the dog."

"That's right," I told him. "But if this is a kind of flank attack initiated by Matthew's to get me to tell you any more, then you might as well save your breath to blow on that coffee."

"Ah well," he said, and began dropping in lumps of sugar. "It shouldn't be long now'. Funny business, though, about that dog. Mrs. Carver was pleased. She gave that dog to her father-in-law as a pup. You know what they're going to do as soon as they've got it repaired? Have it in the bar. It ought to attract no end of custom. Wonder what was inside it, though?"

I didn't even hazard a guess.

"Strictly in confidence, there may be a big surprise for you this morning," I told him. "I'm pretty sure there will be."

He tried to manoeuvre it out of me but didn't have any luck. We sipped the hot coffee and then Matthews came back. He was like a cat on hot bricks.

"They ought to be there by now."

He caught my look.

"All very well for you, sir. You're sitting pretty."

"Not so pretty. What about that bet?"

Fusson had to be told about the bet and so time went on. Matthews sent down for some coffee for himself, and we chatted about this and that with no real heart in it, while the wall clock kept ticking on.

"They ought to be here by now," Matthews said. "Think I'll go down and see."

He didn't re-appear. And it was another quarter of an hour before Jewle came up. I'd thought he might be the least bit annoyed but he was smiling away as if he'd just been promoted.

"That was a hell of a trick. You could have knocked me down with a feather when I saw who they were."

"Who who were?" Fusson asked.

"The Dawsons," Jewle told him. "They weren't the Dawsons at all. They were the Harbans! My old friend Gloria and her husband, Fred!"

"Well, I'm damned," Fusson said. "Then you can hold 'em on an impersonation charge."

"Impersonation charge?" Jewle said, and snorted. "I can hold 'em on a dozen charges."

"Wait a minute," I said. "Are they downstairs?"

"In a room up here."

"And Fusson can have a quick look-see?"

"Why not?"

Fusson was making for the door at once. It wasn't more than three minutes before the two were back. Fusson's eyes were still bulging.

"You talk about a surprise," he told me. "Never had one like it. It wasn't that Gloria Tibball at all. It was Gladys Trent!"

"That's right," I said. "Just like the goddess Diana, one thing in heaven, another on earth and something else down under. What happened at the hotel, Jewle? Everything go off nice and peaceful?"

"Not exactly," he said. "There was a hell of a squawk and Harban tried to bolt out of that other door but we nabbed him. We found the passports all right. British ones. And in their right names. Nothing else of any importance. Hetty's had a peep at Harban, by the way. No doubt about him being the one who pinched that dog."

"And what now?"

"Think I'll have 'em in separately. They've been cooling their heels long enough. Just think out one or two nice holding charges and Bob's your uncle. Everything can be worked out later."

It was a slow business for all that, and it wasn't till almost two hours later that I was back in Jewle's room. I knew I'd have to make a statement myself in the near future, so I'd passed some of the time making notes.

Fusson and Matthews were there and it was obvious that everything had gone pretty well. Jewle said that Gloria Harban had been the more brazen. Her husband had been a badly scared man. Murder hadn't been mentioned. Both thought they were being held for offences connected with that old robbery.

"That damn robbery's going to haunt me the rest of my life," Fusson said. "I slipped up pretty badly over that Gladys Trent business."

"Oh no," I told him. "There was just one thing you couldn't possibly know. If you'd stumbled across that, then you might have found some of the answers. It was a thousand to one against."

"You mean the truth about Speer," Jewle said. "How'd *you* get on to that, by the way?"

I smiled.

"Remember our bet?"

"Damn the bet!" he told me ruefully. "When you get in that box you won't be able to quote bets to a judge and jury."

"True enough. *If* you ever get me in that box. Still, I'll tell you this. I didn't get it from Brittle, who was one of the few who really knew, but I did get it in the course of enquiries about him. Brittle, as you know, isn't mentally fit."

"Look," Jewle said. "We're all friends here and none of us is in a hurry, so why not tell us the way you see everything. You're an older hand than any of us, you know."

"You won't get far by buttering me up with that feet of Gamaliel business," I told him. "Also, we mayn't be such good friends by the time I've finished. For instance, things only got serious as far as I was concerned after Kate Howard disappeared. Up till then I was just amusing myself in a very shameless way on a busman's holiday. Then, when the Kate Howard business broke I couldn't help knowing, as you all did, that it had to be tied up with what happened four years ago. And before I forget it, you'd better have this as an exhibit."

I gave him that cable from THORONESS. They'd been surprised at my statement that I could now get any information direct from the Dawsons in London. The Dawsons, they said, were in Wensburg and hadn't left it, so was I sure I didn't want the investigation to go on?

"But about that old robbery," I went on. "This is, of course, only how I see things and you people may have other ideas, but I think Tibball and his family circle had that job planned well ahead. They were about to commit another robbery and they knew the actual date when that first robbery had to be committed. It was going to put them in possession of something really valuable: a diamond necklace, say, with specially fine stones. I say that because it's about the only thing that might have been stuffed into the belly of that dog."

"I can help you there," Jewle said. "It must have been that Sellbrook Gardens job. You remember it? A big job and we thought it out of the Tibball class. A Mr. and Mrs. Hooper Wright."

I allowed myself to remember. It looked as if I was about to learn something I didn't know.

"That was the job," Jewle told us. "And now I can tell you why. Wait a minute, though. Something else is beginning to tie in."

He thought for a minute.

"I've got it. You remember, Travers, how Gloria used to stay at various posh hotels and pick up friends for business reasons? What she must have done was to learn all about that big do at the American Embassy and the Hooper Wrights and Mrs. Wright's jewellery, so Tibball knew well ahead when the job had to be done."

"Then where's that jewellery now?" Fusson wanted to know. "It wasn't in that hotel. The way you had everything searched you couldn't have missed it."

"Plenty of time yet," Jewle told him. "But you carry on, Travers."

"Where was I? Oh yes. That Tibball knew when that first job had to be done. After that the way I see it is this."

17. Buying a Garden

It was a good thing that I'd had time to get my ideas assembled beforehand or I might have found myself dropping all manner of bricks: such, for instance, as talking about diamonds instead of jewellery. What I had to do was to add a certain amount of trimming to the startling happenings of that morning; events not so startling to me as to the others in that room.

"That Sellbrook Gardens job throws just the right amount of light on things," I said. "In fact it's the key to everything that happened. It, and what was to arise out of it, was to be the biggest and most lucrative job the Tibball gang had ever brought off, and the lucky thing for them was that they had all the time in the world to plan it. The more they began working things out, the bigger possibilities they saw, and ultimately it developed into what I called a treble twist, with Speer as the one to be twisted. The rewards were to be so big that they weren't afraid of ruthlessness: that knocking down of Speer's maid, for instance, so that Gloria could be planted in the house. Her job was to locate the safe, and other things which I'll come to later. And, before I forget it, I think it was something to do with her that Kate Howard remembered and which she was going to tell me when she came to town that day. I think you'll see that when we get to it.

"But to take things in order. The Sellbrook Gardens job was duly pulled off and the next thing, after getting Gloria established as Speer's maid, was for Tibball to make the necessary contacts and to bring the loot personally to Speer on the Thursday afternoon. He must have been the one Kate Howard heard. At any rate, we know that Speer had the cash ready and there must have been a lot of bargaining. If Speer paid the whole seven thousand he'd drawn out he still would have been getting a bargain. What he actually paid didn't matter. The important thing was the timing. Tibball, thanks to what he'd learned from Brittle, was sure the jewellery would be in Speer's safe till at least the Monday.

"And now to the actual Friday. I'd had to ask myself quite a few questions and I'd never been able to get satisfying answers. One was why the whole affair had such an air of certainty about it. Why Conward should carelessly come round to the study windows, for instance, to see how things were going. I know now, of course, that it was because Gloria was in the house and it was all a piece of cake. The other questions were more tricky. Why didn't Speer hear Tibball enter the study? Why didn't he holler when attacked? How did Tibball know that Speer would be working with his back to the windows?

"What I think now is that they're all the same question, and the answer's this. Gloria and Kate Howard were in the kitchen and while Gloria was finishing the washing-up, Kate was preparing Speer's hot toddy. It was child's play for Gloria to drop in a Mickey and then, when she went upstairs, to signal with her lights that she'd done it. All Tibball then had to do was wait a few minutes and go through the doors which Gloria had already unlocked, and there Speer would be, flat out on the floor. That was when

Speer was knocked on the head and the glass removed from the window to give the looks of an outside job."

"Yes," Jewle said. "That was it for a fiver."

"I hope we're right," I said. "In any case there was the second of the twists. Tibball had been paid for the loot and now he had it back, and everything ready to start selling it again; this time in America. And now for the third twist and, frankly, I can't make up my mind about that. I'd asked myself why Speer closed down his house so quickly and why Gloria was paid off as early as the Tuesday night, and you can add the matter of the money Speer drew by arrangement on the Tuesday from the Elmhurst bank. Mind you, I knew Carlotta had gone back to town to get her flat ready for her father and that he wouldn't want the house, but that didn't explain everything. As for the answers—well, there're two choices.

"The first supposition is that Gloria was intended from the very beginning to operate the third twist, which was to blackmail Speer. The other is that it only occurred to Gloria after she knew her father had been killed. That makes it a blackmail of revenge. But in any case, I'm sure Gloria did see Speer not later than the Monday morning, and threaten to give him away to the police. The loss of the jewellery and the money he'd paid for it would have been a small disaster compared with the disclosure that he was a fence. Also, Gloria had to have a good excuse to be out of the house and back in town in case the police wanted to interview her about her father and Conward, so my guess is that forcing him to close down the house so suddenly was just part of the blackmail.

"Gloria, by the way, tidied up everything and hid her trail by writing almost at once to Kate Howard and telling her she was getting married and going to live in Scotland. What she ultimately did, of course, was to lie very low until she'd realised Tibball's estate and then she and her husband went to Canada. That'd be only a stepping-off place to the States and my guess is that the pair proceeded to bleed Speer white. He'd still have a fear of extradition. And though he ought still to have had quite a lot of money, all he left at his death was about three thousand pounds."

"Everything sounds perfectly feasible to me," Jewle said. "The trouble is that Speer's dead and to get any real proof I'd have to see the real Carlotta. If I did that, then I don't see how I can avoid disclosures about her father."

"You'll think of a way," I told him. "Not that it matters as far as concerns the trial. That won't need proof of blackmail. But to get back to what happened next. Speer was dead and so there was no more blackmail, but Conward was coming out in a few months' time and he'd never disclosed the whereabouts of the loot. Hence the new plan. Another fortune was at stake and well worth all the trouble and planning, so the Harbans came to London under their own name and using their own passports. By staying somewhere quiet and shifting quarters as they did a few days ago, he managed to grow a beard and she had her hair dyed. She'd seen Carlotta and it wouldn't be too difficult to darken the skin and fix the hair to give herself that Italian look. I've seen old photographs of Carlotta and I frankly own I was completely taken in. Also I had not the faintest reason to suspect anything. If I'd had, then I might have wondered about a few things that I've never mentioned yet, and because they've only just occurred to me. Why, when I first saw the pseudo-Dawsons, for instance, she didn't want the room lights on. They didn't go on till both of them were sure I'd accepted her as Carlotta Dawson.

"Still, that's no great matter, and to go back to the time when Gloria had everything set, and ten days before Conward was due out. Harban wouldn't risk picking up Conward himself so he had to get hold of a private detective and have a beautifully convincing tale ready to tell. So he had look through the advertisements and happened to choose the Broad Street Agency. An interview was arranged and I turned up. Between ourselves I think they must have been just the least bit surprised."

Jewle laughed.

"I bet they were!"

"Blame nature, not me," I told him. "However, they told me the tale and then they began to ask themselves if they hadn't chosen the wrong man. Strange as it may seem to you people, I had too many scruples, so they hired Scant to keep an eye on me in case I found out a hole in the yarn they'd spun to me. And this will be news to you. Scant reported that he'd been spotted so they called him temporarily off. Then they told me they'd been followed themselves. And since I'd mentioned the Harbans—rather ironical that!—Harban himself rang me one night, practically admitted who he was, and offered me a job that would take me to Vancouver. That was to convince me that Harban was after the jewellery and to lay plans for what was to happen when Conward came out. Then the Kate Howard business broke and I told them flatly that I couldn't take the job, and after that I had that very nice letter from Gloria about her husband going home and all the rest of it."

"That explains Kate Howard," Fusson said. "He drew up alongside her in that car and introduced himself as Carlotta Speer's husband come specially to fetch her."

"Exactly! Gloria daren't let Kate see her. I think I sprang Kate's visit to town and how I was sending her to the hotel so suddenly that Gloria hadn't time to say it wouldn't be convenient, and once she'd committed herself then something drastic had to be done. As for Harban's alibi that morning," I said to Jewle, "you've probably busted that long ago."

"Didn't want much busting. She pretended to be talking to a man who wasn't there."

"Yes," I said. "I was fool enough not to suspect that, but I had formed the opinion that I was being made a tool, so before I refused the job I warned them that they'd probably be questioned by the police about the disappearance. That's another reason why they changed hotels. Also, they were expecting either that Harban could get the jewellery through or from Conward and then they'd have to get out of the country. And that meant they had to resemble the photographs on their passports.

"But that doesn't so much matter. What I want you to listen to is this. *And listen closely.* I don't want to be drawn publicly into any trial but I'm prepared to change my mind on account of Kate Howard. So get this clear. I think it might impress a jury.

"Let's call Gloria Gloria and Carlotta Carlotta and then we shan't get into a muddle. Gloria didn't know that Kate was living at Puckenford. Neither did Carlotta, so when Carlotta wrote to her from America she addressed the letter to her old home and asked the people there to forward it. Now in the course of talking to Gloria about Kate's disappearance I mentioned the letter that had been written to Kate. 'Oh yes,' said Gloria, 'I wrote to her at Puckenford.' *Remember that carefully.*

"But on the night when I saw the pseudo-Dawsons and told them I couldn't take the job, Gloria followed me out to the corridor when I left. She threw in an *arrivederci,* by the way, just to leave me with the thought that she was Italian. But that's not important. This is. She apologised for a mistake she'd made the previous night. Of course she hadn't written to Puckenford! It was just a slip of the tongue. She hadn't even known that Kate was at Puckenford, and what she'd really done was write to the old home for the letter to be forwarded. You see it? Where could Gloria have got that information from?"

All three spoke at once. It could only have come from Harban, who'd met Kate that very morning and, on the strength of being Carlotta's husband, had wormed every bit of useful information out of her before killing her.

"I think it ought to hang him," I said. "It'll certainly help."

"Yes," Jewle said. "If the wizards of Westminster haven't changed their minds again by that time and abolished the death penalty."

"Gloria's the one who should swing," Fusson said. "Alongside him, I mean."

"Plenty of time," Jewle told him mildly. "They'll both have a lot to think about during the next few weeks while we're preparing a case. Anything else?"

"Well, no," I said. "Only that Harban did have a crack at that jewellery, but you know all that."

"We don't know all by a long chalk," Fusson said. "Someone presumably took that dog and something very valuable was in it. You've proved, Mr. Travers, that it was Harban. All right, then. Why did he hang on in England? Why didn't he and his wife leave at once for Canada or somewhere?"

Poor Fusson! For him that damn dog was a regular King Charles's head. And no wonder.

"There you've got me," I told him. "But there might be various reasons. Waiting till Gloria was herself again, for instance. Or trying to dispose of the jewellery over here, knowing he'd take an enormous risk trying to smuggle it through."

"It'll all fit in in time," Jewle told him with the same cheerful patience as he looked at his watch. "I don't know what time you people had breakfast but I'm getting pretty peckish. And I've a conference about all this at two o'clock."

There were mutual congratulations, shaking of hands and out we all went. But I was sent back.

"Just stay for a minute, Travers, will you?" Jewle said, so I went back again. I was feeling hungry, too, so I lighted my pipe to stay the pangs. It was quite a time before Jewle came back.

"Thought I'd never get rid of Fusson," he told me, "but here's something I want to show you."

He slipped the key in the lock and put on the table a box I well remembered. Then he showed me three letters.

"Interesting," I said. "Who do you think he or she was?"

"Remember?" he said. "We thought it was Gloria, but it couldn't have been. But have a look at this."

He slowly trickled those diamonds out of the cotton wool, and separated them with a finger.

"Good lord!" I said. "They must be worth a fortune!"

"Know what they are? They're the stones from that Sellbrook Gardens job. So the experts think. And tomorrow they're going to America. We've been in touch with the son at the Embassy and he wants his parents to make an official verification. They and the New York jewellers they were bought from."

"Wait a minute," I said. "Wasn't there a big reward offered for the recovery of those jewels? Something like five thousand pounds?"

"That's right. But it won't be all that much now. The reward was for the jewellery intact. From what I'm told it won't be more than three thousand five hundred."

"A nice little nest egg for somebody." Then I stared. "But that letter! Whoever sent you the stones says you're to keep them safe because there may be a reward and he has the receipt for the registered package."

"I know," he said. "But it's a she, not a he. And how can she come forward? Who is she? Some other woman Harban was keeping somewhere?"

"Don't ask me," I told him and rose as if to go. "That'll be your headache. And, by the way, are you perfectly satisfied about that little bet we had this morning?"

He grinned.

"I'd like to make one every day like it."

"No hard feelings?"

"My dear fellow! It was a fair bet and I'm the only one who stood to profit by it. Try it on me another time and see what I say."

"That's fine," I said. "All I have to do is bring 'em in and you ask no embarrassing questions."

"That's it," he said. "Money for old iron."

"Yes," I said, and took out my wallet and found that post-office receipt. "In that case you might like to have a look at this."

There were one or two echoes that you might care to hear about. To go a long way ahead—after the trial, in fact—Jewle got a promotion to Superintendent and Matthews to Inspector, and we had a dinner to celebrate, and at, of all places, Tibball's old restaurant. Fusson was there, too. He told us that after all the publicity it had had at the trial, that dog was making the Commercial bar a regular gold-mine.

But, to get back a bit. Long before I was sure of that reward I made up my mind to hand it over to the Agency. If I'd kept it myself, the Commissioners of Inland Revenue would have left me about enough for a cup of coffee and a sandwich, but if it was an Agency affair, then we could put in a pretty stiff expense account.

I don't know if it was exactly that that made me a bit generous, but I did see that Bertha had a good present and I also sent a registered letter to Hooker, c/o The Citadel, Laverock Road, enclosing some notes for use at his own discretion, and saying it was a small gesture of gratitude for a talk he'd once had with a stranger. The other echo was quite amusing.

I hope you haven't forgotten Leonard Stockwold. I'll never forget him, if only because he was the kind of man who could have touched Nasser for a signed photograph and then have sold it to Eden. But be that as it may, this is what happened:

I was at the Agency one morning in the middle of October when Bertha rang through to say a big package had arrived for me. I hadn't the faintest idea what it might be but I took it home at lunch-time as I happened to have come in my car. When I got home I found a letter. It was from Stockwold and with it was an invoice for goods on approval, the price being four pounds ten.

This was the letter:

Dear Sir,

Remember you asked if I could sell you a garden? Well, here's one for you. I had it specially made and hope it gives every satisfaction. Do not hesitate to call on me for any other requirements in the same line.

Yours truly,

L. STOCKWOLD.

Bernice and I opened the package. It was a handsome window box in Canadian red cedar. It stood on little feet and it had holes for drainage and a plastic tray to catch the water. Inside in a bag was the necessary potting soil, fertiliser included.

Bernice kissed me. She said it was a lovely surprise and one of the most thoughtful things I'd ever done. That very afternoon it was stocked with bulbs that were supposed to be out by Christmas. I sent Stockwold a cheque, and recouped myself by working out all the cost of the day I spent in Peterborough, including some double whiskies. Stockwold would be the last person to know it, but I owed him a considerable deal, and at Christmas I could well afford out of that handsome reward to do something about that proprietary brand he'd hinted at.

Curious, isn't it, how the whole thing really began because of a night years back when Norris and I had been kept late adjusting expense accounts, and so I'd happened to run into Jewle? I was still on the same subject, wondering if a possible present to Stockwold mightn't be at the expense of the Commissioners of Inland Revenue, and feeling some faint scruples about it. Me and my conscience. Jewle would laugh!

He was laughing in any case. Only that morning he'd rung me to say that Harban had begun to sing and had fingered Conward as the one who'd knocked down Alice Edwards. So Conward was again under lock and key. And all because, if you really work it out, a motor-coach had happened to be carrying a fire extinguisher. Jewle had laughed again when I'd mentioned that. He'd said it wouldn't be long before Harban was wishing he had one, too!

THE END